Nell Johnson began her career as an actress at the age of sixteen. She spent many years working in theatre, film and television. Performing Shakespeare's *Romeo and Juliet* and many classic plays, musicals, including her favourite, *Gypsy.* In the series *Prisoner,* she played Sarah Higgins for a year in Australia. She realised very early that the imaginary world was the place for her. The shock of her older sister, a prodigy and a concert pianist, cleaning the floors of their parents' home; drove her to vacate and venture where the green grass grew. All was forgiven after her sister presented a sparkling raindrop on a rounded green leaf, as the *Fairy Queen*. A vivid memory on her third birthday that survived the passage of time. After writing many film scripts and producing, directing and writing a short film, she progressed to writing an older children's book followed by the classic novel *Goodbye William.* The late Roy Dotrice encouraged her work as a writer.

I would like to dedicate *Goodbye William* to my son Oliver Jao Smith for his love, inspiration and support.

Nell Johnson

GOODBYE WILLIAM

AUSTIN MACAULEY PUBLISHERS™

LONDON • CAMBRIDGE • NEW YORK • SHARJAH

A CIP catalogue record for this title is available from the British Library.

ISBN 9781528929950 (Paperback)
ISBN 9781528930840 (ePub e-book)

www.austinmacauley.com

First Published 2023
Austin Macauley Publishers Ltd®
1 Canada Square
Canary Wharf
London
E14 5AA

I would like to thank Roy Dotrice (late) for his unrelenting encouragement for my work as a writer. I would also like to thank Austin Macauley Publishers for the opportunity to have my book read by the public throughout the world.

Chapter 1

The redbrick Georgian manor standing majestically on a hill above the river had been home to the Harper family in Devon for many years. A picturesque rose garden was one of the many colourful flowerbeds surrounded by a well-clipped hedge. The oak trees were just far enough apart to enable a shady stroll down the gravel path to the fields where the daffodils were already in bloom in the spring of 1920. The broodmares and their foals galloped where the sun-drenched meadows met the shadows of the tall trees; the wild woods were heavily populated with bluebells.

Isabelle Harper, a willowy fifteen-year-old, woke from a remarkable dream about Romani people, and climbed from her four-poster bed. Delightfully haunted but fully awake, Isabelle realised that the late Granny Harper may have been to blame; she used to tell intriguing mystical pagan tales while they were on their blissful long walks together under the shade of the ancient oak trees. A cherished memory of her grandmother's scandalous adventures inspired a generous smile. Granny Harper had eloped with the man of her dreams—a commoner—and sailed to America. After returning to England many years later, having made a fortune, she alarmed the ruling class by allowing gypsies to settle on the estate.

As an only child, Isabelle's many invitations to the fine houses of England were happily received by the Harper family. Isabelle embraced her love of music, art and literature, although her mother misunderstood the passion and blamed it for the numerous marriage proposals declined by Isabelle from the carefully chosen suitors. If Granny Harper was alive, she certainly would have settled the argument.

Isabelle's maid, a homely woman with a kindly face, dressed her in the fashionable frock that she had chosen. Brushing the head of flame-red hair that framed Isabelle's delicate beauty, Elsie struggled to free the knots.

'You haven't touched your breakfast, miss,' Elsie commented.

'I'm not hungry,' Isabelle replied, tying her rose-pink hat under her chin while waiting patiently for Elsie to finish her hair.

'I'm to remind you that the tall trees and the gypsy dwellings are forbidden. I would take heed if I were you, as Mrs Harper's mood is an impatient one.'

Isabelle collected her easel and paints then hurried down the hall. An unusually warm morning enchanted her; she ambled through a field of daffodils blaming her obsession with the mystical pagan tales for her failure to create the masterpiece that she had envisaged. Her curiosity about life beyond the shadow of the tall trees was overwhelming.

Mother's threat of pagan witches and gypsy voodoo did not deter Isabelle as she stood at the foot of the hill where the gypsies dwelled. Worried about life's adventures passing her by, she bravely entered the eerie woods. Her heart pounded from the suspense. She heard whispers through the trees. The gypsy children climbed silently onto wagons, with their big brown eyes peering through mops of unruly black hair. A human skull became visible to Isabelle through the leaves. A closer inspection revealed dried blood on what appeared to be a sacrificial altar where the skull rested. Beginning to believe that her mother was right about witches, she muffled her gasp and remained hidden amongst the trees.

Isabelle peered through the leaves and watched the older girls and boys playing a rowdy game. A ball landed near her feet. She dropped the easel and paints, bravely stepped from behind the tree, and grabbed the ball.

The girls and boys stared inquisitively.

'Catch!' Isabelle instructed as she threw the ball into play.

Sixteen-year-old Jimmy Williams caught the ball, hesitated and smiled. His rugged good looks and black curly hair appealed to Isabelle. She noticed a girl she recognised—Lorna, a servant from the family estate—scowling in her direction. Isabelle quickly picked up her easel and paints, worried that her little adventure had been exposed.

Isabelle heard a steam train in a far-off meadow; it immediately brought to mind the much-talked-about arrival of the new vicar, Charles Durn.

She hurried down the hill to meet the train and noticed the gypsy children were following. The passengers' faces appeared faintly at the windows but, to Isabelle's keen eye, no vicar was on board. Arriving at the pretty little railway station, the train shunted to a stop. A cloud of steam expelled from the engine, and when it evaporated, the new vicar Charles Durn appeared.

'Gracious!' Isabelle exclaimed, wishing the word hadn't escaped her lips.

The vicar had taken her by surprise. His blond hair framed a pleasant, handsome face, and his unconventional cream suit met with Isabelle's approval.

She noticed a violin tucked firmly under his arm as he staggered to the roadside. After securing his stylish Panama hat, Charles caught a glimpse of Isabelle before she darted behind a tree.

'Hello,' he greeted in a deeply timbered voice. Isabelle remained silent as the middle-aged conventional vicar from her church, Martin Harris, arrived in a Bentley sports car. He had the hood down to enjoy the perfect summer's day.

'Welcome, Charles,' Martin announced as he stepped from the car.

'Thank you, sir,' Charles replied, with a polite tipping of his hat. After exchanging a warm handshake, they loaded the luggage into the car and climbed on board. Martin drove down the gravel road at quite a speed, making Charles a little uneasy.

Apart from movement in the long grass, the gypsy children were almost invisible as they crawled behind Isabelle. After resting her easel and paints against the trunk of her favourite oak tree, Isabelle stood proudly in possession of her adventure. The surrounding wildflowers were plentiful. As she picked three or four to thread through her hair, swishing footsteps aroused her curiosity.

'Isabelle!' Mrs Harper called impatiently.

'I'm coming, Mother,' she replied reluctantly. The gypsy children, who were well hidden in the field, scurried away after hearing the sternness of Mrs Harper's voice. Isabelle picked up her easel and paints and hurried through the field.

~

The usual black-tie dinner took place in a plush, Edwardian dining room that featured a majestic oak table and chairs. Green velvet curtains framed the grand Georgian windows gracefully. The chandeliers hung in just the right places to enhance the French Impressionist paintings on the wall.

The servants were attentive, including Lorna, the gypsy girl from the tall trees on the hill. She glanced at Isabelle with a smirk. She looked different—elegant—with her black hair swept smoothly into a twisted knot at the back of her head. Isabelle sat quietly with her parents as dinner concluded. She avoided eye contact with her mother, fearful that Lorna would expose her glorious adventure. Isabelle's father presented as a suave and worldly gentleman. He smiled at the wildflowers threaded through her hair.

'You look lovely,' he complimented graciously.

'Thank you, Father.' Mrs Harper bristled; her poised elegance became ruffled.

'Pleasing your father will do you no good. You'll not leave the house for a week,' Mrs Harper instructed with austerity. Isabelle glared at Lorna who was leaving the room with the servants.

'But I'm expected at church on Sunday,' she informed her mother with a sense of urgency.

'God will forgive you.'

'He won't! Please! Father?' Isabelle pleaded.

Mr Harper remained silent. He observed his wife disapprovingly; she appeared a little dishevelled after a second glass of gin. The grandfather clock chimed nine o'clock.

'Please, excuse me,' Isabelle requested politely.

Mr Harper stood and placed his serviette on the table. 'You're excused, my darling girl,' he answered affectionately as she left the room.

~

The sun peered through the bedroom window and the birds competed with their morning calls. Isabelle took care to wear a glamorous white hat that matched her stylish frock. After dabbing a little too much perfume behind her ears, she picked up her prayer book and tiptoed past Elsie, who had fallen asleep in a chair. Elsie woke up with a start, alarmed to see Isabelle dressed for church.

'Please, miss!' Elsie pleaded.

'You haven't seen me,' Isabelle whispered.

'Pray for both of us,' Elsie declared nervously.

Taking a short cut through the woods, Isabelle stumbled upon a pagan Celtic ritual being performed by the gypsies at the sacrificial alter, well hidden by the tall trees. The chanting and frenzied voices made her uneasy. Jimmy appeared in a canoe with the gypsy boys, paddling down river to the beat of a Celtic drum; she found his smile comforting.

Isabelle sprinted across the meadow and climbed over the fence as the broodmares and their foals were stirring into a morning gallop. Isabelle arrived short of breath after the church bells had ceased ringing—indicating the last of the congregation had entered the fifteenth century church—and saw the doors closed. Disappointment prevailed. She made the decision to climb the oak tree beside the stained-glass windows of the church, a difficult task in her Sunday best. She found a perfect viewing place for latecomers. Isabelle climbed onto a suitable branch so she wouldn't be seen by the congregation. She stared despairingly at the vicar, Martin Harris, as he appeared in the pulpit. A gusty breeze made his sermon inaudible, so she waited patiently. The gypsy children who had followed her gathered around the tree trunk, trying to muffle their laughter.

'Be quiet!' Isabelle instructed anxiously.

The children obeyed. Then, the moment Isabelle had been waiting for arrived. The new vicar, Charles Durn, entered the pulpit, in possession of his fine good looks and commanding demeanour. His rich voice resonated over the wind. She smiled warmly as the man of her dreams preached his sermon.

> 'Love is patient. Love is kind. Love isn't jealous. It doesn't sing its own praises. It isn't arrogant.
>
> But the fruit of the Spirit is love, joy, peace. Kindness, goodness, faithfulness.
>
> Be kind and compassionate to one another, forgiving each other, just as Christ God forgave you.'

The children were becoming restless and their jolly laughter could be heard.

'Be silent,' Isabelle whispered nervously. The congregation sang the hymn Abide With Me. She slid down the tree trunk in her white Sunday best; the children strove to suppress their hilarity as they observed her dirty dress.

With the church doors opening in readiness for the congregation's departure, Isabelle and the gypsy children hurried across the meadow, passing the broodmares who had settled to graze with their foals. Floating on air she stepped lightly through the grass.

Chapter 2

A violin rested on the lid of a grand piano; a bugle stood on the mantelpiece next to a wall of books. Isabelle's cosy room was in disarray. After she had gazed into the full-length mirror, pre-occupied with her naked body, she slipped into her dressing gown then sat at the easel and diligently mixed the oils in readiness.

As the morning drifted peacefully into the afternoon, Elsie tidied the room and then changed Isabelle into a stylish frock.

'Oh, Elsie,' Isabelle swooned before she mentioned the unmentionable.

'I don't wish to hear,' Elsie replied quickly as she left the room.

Distracted by her thoughts, Isabelle gazed out of the window at the empty field, wondering if she lived in the quietest house in Devon. While beautiful antiques and fine decor were pleasing to the eye, they did not stimulate the mind for long. Vicar Charles Durn appeared in the field. Flushed with excitement Isabelle opened the window.

'Hello!' she called in rapturous tones.

Charles disappeared from view. Disheartened, she slumped onto the bed. Mrs Harper entered as the mantelpiece clock chimed five o'clock.

Isabelle stood to attention quickly, brushing the creases from her frock.

'Your father would like you to dine with us tomorrow night,' Mrs Harper informed her in mellow tones.

'Thank you, Mother,' she answered politely.

Curious as to why a cloth covered the painting on the easel, Mrs Harper attempted to remove it.

'Don't!' Isabelle urged.

Mrs Harper raised the cloth to reveal a painting of a woman's breasts. Astonished by her daughter's art, she quickly covered the painting.

'You need to take heed of your audacious behaviour,' Mrs Harper scolded as she strutted from the room with a forbidding glance in Isabelle's direction. When Isabelle had closed the door firmly behind her, Charles became visible through the window. Striving to endure her disappointment as he disappeared into the sunset, she prepared the easel with a life-size canvas.

A small lamp cast a soft light onto Isabelle, who had fallen asleep at the easel with a paintbrush still poised in her hand. Mr Harper entered the room with many gift-wrapped boxes, looking smart in his elegant tails. After the gifts were carefully stacked onto the table, he gently removed the paintbrush from her hand.

'Isabelle,' Mr Harper whispered with no response. The many hours spent longing to meet Charles had exhausted her.

'Sweet dreams,' Mr Harper said quietly as he draped the cloth over the painting and carried her to bed, covering her with a soft satin quilt. He drew the curtains, then noticed his wife entering the room in her nightgown. She observed the gifts disapprovingly, but he ignored her reaction.

'You've been to London,' Mrs Harper commented with an edge to her voice.

'I have indeed, madam. Good night,' Mr Harper replied brusquely, walking from the room. Mrs Harper tried to suppress her tears as she turned down the lamp.

~

The next morning Isabelle stepped over the empty gift boxes and wrapping paper strewn about the room, parading in a charming red hat. Hugging an exquisite new dress against her body, she twirled joyously. Noticing Charles through the window, she threw the dress aside.

'Hello!' Isabelle called in full voice.

Charles didn't respond. Being an accomplished violinist, she grabbed her instrument and played a dramatic piece. Panicking as Charles walked away, she threw the violin onto the bed, picked up the bugle and played an energetic fanfare. Charles stopped, turned around and walked towards her. She presented a life-size painting of herself in the nude from the upstairs window. Astounded, Charles tipped his hat politely to Isabelle and walked on with a quick light step.

The official punishment had been dealt with and Isabelle spent a great deal of her time in a favourite getaway by the river. A sun hat shaded her fair complexion from a warm summer's day while she prepared her easel and paints on the riverbank. At last, a swan—the subject of her new painting—appeared through the reeds. She also glimpsed Jimmy, well secluded in the long grass. After she'd looked around to study the light, her hat blew off in the strong breeze. Jimmy darted from his hiding place and joined Isabelle in the chase. He grabbed the hat and handed it to her graciously.

'Thank you kindly. I'm Isabelle.'

Putting on her hat and tying it firmly under her chin, she kept a keen eye on him as he admired her art.

'Call me Jimmy. My Romani name doesn't roll off the tongue so easily.'

After wild gusts of wind made it too difficult to continue with her art, she strove to pack the paints. Jimmy stepped in and carried the easel for her. The appearance of Lorna in the field disturbed a blissful silence.

'Is Lorna your girlfriend?' Isabelle enquired.

'No!' Jimmy answered abruptly as he studied her eyes inquisitively. He handed her the easel and hurried across the field.

Isabelle's thoughts of Jimmy diminished as Charles Durn appeared on the horizon hanging onto his hat in the gusty wind. She dropped her easel and paints eagerly.

'Hello!' Isabelle yelled with as much finesse as she could muster. Charles disappeared through the trees and Isabelle sank to her knees in despair, feeling secluded in the long grass. She dreamed of Charles holding her in his manly arms, his heavenly kiss transcending her to a beautiful place. Mrs Harper's voice jolted her from such romantic imaginings.

'Isabelle! Your father's guest is waiting,' Mrs Harper instructed in a brusque manner.

'I'm sorry, Mother,' Isabelle replied. She quickly buttoned up her dress then scrambled to her feet and hurried across the field.

The servants, including Lorna, were standing in position waiting to serve. Mr and Mrs Harper admired Isabelle's beauty and poise as she entered the dining room with a flourish. She had adorned herself in a glorious shell-pink evening gown that made a charming rustling sound as she swept across the room. Looking even more handsome than Isabelle remembered, the suave young vicar waited to greet her in his elegant black tails and she endeavoured to remain composed.

'Meet Vicar Charles Durn. He's eager to hear you play,' Mr Harper said.

Isabelle curtsied and lowered her eyes demurely. After Charles had kissed her hand, she found the courage to look him straight in the eye.

'Delighted,' Charles complimented with a smile.

Isabelle knew she had an ally. The maid Elsie entered with Isabelle's violin and placed the instrument onto the piano lid.

'That will be all,' Mrs Harper instructed.

As Elsie left the room Mrs Harper struggled to hide her impatience as Isabelle tuned the instrument.

'My dear, we're waiting to serve,' Mrs Harper whispered.

After Isabelle had played a beautifully executed piece on the violin, the vicar applauded her fine talent and the servants began to serve.

~

Breakfast remained untouched the next morning as the wonder of the previous evening had taken Isabelle's appetite. After searching for a particular piece of music in an agitated manner, she packed the sheets into her violin case.

'Can I help?' Elsie enquired, endeavouring to calm her.

'No, but you can wish me luck.'

'You don't need any luck, miss. I've often listened to your lovely playing,' Elsie praised. Isabelle smiled, but her violet blue eyes were a little sad that her mother was not the one wishing her well.

While hurrying through a field, Isabelle became distracted by the sound of joyous laughter. Jimmy and the gypsy boys were running naked through the willow trees, shouting inspiring words of passion in their Romani language, before diving into the river with a loud splash. Isabelle paraded through the trees, making sure she'd been noticed; her mischievous smile expanded as the boys panicked to dress hastily.

Isabelle arrived at the vicarage to be greeted by a little gypsy girl, Lola, swinging back and forth on the gate. Her big brown eyes observed Isabelle accusingly.

'You're late, miss,' Lola chastised with authority as she jumped off the gate, dressed in a frock rather large for her small size.

'I am indeed,' Isabelle declared with a chuckle as she hurried across the lawn.

Jimmy and the boys gathered in the picturesque garden, taking turns to peer through the Georgian windows at Isabelle and Vicar Charles Durn, playing a stirring duet on violin and piano. A schoolboy, William Stephens, arrived clutching his viola and waited outside. The gypsy boys stared in his direction standoffishly.

After a long silence, Charles opened the front door for Isabelle to leave. He noticed Jimmy and the boys scurrying through the trees.

'You've been blessed with a great gift, Miss Harper. I thank you for the privilege,' Charles complimented.

William caught the vicar's eye as he glanced slyly at Isabelle's feminine beauty.

'William, you're early,' Charles exclaimed as he ruffled the boy's mop of red hair fondly.

A rapturous squeal escaped from Isabelle as she skipped down the gravel path, treasuring the sublime moment when she had looked into Charles's serious blue eyes and strove to bewitch him with a scandalous smile.

She arrived at her favourite oak tree and rejoiced in her daydream. The precious memory of such a wonderful morning had been interrupted by the discovery of a roll of cloth in the hollow of the tree. She unravelled a painting with a remarkable resemblance to herself, and knew that Jimmy was the artist. She packed his painting into her violin case as he appeared on the river in his canoe. Isabelle hurried to meet him.

'I'm flattered to be the subject of your fine work,' Isabelle told Jimmy flirtatiously.

Paddling downriver, he waved to Isabelle. Lorna appeared through the trees, and—knowing her jealous demeanour—Jimmy and the gypsy boys paddled away hastily.

'Jimmy! Wait for me,' Lorna shouted. She dived into the river, attempting to follow the canoes that had disappeared around the river bend.

On the way home, Isabelle's happy thoughts about her new friend Jimmy were distracted by a movement in the tall trees. Lorna stepped from the shadows, blocking her path.

'Keep away from my Jimmy,' Lorna threatened. Her wild brown eyes flashed a chilling stare as the water dripped rhythmically from her hair and clothes. Isabelle ignored her and detoured from her path.

Chapter 3

Mrs Harper stood grim-faced as Isabelle practised the violin at a feverish pitch. She hadn't noticed her mother until the loud banging of a book being thumped onto the table alerted her attention. Isabelle stopped playing and endured a penetrating look of sternness from Mrs Harper for what seemed an endless time.

'Society can be very cruel to a woman who wishes to be different. Art is not life. I had married by sixteen, and your grandmother before me,' Mrs Harper informed with contained frustration.

Isabelle caught a glimpse of Lorna scurrying through the garden gate. She was indifferent to her mother's concerns, and she made no apology for her behaviour. Isabelle resumed her practice and Mrs Harper left the room in despair.

Following Isabelle's arrival at the vicarage, a dramatic violin and piano duet could be heard. Charles applauded her emotional playing.

'Bravura,' he praised with enthusiasm. Being an enchantress, Isabelle's music transcended her earthly being, for love and passion flowed through her veins.

'Thank you for such a fine compliment, Reverend Durn,' Isabelle said demurely, filled to the brim with desire.

Charles caught sight of Jimmy who was peering through the window.

'You have an admirer,' Charles advised. She looked to the window, but Jimmy darted out of sight.

'Yes,' Isabelle nodded with a girlish smile.

She diligently packed her violin into its case as Charles walked down the hall. He unlocked the door of a cabinet and removed the violin made by the famous Antonio Stradivari.

'My grandfather's violin is wasted on me. This instrument needs a fine musician to enhance its craftsmanship,' Charles said. Impressed by her talent, Charles returned to present the instrument to Isabelle. The shock of seeing her in a state of undress took his breath away. After an awkward silence Charles carefully placed the violin onto the table. He dragged the silk cover off the lounge and gently wrapped it around her.

'I love you,' Isabelle whispered with a tear in her eye.

Charles fell silent. He blamed the emotional music for her sensual passion.

'Practice the Brahms duet for next week,' Charles advised in a nonchalant manner, kindly erasing the moment of embarrassment as he closed the door behind him. Isabelle dressed quickly. She grabbed her violin and left the gift from Charles on the table.

Walking by the riverbank, Isabelle's tears flowed uncontrollably. A swan taking flight caught her attention and she ran in its direction.

Unexpectedly, Jimmy scrambled from the long grass and joined the chase. They both collapsed in the field from exhaustion. Jimmy gave her a caring look and dried her eyes with his shirtsleeve. Alerted by marching footsteps and shocked to see his father, Sam Williams approaching, Jimmy stood quickly to attention.

'Keep away from that girl!' Mr Williams bellowed as he hit Jimmy over the head.

Distressed by the violence, Isabelle stood tall and stared disapprovingly. Mr Williams was hitting Jimmy repeatedly while leading him across the field and Isabelle noticed Lorna watching from behind the trees.

~

A recording of the opera *"Madame Butterfly"* played on the gramophone as Isabelle kept a keen eye on the window in case Charles walked by. After mixing her oils to create a rich colour, the sound of a car on the dirt road outside alerted her. She looked through the window and saw the vicar Martin Harris driving past in his Bentley sports car, accompanied by Vicar Charles Durn and the fashionable lady that Isabelle had learned was his fiancé, Sarah Howard. The luggage, visible on the back seat, spun Isabelle into a whirlwind of curiosity. Elsie entered the room as Isabelle adjusted her stylish hat to flatter her well-groomed hair.

'Please, miss! You're not allowed to leave the house until Mrs Harper has given instruction,' Elsie advised firmly.

'I won't be long, I promise,' Isabelle answered reassuringly, rubbing a little rouge on her cheeks.

'Your mother will dismiss me,' Elsie said, reluctantly handing Isabelle her violin case.

An eerie silence—apart from the occasional croak from a frog in a pond nearby—had fallen on the vicarage garden. Isabelle stared at the empty Bentley parked on the lawn; her thoughts were filled to the brim with speculation. The hood being down the gypsy children were able to climb into the car. The little girl Lola sat in the front seat observing Isabelle with a cheeky grin.

'Hello,' Lola said.

'Have you seen the vicar?' Isabelle questioned, striving to appear calm.

Lola and the gypsy children sniggered amongst themselves. Being in no mood for dallying, Isabelle marched across the lawn and knocked on the front door. After waiting for what seemed like an eternity, she peered through the parted curtains of a closed window. She saw Charles kissing his fiancé, Sarah Howard. Isabelle's devastation was such, that if her heart had stopped beating at that moment, she would have been glad of it.

Charles caught a glimpse of Isabelle with tears spilling down her cheeks. Sarah, a tall elegant beauty, felt a little bewildered by his sadness.

'Is anything wrong?'

'Please excuse me,' Charles replied.

When he opened the front door, he could see Isabelle running from the vicarage.

The gypsy children followed Isabelle through the field as she threw her violin case away with all her might. Sprinting from his hiding place, Jimmy jumped into the air to catch the flying missile.

With the sun barely filtering through the leaves of her favourite oak tree, Isabelle woke to a warm breeze blowing across her face. Surprised to see her violin case in the hollow of the tree trunk and distracted by two dirty feet nearby; the sight, surprisingly, brought a smile to her tragic face.

Jimmy had joined her and they sat in a tranquil silence, each holding on to their muted thoughts.

'Do you swim?' Jimmy enquired mischievously, disturbing the silence.

'Certainly not,' Isabelle replied.

'One day you may fall into the river and drown. Then, I would spend the rest of my sad life missing you,' Jimmy declared as he took off his shirt and threw it into the air. Amused by his antics, Isabelle laughed heartily. He ran to the river and dived into the water with a loud splash.

Isabelle's frock was hanging precariously from a nearby tree branch as she attempted to emulate Jimmy's swimming stroke.

'I can do it,' Isabelle insisted, coughing and spluttering while swallowing water. Persisting with the stroke and realising that she'd actually stayed afloat, Isabelle squealed with joy. After she'd climbed from the river, exhausted from her great accomplishment, Jimmy strove to muffle his hilarity at the sight of her frilly petticoat billowing around her.

Charles joined the gypsy children in a serious game of football by the vicarage. A gusty wind blew the tree branches to and fro, nearly exposing a well-hidden Isabelle as she shivered from her damp hair and wet clothes. She observed Charles with tears in her eyes and longed for the day when he would reciprocate the glorious passion she held prisoner in her heart—only then would she know true happiness. The vicar Martin Harris disturbed her blissful but impossible imaginings when he arrived in his Bentley with a sense of urgency.

'There's trouble on the hill,' Martin bellowed.

Charles threw the ball to one of the boys and grabbed his coat from the fence post. After he'd stepped into the Bentley, Martin drove down the road at speed. The gypsy children knew the seriousness of the alert and sprinted towards the hill.

Martin and Charles hurried through the woods towards the screaming Rosa Williams, Jimmy's mother, who was bleeding profusely from the head. Lorna had joined the elderly women surrounding Rosa. Jimmy stepped from the wagon with his baby brother cradled in his arms. He handed the baby to the elderly women to keep him safe from their father, Sam Williams. After his drunken rage, he raised the stick to hit his wife Rosa again. The children screamed. Charles marched up to Sam and hit the stick out of his hand. Sam tried to grab the weapon, but Charles kicked it out of reach. Standing face-to-face, Charles stared Sam down with deep blue eyes full of determination. Sam walked away.

Isabelle had been hiding in the forbidden woods as a consequence of her vivid imagination, still shivering from the damp clothes. She wished that her curiosity had not led her to be a spectator of such terrible violence.

Charles's heroic resolve, and his compassion for her friend Jimmy, brought tears to her eyes as she quietly walked home through the woods.

Charles shouted to Martin and Jimmy when he saw the bloodied state of Rosa.

'Bring a full bowl of water, quickly!'

Martin hurried to Rosa with a Gladstone bag full of bandages open in readiness. Jimmy handed Charles a bowl of water and comforted his mother.

After Martin had bathed the blood from Rosa's face, he examined her eyes with a serious concern.

'It looks like she might have lost the sight in her right eye,' Martin advised.

Surprised by Martin's medical skills, Charles observed the bandaging of Rosa's head while he kept an eye on Jimmy and his father in case of more violence. Martin admired the new vicar as he packed the medication, pleased by his kindly compassion for the parish.

'Your medical skills are impressive,' Charles praised.

'I trained in the army,' Martin informed proudly.

'Thank you for saving my mother,' Jimmy said, shaking their hands firmly to express his gratitude.

'You know where we are if you need us,' Charles reassured, worried about the responsibility bestowed upon Jimmy.

~

Isabelle retired early that evening. After the trauma of the afternoon, she'd decided that a formal dinner would not be possible for her; she did not have the energy to pretend the day had been different. Isabelle strove to relax in a warm bath, prepared by Elsie, and the rising steam assisted her to drift peacefully. She wondered what had caused the vengeful blame on Sam's loved ones. There again, she'd read about many violent men in her history books.

~

After the mist had lifted from the vicarage, the warm glow from the sun filled the room where Isabelle's delicate virtuoso playing on the Stradivari violin had certainly enchanted Charles. Delighted with the gift she prayed for the power of her music to bond their souls and create a place where Sarah Howard could never venture.

Relieved to see Isabelle and Charles enter the garden after the lesson had concluded, Sarah greeted Charles keenly. He noticed the book entitled Weddings that she carefully placed onto the table. Isabelle attempted to hide her envy when Charles embraced Sarah affectionately.

'Reverend Durn, Miss Howard,' Isabelle farewelled standoffishly performing a little curtsy.

'How lovely to see you,' Sarah announced with caution. She noticed a doting glance from Charles as Isabelle left the vicarage. Sarah recognised her at once to be a young lady of her own mind and made it clear that youth played no part in her desire to bewitch the man of her dreams.

Sarah admired the courage in one so young, but felt a dark cloud may be gathering.

'I believe we'd be happier in London,' Sarah mentioned to Charles.

'My work is here,' he reminded her gently.

The gypsy boys charged through the garden with their boisterous play and careless footing destroying the colourful flowers.

'Watch out!' the boys shouted as they ran past Sarah to catch the ball.

Amused by the spirited game but surprised by Sarah's tears, Charles held her hand reassuringly. He could see Isabelle and Jimmy in a field in the distance.

~

An eerie mist hovered over the majestic trees that lined the riverbank. Their twisted roots entwined above the ground taking on a medieval appearance. A Celtic drum could be heard in the distance as Isabelle and Jimmy paddled upriver. He pointed out an eagle swooping on its prey.

'Where are we going?' Isabelle queried curiously.

'My secret river,' Jimmy whispered.

Intrigued by Jimmy's answer, Isabelle smiled mischievously as they continued paddling around the river bend and into the dense willow trees.

'Does Lorna know about the secret river?'

'No,' Jimmy answered firmly.

Isabelle waded into the water after a gusty breeze blew her frock into the waterfall. She was spellbound by this mysteriously tranquil place of nature's splendour. After tying the frock to a tree trunk, she dived into the river. She watched Jimmy gliding through the water; he had the grace of a dolphin as he reached out and caught a fish with his hands. Jimmy showed Isabelle how to fish and she tried to emulate his skill. Finally, she caught a fish excitedly in her hands. Jimmy came to the rescue and secured it for her. After inhaling a deep breath of forest air as they surfaced, Isabelle squealed from the thrill and he handed her the fish.

Isabelle struggled into her wet dress, then stood on the riverbank hoping the warm breeze would dry the fabric. She hadn't mentioned the safety of Jimmy's family, but felt she'd earned his trust.

'How is your mother?' she enquired as he joined her on the riverbank. The question struck a chord with Jimmy and tears welled in his eyes.

'Mother will be all right,' he replied bravely.

Isabelle held his hand gently to show that she cared.

The aroma from Jimmy's cooking at a makeshift campfire had enhanced Isabelle's appetite. She smiled appreciatively as he fussed caringly while preparing her fish on a large leaf.

'Lunch is served, ma'am.'

'Thank you,' she replied graciously, trying not to burn her fingers.

'Is the flavour to your liking?' Jimmy enquired eagerly.

'Delicious,' Isabelle enthused, striving to maintain her usual etiquette as the afternoon drifted away blissfully.

Isabelle looked bedraggled, sitting in the field and putting on her shoes. She disguised her wet hair by tying two plaits that fell past her shoulders. Her best-laid plan faltered, however, when Isabelle heard horse's hooves galloping through the field. She scrambled to her feet quickly to see her father and his business partner, George Hoskins—a distinguished young gentleman with a kindly face—riding their horses towards her. Realising that it was too late to hide, she stood confidently as they approached.

'Isabelle!' Mr Harper bellowed, startled by her appearance.

'I fell in the river. Don't tell Mother,' she pleaded.

Mr Harper and Mr Hoskins seemed to find the situation amusing.

'Isabelle, you remember my partner, George Hoskins?' he enquired. She nodded demurely and performed a quick curtsy.

'Good afternoon, young lady,' he greeted, tipping his riding hat.

'Mr Hoskins,' Isabelle replied, performing another curtsy.

'I believe you're an accomplished artist?'

'I dabble to make some sense of life.'

'An adventurous young lady like yourself should learn to swim.' Isabelle smiled at Mr Hoskins as her father offered his hand and assisted her to mount his horse.

'I'll take you home.'

Intrigued by such a lovely young temptress, George Hoskins felt that her spirited nature could seriously challenge a creature of habit such as himself.

Elsie tidied the new dresses strewn across the room while Isabelle indulged in a warm bath. As she rinsed the soapsuds from Isabelle's hair, her loud sneeze alarmed her maid.

'I hope you haven't caught a chill, miss,' Elsie warned as she fussed to lay out Isabelle's dress for the ball.

Isabelle smiled proudly as she peeked at the portrait Jimmy had painted. Rubbing a little rouge on her cheeks and keeping a keen eye on Elsie, she slid the signed artwork under her bed.

'You're a miracle worker,' Isabelle praised. She looked in the mirror and twirled in her exquisite ball gown, feeling the skirt flow.

'I am indeed, miss,' Elsie agreed earnestly.

She placed a recording onto the gramophone and danced around the room to the delicate waltz. A sudden sneezing attack worried Elsie as Isabelle picked up her fan then opened the door to go downstairs.

'Before I forget... Mrs Harper would like you to choose one of these new dresses for the vicar's wedding,' Elsie instructed.

Shocked by the news, Isabelle turned sharply to face her maid. 'Reverend Durn?' she enquired, striving to remain calm.

'The date was announced downstairs,' Elsie explained.

Isabelle sat back down at the dressing table, unable to breathe for her heart had been broken. She climbed onto the bed and coughed continuously. Elsie panicked and fetched a glass of water, but Isabelle showed no interest.

'I'll let Mrs Harper know you're ill, miss.'

After Elsie had hurried out of the door, Isabelle shed tears of despair.

The music and gaiety from downstairs woke Isabelle. Mr Harper entered the room dressed in his stylish black tails, waited for Isabelle's coughing fit to finish, then felt her forehead with concern.

'My darling girl, a day in bed should put you right. I promise not to mention the river,' he whispered and kissed her goodnight.

Chapter 4

Isabelle rested under the oak tree with no improvement to her dismal mood; her broken heart showed no signs of being mended and her cough persisted. A pair of dirty feet caught her eye. Jimmy had noticed her dark mood and picked wildflowers to thread through her hair, which had caused a glimmer of a smile to appear on her tragic face.

Jimmy carried Isabelle's violin across the meadow with pride in the knowledge that Lorna was following through the trees.

'Jimmy!' Lorna yelled in a distressed voice.

Taking Isabelle by the hand to show his affection, he ignored Lorna. 'Are you going to marry Lorna?' Isabelle asked.

'Not ever!' Jimmy replied.

'I'll mention your mother in my prayers tonight,' she promised as they approached the vicarage.

Jimmy blinked away a tear and spoke quietly, trying to control the emotion in his voice. 'Mother's spirit is preparing for death.'

Jimmy handed her the violin, and she embraced him warmly. The little gypsy girl Lola greeted them by jumping off the gate with enthusiasm.

'Hello Isabelle. The vicar is inside with William, and Jimmy is supposed to be at home,' Lola informed them in a direct manner.

'You're a cheeky girl for a six-year-old,' Jimmy replied.

~

Confused by his growing feelings for Isabelle, Charles peered through the window to observe her at play with the gypsy children. As William's lesson had concluded, he joined Charles at the window.

'Isabelle's beautiful,' William commented, watching her keenly.

'Yes, she is,' Charles agreed, deep in thought.

'Mother said that you're getting married.' William announced with a touch of jealousy in his voice.

'Did she indeed? Send Isabelle in like a good lad,' Charles instructed, being aware of William's boyish infatuation.

'Yes, sir!' he replied eagerly.

Charles's heart was beating loudly in anticipation of Isabelle's arrival. While choosing the music for her lesson, he became aware of her presence in the room.

He broke the tension in the silence between them. 'I'm sorry you haven't been well.'

'I suppose you've heard the news about Jimmy's mother Rosa,' she remarked nonchalantly. Charles realised Jimmy had informed her of the news.

'Be careful. Not everyone thinks as we do,' he warned. 'Rosa is dying. Jimmy needs you,' Isabelle pleaded quietly.

'You seem so grown up today,' Charles remarked; determined that his emotions remained concealed. They were interrupted by Vicar Martin Harris's voice from the garden.

'Charles! We're needed on the hill,' Martin bellowed.

He grabbed his coat, hesitated, then gently touched Isabelle's cheek. 'Please, Isabelle. Don't be seen on the hill,' Charles pleaded.

'Go quickly,' she urged.

~

The beat of a Celtic drum sounded rhythmically through the tall trees while the gypsies chanted their pagan ritual. Lorna joined the elder women as their frenzied voices rose to a crescendo. Martin and Charles attended to Rosa inside the wagon while Jimmy and his father Sam sat silently. Martin handed a bottle of medicine to Charles.

'Make sure Rosa drinks every drop,' Martin urged, alerting Charles to the seriousness of the situation. Charles persevered with kind words of encouragement. Martin changed the bloodied bandages and examined her eyes with deep concern.

'If Rosa makes it through the night, we have a fighting chance,' Martin remarked quietly to Charles.

Jimmy lit a lamp as dusk became night. Charles and Martin did what they could to save Rosa's life. Jimmy held his mother's hand and whispered a prayer to his God to save her.

At the first glimpse of dawn and the beautiful sunrise that followed, Charles and Martin waited patiently for any change in Rosa's diminishing pulse. Charles was not a man who believed in miracles, and yet he seemed to be the only one who noticed Rosa's lips move. 'Jimmy,' Rosa muttered, struggling for breath.

'I'm here, Mother,' Jimmy whispered. His eyes filled with tears and he held her hand a little tighter. Martin looked at Charles with a sense of relief after checking Rosa's pulse.

'Rosa, you're going to be all right,' Martin reassured her.

Jimmy's father nodded to show his appreciation then left the wagon.

'Congratulations,' Charles praised, in awe of the miracle he had just witnessed.

'I must thank you for your assistance, patience and dedication, Charles. We make a good team,' Martin replied.

A steam train appeared through the woods as Isabelle ambled along the railway line happily carrying her violin case. She jumped excitedly from the tracks and read the sign on the carriage A Touring Theatrical Troupe. Isabelle had read about the travelling theatres in Europe, but this would be her first encounter in rural England. Being an avid reader of Shakespeare's great work, the thought of seeing his plays performed inspired her. The actors appeared at the windows of the carriages waving to any fellow thespians; even the sheep and cows would suffice. Isabelle waved and cheered enthusiastically, intrigued by the theatrical train and the life it represented. Even though Granny Harper's first cousin had been an actor and performed at the Old Vic Theatre, she knew that her father—although more broadminded on such matters than her mother—would not approve of the theatre for his daughter.

Isabelle performed a Shakespearian sonnet to the sheep in the field, and Jimmy applauded her recital as he arrived quietly and lay down beside the oak tree. Having developed a fascination with Isabelle's violin, Jimmy seized an opportunity to test his skills. She smiled mischievously as he picked up the violin and ran the bow across the strings, creating—to his dismay—a screeching sound. A little embarrassed by his feeble attempt, he looked at Isabelle with a smile.

'I'm so grateful to Reverend Harris and Reverend Durn for saving my mother's life.' Jimmy looked at Isabelle with concern when he mentioned Reverend Durn's name. She dismissed the look, then gently took him by the hand.

'Allow me to escort you to your lesson,' Jimmy offered.

'You may, but we must hurry. Reverend Durn insists on punctuality.'

~

William's lesson had concluded but he waited patiently at the vicarage gate, listening to Isabelle's magnificent performance on the violin and dreaming of the day that he could master the instrument well enough to accompany her. He prayed that she would accept his gentlemanly offer to walk her home.

After Isabelle had joined William on the gravel road near the vicarage, Sarah took the opportunity to show Charles the wedding invitations and her new dress. Placing the cards onto the table, she twirled a little.

'Very attractive,' he flattered, distracted by the elaborately decorated wedding cards.

'Thank you, darling. I thought we should complete the guest list.'

'There's plenty of time.'

'Not everyone is like you, Charles. People like to plan ahead,' Sarah declared with a slight edge to her voice.

Confused by his emotional state of mind and feeling quite vulnerable, Charles embraced Sarah warmly and returned to the music room to seek solace in his work.

~

Endeavouring not to show his elation, William walked Isabelle along the riverbank in a nonchalant manner. He pondered upon a curiosity that had been troubling him.

'Reverend Durn is sweet on you,' William remarked.

'How do you know?' Isabelle enquired, intrigued and pleased by his observation.

'I also know that a gypsy girl follows you,' William announced confidently. Isabelle turned around quickly to catch a glimpse of the girl he was talking about—she presumed he must mean Lorna—but there was no one there. She looked to William for an answer.

'I can assure you that she's there. Gypsies have magical powers and can disappear at will.'

'Rubbish!' Isabelle scoffed.

'I speak the truth,' he said, being direct.

William's school friend Peter Low approached on the river in his rowing boat, and William acknowledged him by waving in his direction.

'I'm fishing upriver if you wish to join me?' Peter smiled when he noticed Isabelle.

'Can I bring a friend?' William enquired.

'Of course,' Peter replied.

'Today is not possible, but I'll see you next week,' Isabelle said.

After the thrill of spending time with her, William's thoughts were all over the place. He waded into the river in his smart suit and tie with his violin tucked under his arm, then strove to regain composure after climbing into the boat and bidding Isabelle a fond farewell. Amused by his antics, she continued her journey diligently.

William and Peter were pleased with their catch. The sound of paddles churning through the water distracted them as Isabelle and Jimmy appeared through the late afternoon mist in a canoe. William stared in disbelief; the girl of his dreams was with a gypsy boy.

'Isabelle!' Peter exclaimed.

'If you so much as utter a word to anyone, the gypsies will get you in the night. They'll cut your tongue out and boil you alive!' William threatened Peter, being protective of Isabelle.

Peter's curiosity and desire to seek an adventure drove him to follow them through the overgrown river, even though the terror of the gypsies haunted him. They rowed around the bend, diligently searching, but Isabelle and Jimmy had mysteriously disappeared.

'A canoe cannot vanish,' William said, bewildered.

'I agree, my good friend. There must be an entrance amongst the willow trees,' Peter advised.

The scary sight of Lorna watching them through the trees startled William.

'There's the witch!' he warned in a whisper. Panicking, they rowed down the river in haste.

Isabelle respected the fact that Jimmy displayed privilege and trust. She felt blessed in his company on the secret river: a place of their own, where uninterrupted daydreams could flow with the rhythm of the waterfall and plain thoughts could be spoken out of earshot. Her recently acquired swimming skills she continued to enjoy as Jimmy whittled a sculpture in Isabelle's shape. Their time spent together was as precious as the air they breathed; their feelings were blossoming into a new beginning.

The gypsy girls were playing a boisterous ball game by the railway line when Lorna caught a glimpse of Isabelle with dripping wet hair hurrying through the trees. She waited suspiciously, expecting Jimmy's arrival; after Lorna had been following Isabelle for a short distance, Jimmy made a sudden appearance and scowled in Lorna's direction.

'Jimmy!' Lorna cried out as she hurried towards him.

'Stay away from me,' Jimmy urged as he made a hasty departure.

~

Her fashionable evening gown made a glorious rustling sound as Isabelle swept across the room with a completed portrait of Jimmy that she'd removed proudly from the easel. As she bent down to hide the painting under the bed, she'd noticed that all of Jimmy's artwork had gone.

Crouching under the bed, Isabelle saw Elsie enter the room followed by Mrs Harper.

'Isabelle must be downstairs on time so that George Hoskins can escort her into dinner. Mr Hoskins is Mr Harper's partner in law and comes from a fine family indeed, so punctuality is of the utmost importance.'

'Yes, ma'am,' Elsie replied.

After Mrs Harper had left the room, Isabelle struggled from under the bed and Elsie showed a look of surprise.

'Who's been in my room today?'

'Young Lorna delivered the linen this morning,' Elsie answered. 'Nobody else is allowed to enter,' Isabelle instructed firmly.

'When I arrived, Lorna was closing the linen cupboard. She left the room without a word being said, miss.' Elsie began to arrange Isabelle's hair into an exotic style.

~

After a dinner of elegance and fine conversation, Mr Harper changed the mood of the evening by telling the story of Granny Harper's estranged cousin's performance at the Old Vic Theatre. The audience had sat in breathless silence as his blond wig slid slowly down his face during the famous Hamlet soliloquy and then, with a grand theatrical gesture, he'd removed the item in question and concluded the performance as a balding Hamlet. Even though Isabelle had heard this story many times, she laughed heartily along with George Hoskins and the other guests. Mr and Mrs Harper were pleased with Isabelle's graciousness, not knowing that her thoughts were concentrated on Vicar Charles Durn and his fiancé Sarah Howard. Isabelle's occasional glances at Charles were subtly received; he peered from under his blond eyebrows with kind blue eyes and managed a smile that Isabelle would treasure forever.

The visiting London quartet played the first waltz of the evening. George escorted Isabelle to the dance floor along with many other elegant guests, including Charles and Sarah. As George guided Isabelle around the room with grace and style, she smiled flirtatiously at Charles.

Chapter 5

The sun had just broken through the morning showers as Isabelle acknowledged the dozens of red roses that had arrived after morning tea. Elsie struggled to find enough vases to display such beauty.

'Mr Hoskins is certainly showing a keen interest. A man who expresses his heartfelt attraction through flowers is usually kind and thoughtful,' she advised. Elsie had been a little worried about Isabelle's infatuation with Reverend Durn.

'Do you think so, Elsie?' Isabelle said as she stared out of the window.

'I do indeed.'

Isabelle indulged in another scone with jam and cream. She saw Charles drive by in Martin's Bentley. Without dallying, she wiped her hands with a serviette and put on a fashionable hat.

'You're leaving early, miss,' Elsie remarked, handing Isabelle the violin.

'I need to practice the Bridal Waltz for the vicar's wedding,' Isabelle replied, hurrying out of the door.

~

The elm trees in the vicarage garden gave adequate shade for Sarah Howard's fair complexion. The gypsy children were bemused by her disdainful disinterest in their joyful games. Not even reading her book—entitled Weddings—could ease her jealousy about the beautiful music that Isabelle and Charles were playing together.

The music room door being ajar as a violin solo concluded Charles mopped his brow with a handkerchief; on such an unusually warm afternoon. Charles hesitated, puzzled by the long silence. He turned around to see Isabelle removing her blouse. With the knowledge that Charles was watching, she mopped her breasts with a delicate lace handkerchief and closed the door a little.

'I won't play at your wedding,' Isabelle said.

Charles fumbled awkwardly and strove to resist the sublime temptation. She buttoned up her blouse. The gypsy children's laughing faces appeared through a gap in the curtain.

'Charles!' Sarah called from the garden, sounding distressed.

'You'd better hurry. Your mother's waiting,' Isabelle remarked sarcastically.

~

As the Bentley arrived through the woods, the gypsy children squealed with joy. They scrambled into the car before Reverend Durn and Reverend Harris could close the doors. Rosa looked much improved as Charles attended to her medication.

'I'm afraid my father is still sleeping,' Jimmy advised.

'We have no need for him here. Throw the dirty bandages into the fire,' Martin instructed as he handed him the bowl.

'Jimmy is a good boy,' Rosa praised as her son left the wagon.

'He knows to alert us if there's trouble,' Charles reassured her.

Martin observed Charles more closely and noticed that he looked drawn and pale.

'You've lost weight. You need a good woman to look after you. What do you think, Rosa?' Martin remarked as he put the drops into her eyes.

'I agree,' Rosa replied with a smile.

'How long have you been engaged?' Martin enquired, trying not to be too intrusive.

'Three years,' Charles answered hesitantly, curious as to where the conversation may be leading.

'What are you waiting for? If it's something to do with Isabelle, I would think again,' Martin remarked directly.

Charles remained silent; he was a little surprised by Martin's comment and yet, in a strange way, he felt relieved to hear it said.

'We'll make a doctor of you one day,' Martin declared, hoping that Charles had listened to his advice about Isabelle.

~

She woke to the early morning sunrise with disinterest. At morning tea, her favourite scones, jam and cream remained untouched as Isabelle gazed wistfully through the window at a steam train travelling by the meadow. She looked a picture of fashion in her glamorous dress and hat, yet her sullen mood displayed her unhappiness. Her only wish being that time would stand still forever, or that her heart would stop beating and never start again. Isabelle put on her gloves and picked up her prayer book, as Elsie observed her mood.

'You're quiet, miss. I'm a little teary myself. It reminds me of my own wedding day.'

'Is he a good man?' Isabelle enquired.

'He is indeed,' she answered proudly.

Alerted by a car horn from downstairs, Elsie handed Isabelle her violin. Isabelle threw the instrument onto the bed, and hurried out the door with Elsie chasing after her.

'But you're to play the Bridal Waltz, miss!' Elsie urged to no avail.

'Don't fuss,' Isabelle instructed impatiently.

The brass band played the Wedding March as the radiant bride and groom walked down the picturesque fifteenth century church steps. Isabelle found it difficult to disguise her devastation as the gathering of wedding guests cheered and tossed confetti over the handsome couple, Sarah and Charles. The vicar Martin Harris and his wife Edith joined Mr and Mrs Harper as they took part in the festivities. Isabelle walked away after her father had observed her tears.

To ease the pain of her devastating loss, Isabelle ran hard through the field. Struggling for breath, she waded into the river fully clothed; the water lapping against the jetty had a calming effect on her as she floated in the river. Comforted by the warmth of the sun on her face, she opened her eyes to see Jimmy observing her from the jetty. After being rescued from the river, he sat beside her in the quiet of the morning and found that his affectionate smile soothed her broken heart a little. The dripping water from her hair and clothes didn't matter with her friend Jimmy, who was near and dear to her. He took Isabelle's hand and embraced her tenderly, then he noticed his father looking sternly in his direction. Jimmy leaped to his feet and sprinted towards him. Sam grabbed a solid tree branch, ripped it off the tree in rage, and belted Jimmy hard.

'Keep away from her!' Mr Williams bellowed as he dragged Jimmy across the field.

~

The magnificent sunrise could not improve Isabelle's dismal mood as she lay on the bed and wondered if her broken heart would ever mend. She reached for the violin—her gift from Charles—and caressed the instrument with her elegant fingers. A seemingly long morning followed. She opened the window to breath in the crisp morning air, seeing the thoroughbred horses and hearing their thunderous hooves galloping across the meadow.

With the blood pumping through her veins, Isabelle rode her horse Tiger, who had been sadly neglected since the arrival of Charles Durn. Tiger, a gift from her father, was just the right medicine for Isabelle to regain her spirit. She galloped hard across the meadow and revelled in the wind blowing wildly through her hair.

An unknown horseman appeared through the trees as Isabelle entered the woods. She slowed down and discovered Jimmy's father, Sam Williams, to be the rider. His aggressive approach made her anxious.

'Don't come any closer,' she warned. Her nervous state made Tiger spirited and difficult to manage.

'You leave my son alone!' Mr Williams shouted aggressively, taking another swig of whisky from the flask.

She attempted to ride away, but he blocked her path with his horse and edged forward to grab her skirt. Isabelle whipped him across the face with her riding crop until he let go. She rode away at speed, jumping the fence at the same time as his horse shied, reared up and threw him to the ground with a loud thud.

'You bitch!' Mr Williams shouted in a manic rage as he staggered to his feet.

Isabelle rode along the railway line worrying about Sam Williams. After much pondering, she decided to remain quiet about the situation as she feared repercussions from her family. Relieved to see George Hoskins approaching on his horse, she returned his smile.

'It's late. Your father's been worried.'

'You found me.'

'Do you believe in chance?' he enquired.

'Maybe I do…'

'My orders are to escort you home,' George instructed as he turned his horse around.

'Then what are we waiting for?'

Isabelle galloped across the meadow and George made savage use of the riding crop, trying to catch up with her.

~

Isabelle stared at her breakfast with no appetite. Through the window she saw Sam Williams walking briskly from the manor. She anxiously mixed flowers to her paint for a richer colour when Mr Harper entered the room; he'd been knocking on the door with no response. Managing a smile, Isabelle moved away from the easel to greet her father.

'My darling girl, George Hoskins has asked for your hand in marriage,' Mr Harper announced proudly.

Isabelle stood silently, as her worst fears had been confirmed. Mr Harper became emotional and strove to protect his daughter from a relationship that she would regret. Her father embraced her.

'I love you, Father,' Isabelle said with warmth.

'There's no need to upset your mother by mentioning Jimmy. You and I will not converse on the matter again.'

Chapter 6

Isabelle sat in a majestic wicker chair looking a picture of elegance and refinement. Mr and Mrs Harper were pleased with the attention George displayed to Isabelle as a young lady engaged to be married.

'We welcome you as our future son-in-law and look forward to a splendid spring wedding,' Mrs Harper said joyfully.

'I too look forward to the day,' George replied, admiring his beautiful bride-to-be.

Mr Harper frowned disapprovingly at Lorna as she served a second glass of gin to Mrs Harper. Being fearful that his wife's eloquence could be on the decline, Mr Harper looked at his watch and signalled for Lorna to approach.

'Why isn't Cummings on duty?' Mr Harper enquired.

'Mr Cummings is ill, sir,' Lorna explained. She performed a little curtsy before making her exit.

After glancing at the gathering clouds, Mr Harper turned to Isabelle and George.

'If you're going to ride, I'd keep an eye on the weather,' he advised. 'Can I interest you in a game of billiards this evening, sir?'

'If the glint in your eye is any indication, I'd better have my wits about me,' Mr Harper answered.

~

The sound of thundering hooves in gallop stirred the blood as Isabelle and George rode across the field. They could hear the Celtic drums which reminded Isabelle of the extraordinary time she had spent on the river.

Jimmy and the gypsy boys appeared through the mist, paddling to the rhythmic beat of the drums. After being mesmerised by the erotic ritual, Isabelle felt distanced from George and the life he represented. Sensing his momentary loss, he smiled reassuringly. He took her horse by the reigns and walked her away from the river.

'I love you with every fibre of my being. I promise to make you happy,' George reassured her.

~

Isabelle looked tirelessly through the sheaths of flowers that celebrated her engagement, in search of a note of congratulations from Vicar Charles Durn. After finding the card, she quietly sat by the window. She longed for Charles to be so jealous of her fiancé that his desire to be with her would urge him into her welcoming arms.

'A penny for your thoughts, miss,' Elsie commented as she entered the room with more congratulatory gifts.

'Did you have a long engagement?' Isabelle asked curiously.

'No, miss. My parents couldn't afford much but I was blissfully happy and in love all the same. I must say Mr and Mrs Harper are the happiest I've seen them in years,' Elsie exclaimed, as she organised vases for the spectacular displays of flowers.

'I'm pleased to be the one bringing them joy,' Isabelle replied wistfully.

Painting at the easel by the river, Isabelle had chosen a well secluded hideaway, with the knowledge that Charles Durn would at some stage appear down the path, on his way to discuss future lessons with her father. She'd be inconsolable if the opportunity to see Charles had been lost. Her obsessive thoughts were distracted by Jimmy who arrived from across the field playing a hauntingly beautiful tune on the flute.

'I wrote the song for you,' Jimmy greeted her with a loving smile.

'It will play in my mind forever,' Isabelle replied, welcoming his generous spirit. The thought of Charles faded from her mind.

Well hidden by the overgrown trees Jimmy laughed heartily as Isabelle floated in the river fully clothed. He suddenly alerted her to Lorna who had been watching through the tall trees. He signalled to Isabelle and assisted her to climb on board the canoe. Drifting blissfully, an eagle caught their eye; it dived on its prey without mercy as Mother Nature had intended.

~

An easel and paints stood amongst the trees with no sign of Isabelle. An eerie breeze blew softly as Mrs Harper approached, followed by the servant Lorna.

'Isabelle!' Mrs Harper shouted, full of impatience.

'I saw Miss Harper swimming in the river with her clothes on, ma'am,' Lorna said vengefully.

'Thank you. Please return to the manor,' Mrs Harper instructed. She strove to contain her anger while searching for Isabelle to no avail.

Later, the seriousness of the mood in the dining room was apparent. Isabelle sat quietly with Mr and Mrs Harper while Lorna glanced gleefully in Isabelle's direction. Mrs Harper signalled for the servants to leave.

'I've been very patient up to this point, young lady, but I am warning you not to push the boundaries. What do you have to say for yourself?' Mrs Harper questioned.

'I'm sorry,' Isabelle said demurely.

'I should think so. You must take responsibility for your place in society. Believing that you are an artist is no more than an outrageous arrogance!'

Mr Harper banged his fist onto the table, annoyed by Mrs Harper's belittling remark.

'Isabelle's arrogance, as you so quaintly put it, is an expression of her wonderful and extraordinary ability, ma'am,' Mr Harper said as he defended his daughter passionately.

With a stern eye on her husband, she sipped her glass of gin. Mr Harper continued with his dinner and nodded for Isabelle to do the same.

~

Mrs Harper raised her head off the pillow, pleased to see that Lorna had entered her dimly lit room and carefully set up a bottle of gin on the table with a crystal glass from the cabinet. Mrs Harper's usual beauty and elegance seemed to have failed her that evening; a mop of tangled and unruly hair portrayed her tragedy.

'Until further instruction, I will be dining in my room.' Mrs Harper stated firmly.

'Yes, ma'am,' Lorna replied, smiling sweetly as she performed a curtsy.

Mrs Harper stared with muddled thoughts at her lovely wedding photograph hanging on the wall. The happy memory brought a tear to her eye.

Noticing that Lorna had been in the pantry with the flour bags the day before, Elsie waited for the servants to leave the kitchen, then searched diligently. She moved the heavy flour bags aside and delighted in finding Jimmy's signed artwork that had gone missing.

Isabelle was relaxing in a warm bath gazing at the extraordinary collection of birthday cards and gift-wrapped boxes displayed on the table. Her thoughts were of Charles and when her next music lesson would be. Elsie entered, carrying a spectacular bunch of pink roses.

'Reverend Durn delivered the roses for your birthday.'

'Is he downstairs?' Isabelle enquired, flushed with heartfelt joy.

'No, miss. Reverend Harris and Reverend Durn were running late for church.'

Isabelle was disappointed, but also curious as to why Elsie had locked the door. Her maid pulled Jimmy's paintings from her skirt pocket. The knowledge that his art had been returned and safe in her possession, cheered Isabelle.

'Thank you,' she rejoiced.

'Find a good hiding place. That girl should be dismissed.'

After putting on a glamorous new dress, Isabelle climbed onto a chair and hid the paintings in a suitcase on top of the wardrobe. Locking the case, she jumped off the chair and hid the key in her dressing table drawer. She saw Charles through the window leaving the manor; his presence meant that her father had sent for him and had approved the continuation of her lessons. She rummaged through her sheets of music in preparation. As Isabelle concluded the sonata on violin, her emotional playing moved Elsie to tears.

A dozen red roses and another gift arrived; Isabelle impatiently opened the box. She struggled to fasten the clip of a pretty diamond necklace, so Elsie hurried to assist.

'Your fiancé is a generous gentleman, miss,' Elsie complimented as she admired the jewellery.

'Yes, he is,' Isabelle replied. She knew how much easier life would be if she loved George Hoskins.

Isabelle admired the colourful vicarage garden as she arrived for her lesson. She'd paid a great deal of attention to her alluring appearance; her stylishly groomed hair was threaded with the occasional wildflower that matched an elegant straw hat for shade.

'Thank you for the roses,' Isabelle said gratefully.

'Sweet sixteen,' Charles replied with a wistful smile.

Isabelle and Charles remained on a professional level during her lesson, but as they said a fond farewell in the garden, he found the courage to look into her violet blue eyes and be vulnerable to a glorious silence between them. A temptress stood before him, possessing a smile so sweet and skin so fair that her rosy cheeks glowed pink in the morning sunlight.

'I pray that my lessons continue next year as my fiancé may not approve,' Isabelle advised, bringing Charles's attention to her engagement, hoping to make him jealous.

'Congratulations, Isabelle. How remiss of me not to mention such a happy occasion. I'm afraid your music held me spellbound for a time.'

'Thank you,' Isabelle said pleasurably.

'I couldn't imagine a life without music, for that would be no life at all,' Charles remarked.

Young William had been waiting in the garden with his violin. He took a jealous lover's stance as Charles gently caressed Isabelle's cheek.

'Are you walking with me today?' William said, in a serious tone of voice for a twelve-year-old.

'Yes,' Isabelle replied.

'Surprise me with your choice of Beethoven for next week,' Charles suggested.

Sarah entered the garden just in time to see Isabelle blowing farewell kisses to Charles as she walked down the road with William.

'You look tired, Charles. The students are taking up too much of your time. Surly there's another teacher in the village,' Sarah encouraged, wanting to spend more time with him.

'I'd have chosen music as a career if it wasn't for my father,' Charles said.

'You never mentioned that before,' Sarah replied, surprised by his change of mood.

'Maybe you weren't listening,' he remarked quietly.

William played Offenbach's Can-Can music on the violin as Isabelle danced her version in the woods. She lifted her skirt and kicked her legs high into the air, dancing herself into a frenzied state. William stopped playing when Isabelle collapsed into the grass laughing heartily.

'Where did you learn to dance?' William asked, bewildered by the performance.

'Paris! Even the Parisians are shocked by the depraved Can-Can.'

A steam train travelled by, Isabelle snatched her violin from the grass and chased the train.

'I'll see you in Paris!' Isabelle teased as she ran after the train, vanishing through the trees.

'Isabelle!' William called anxiously, after following her and searching through the woods to no avail. He was beginning to wonder if she'd caught the train. Suddenly, and without warning, she appeared from behind a tree.

'Very funny, Isabelle,' William chastised in a startled state. His sulky mood amused her and they continued their journey in silence.

The thought of Charles being foremost on Isabelle's mind when Elsie struggled through the door holding dozens of red roses; for a fleeting moment she believed they were from him.

'Your fiancé, George Hoskins, is your guest at dinner this evening,' Elsie clarified earnestly.

'Who sent the roses?' Isabelle enquired eagerly.

'Your fiancé, I presume. Mrs Harper gave no other instructions,' Elsie replied, a little bewildered by the question. Isabelle smiled, but the disappointment showed on her face.

'Always remember that a kind and thoughtful gentleman is a reliable one. Romantic ideals may let you down.'

'Thank you for your wise words,' Isabelle replied wistfully.

She saw Jimmy and the boys through the window when they appeared on the river in their canoes. Elsie strove to intervene, but Isabelle quickly changed into her riding clothes.

'Mrs Harper has advised a quiet afternoon.'

'To ride my horse will be good for the soul,' Isabelle insisted.

Resisting the temptation to visit the vicarage—as Isabelle felt so compelled to do—she found pleasure in riding her horse across the field to the river. The water was just too inviting, so she removed her riding boots and waded into the river while Tiger grazed contentedly. She heard the sound of the Celtic drum beating amidst boisterous cheers of joy; Jimmy and the gypsy boys appeared around the river bend, taking part in a competitive boat race.

'Come on, Jimmy!' Isabelle shouted as they passed her in first place.

Isabelle squealed jubilantly as she waded to Jimmy's canoe and congratulated him on a triumphant win. William and Peter had been observing the event from their rowing boat, well secluded by the overgrown trees. They'd noticed Lorna observing Isabelle's fiancé George Hoskins as he appeared through the trees and that brought a smirk to her disgruntled face.

'The witch,' William warned.

Peter grabbed the oars and rowed hastily from her view. After Isabelle had farewelled Jimmy and stepped onto the riverbank with her riding skirt dripping with water, she strove to hide her look of astonishment when her fiancé George appeared, holding Tiger by the reigns. Having no place to hide, she stood tall, relieved that her father had not accompanied him.

'Good afternoon, Miss Harper,' George greeted with a slight edge to his voice as he tipped his hat politely.

'Please excuse me, Mr Hoskins, I didn't expect you this early.'

'To change the spirited young lady who I fell in love with would be foolish, and there'd be little to gain. In fact, the very idea is preposterous.'

Concerned that George may mention the adventure to her father, she felt the need to appeal to his good nature.

'Discretion is one of the great virtues in a gentleman and for those who possess such a fine quality, I cherish their gift,' Isabelle praised, hoping that flattery would be enough to silence him.

George dismounted to assist Isabelle, who strove to pull on her tight boots.

'The matter at the river has been erased from my mind,' George reassured her, stepping into an intimate position to pull hard on the boots.

'We're creating a scandal,' Isabelle teased.

'I'd like to throw caution to the wind and kiss you, but I'll refrain from doing so as your father may appear at any moment and chastise me for failing to deliver you on time and present you at dinner. Kindly let us ride before I change my mind,' George said, assisting Isabelle to mount her horse.

As Elsie sprinkled rose petals into the bath water, Isabelle wondered what it would be like to kiss George. She had only imagined kissing Charles.

'You were right to take an afternoon ride. Your cheeks are positively glowing, miss. Although, I must say, the surprise of seeing such a handsome couple without a chaperone is a little disconcerting,' Elsie remarked, criticising George's lack of tradition.

'Don't judge too harshly. Mr Hoskins may have had a valid reason for doing so,' Isabelle defended.

Chapter 7

George Hoskins looked handsome in his stylish black tails. The altered vision of Isabelle quite startled him as she appeared in a magnificent rose-coloured evening gown; the girl he had seen with the gypsies had been transformed.

Mr and Mrs Harper were enchanted by their matchmaking with Isabelle and George. After flashing her exquisite diamond engagement ring, Isabelle appreciated her mother's warm smile, pleased to be the one bringing her such joy.

However, she became distracted by Charles. Isabelle smiled demurely as Charles faltered in conversation with a guest and then returned a generous smile. But she must distance herself from the man of her dreams. The look from Sarah had been barely tolerable and Reverend Harris only greeted her with a nod of the head followed by a steely glance. Isabelle certainly needed George as an ally so that he wouldn't mention the river.

Mr Harper instructed the guests to stand and raise their glasses, while Isabelle smiled pleasurably.

'To the happy couple, Isabelle and George,' Mr Harper announced proudly.

~

Isabelle practised Beethoven's Moonlight Sonata on the piano as a surprise for Charles. Her lesson was after lunch, but she'd dressed early. She looked a picture of fashion when Mrs Harper entered, grim faced, and waited for Isabelle to conclude the piece.

'Your father has been to see the vicar, Charles Durn, early this morning to cancel your music lessons until further notice. Also, you're confined to the manor as you need time to consider your behaviour,' Mrs Harper said firmly as she closed the door behind her.

Believing that George had betrayed her, Isabelle fell into the depths of despair. The loss of her beloved Charles and the music that they shared so beautifully was more than she could endure. She tried to practice without success. Watching a steam train travelling through a far-off meadow calmed her;

she imagined herself on board the train arriving in a faraway place. Elsie entered, interrupting her thoughts with more roses.

'Sorry if I startled you, miss,' Elsie remarked, observing Isabelle's mood.

'I find my thoughts comforting,' Isabelle replied, looking at the roses with disdain.

'Don't worry. You'll forget all about the upsetting times once you're happily married,' Elsie reassured her kindly.

'I may have changed my mind about marrying Mr Hoskins.'

Worried by the depths of darkness that Isabelle portrayed, Elsie prepared a bath.

'There's nothing like relaxing in warm water to take your cares away,' Elsie insisted with a smile.

~

Isabelle mixed oils at the easel in her room with a renewed enthusiasm. She had noticed Jimmy and the boys near the river. Surprised by Isabelle's pleasure at seeing the gypsies, Elsie observed her with serious concern.

'Keep away from those heathens. They practice witchcraft in the night.'

'You may find that to be a myth handed down through the ages.'

'No, miss! People have disappeared in the woods, believed to have been boiled alive. Their screams were heard in the night,' Elsie insisted.

'Your imaginings have surpassed mine, I can assure you,' Isabelle declared, with a hearty laugh.

'Well, at least you're laughing and that has been a rare occurrence of late,' she remarked fondly.

Isabelle snatched her hat off the dressing table and hurried out of the door.

'Miss, I'll be dismissed!' Elsie warned.

'Be an angel and cover for me,' Isabelle pleaded.

Tempted to sleep under the stars and wake up with the sunrise, Isabelle embraced a wonderful sense of freedom while resting under the oak tree—a home that she could call her own. After hearing the flute, she looked for Jimmy and waved keenly to attract his attention. He ran to greet her, out of breath when he arrived.

'I've missed your beautiful spirit in the field,' Jimmy said, looking wistfully into her violet blue eyes.

'Sadly, my punishment continues. But I'll be free one day soon to join you on the river, my dearest friend, for I miss you too.'

Relaxing peacefully in the afternoon breeze, their blissful thoughts found a place to dream; Jimmy alerted her as a remarkable sunset appeared through the trees. Realising the late hour, he escorted her to a secluded path near the overgrown river, well hidden from accusing eyes.

~

Dozing in a chair near the window, Elsie woke as Isabelle entered the room with caution.

'Thank God, miss! I've said that you've been unwell and suggested dining in your room.'

'Thank you.'

'Mr Harper dismissed Lorna for serving a bottle of gin to Mrs Harper without the butler's permission. Mrs Harper screamed abuse at your poor father, defending that gypsy who reported you at the river and stole your paintings. Screaming like a woman possessed, your mother demanded that Lorna be reinstated. I'm afraid your father gave in under extreme duress, miss,' Elsie advised in a whisper.

'How remiss of me to think it was George Hoskins who betrayed me,' Isabelle answered with a melancholy tone to her voice.

Shaded by the trees amongst the wildflowers, Isabelle looked across the table at lunch and wondered about her marriage to George, questioning if she loved him at all—certainly not in the same way that she loved Charles, but she did find him likeable and felt protected in his presence. She imagined his physique to be like Michelangelo, tall in stature with well-groomed dark hair. The sun filtered through the leaves causing him to squint a little; his kind face appealed to her as she observed him more closely. Once married, the enjoyment of travel and the theatre awaited her, and, more importantly, no punishment would be endured after spending a wonderful time on the river—a serious consideration indeed.

'You're quiet,' George remarked as he lowered his newspaper, The London Times.

'Marry me! Marry me now!' Isabelle declared impulsively with a smile. Astounded and flattered by the offer, George took her gently by the hand.

'If only the decision were mine, my darling. Your father has arranged a spring wedding, a good nine months away. However, I believe that somewhere in the world an engaged couple would be allowed to kiss.'

He escorted Isabelle behind a tree, where she made no objection to such a lovely long kiss.

'Thank you for such a glorious kiss,' George praised.

'We could make a habit of kissing if you marry me now.'

'I love you. I'd marry you tomorrow if it were possible.'

Isabelle smiled blissfully, proudly reminiscing about her first kiss.

At dinner that evening, Isabelle and George guarded their secret. Isabelle was wearing a gorgeous pastel-pink, lace evening gown, a favourite with Mrs Harper. She'd also given an eloquent speech about their much-desired wedding next spring, hoping to dismiss the upset at the river so that her music lessons with Charles could continue. George had been loyal, another quality she admired besides his adorable kissing.

Isabelle appreciated her mother's warm smile after she'd played the piano at her father's request.

'A charming sonata,' Mrs Harper complimented.

'Thank you,' Isabelle replied, enjoying her mother's approval.

Mr Harper nodded to the butler Mr Cummings, who served the first glass of gin to Mrs Harper as the grandfather clock chimed nine o'clock.

'My dear George, have you any artists hidden away in the closet? I've already owned up to Mother's estranged cousin,' Mr Harper remarked in a goading fashion.

'No, sir, I can't say that we have. Although I did have a great aunt who ran away to become an opera singer in Italy,' George replied.

'My darling, how I adore to hear dark family secrets,' Isabelle teased.

'I'm afraid we have a family of landowners and lawyers, dull and unimaginative,' George replied, amused by her mischief.

She caught her mother's cold stare and quickly regained her demure composure.

'My dear chap, I feel the need to restore my reputation as a billiards player,' Mr Harper insisted, happy to see his family harmonious again.

~

Isabelle observed Jimmy and the gypsy boys from her window; they entered the field as the moon appeared from behind the clouds. She wondered about Elsie's warnings but the thought of her dear friend brought a smile to her lips. She closed the window and climbed into her soft, warm bed. Isabelle had fallen asleep before she'd finished her prayers.

The woods were plunged into darkness that night after the moon disappeared from view. After searching for Jimmy in a distressed state, not able to accept his rejection, Lorna found him by the smouldering campfire with the gypsy boys. She lay down quietly beside him.

'Go away!' Jimmy demanded harshly.

Scrambling to her feet and running through the woods until she reached the river, Lorna dragged a wooden box from a rotting log and lifted the lid. Inside there was a voodoo doll in the image of Isabelle. She began jabbing at the doll with an altered mind. The ritual drove her into a frenzied state. Jimmy heard her manic chant echoing through the woods. He knew the pagan ritual and what it represented. Leaping to his feet, he sprinted through the trees as her chanting reached a crescendo of deranged madness. Jimmy snatched the doll from Lorna's hand to protect Isabelle from the curse. As Lorna fought ferociously, he shoved her to the ground and threw the doll into the river. Struggling to her feet, she surged forward into the water, but he dragged her to the riverbank as the doll disappeared from view.

~

Waking to the rain pelting against the window, Isabelle pulled the bedclothes around her. She was a little disappointed as George would have left in the early hours with her father. She had enjoyed his adorable kiss and wondered when there might be another. She saw breakfast on a tray beside her. Elsie turned around from preparing Isabelle's bath to notice her bewildered look.

'Mrs Harper's instructions, miss. Now that you're engaged to be married, breakfast in bed is one of the privileges.'

'How decadent and lovely,' Isabelle replied, pleased that her mother appeared to have forgiven her.

'Good morning, my darling girl,' Mrs Harper greeted as she entered with a flourish.

'Your new dress becomes you, Mother,' Isabelle flattered as Mrs Harper looked approvingly at Isabelle's unfinished painting of daffodils in the field.

'I can see why George is impressed by your art, so keep up the good work. As your behaviour is much improved, we've decided that your music lessons can resume,' she said agreeably.

'Thank you, Mother,' Isabelle replied as Mrs Harper made a graceful exit.

Deliriously happy and struggling to catch her breath, Isabelle impatiently took her violin from its case.

'You'll be pleased to know that Lorna will no longer wait at your table and her duties have been restricted,' Elsie advised in a whisper.

'Thank goodness,' Isabelle answered in a vague manner. Her thoughts were on far more important matters.

~

Arriving early for her music lesson, Isabelle entered through the gate and Charles approached to welcome her. Flushed, she looked into his sensitive blue eyes and felt the need to fall into his manly arms and kiss him passionately.

'I've dreamt this moment over and over until sleep intervened,' Isabelle said with a smile.

Charles failed to hide his emotion. He looked into her eyes with love in his heart and struggled to blink away a tear.

'Before we enter the vicarage, there's a matter I need to make clear. I'm a vicar and must honour my marriage vows in the name of God, but you take my heart, dear Isabelle. George Hoskins is a good man and he can offer you a better life.'

'You say that, Charles, but you have tears running down your cheeks. Please, let me take care of you, just this one time,' Isabelle pleaded as she wiped away his tears.

Charles was humbled by Isabelle's brilliant, emotional rendition of Beethoven's Moonlight Sonata on piano. Passion stirred through his veins. As Isabelle concluded the piece, Charles gazed at the young lady whose beauty transcended him beyond his wildest expectation. She kissed him gently on the lips. Charles, being powerless to withdraw; her lovely temptation had overwhelmed him to the very brim of desire.

'I love you, my darling,' Isabelle whispered as she prepared to leave.

'I love you too,' Charles replied quietly.

After he'd closed the door behind her, Charles stood alone in the empty room with a desolate despair haunting him in the silence as a glaring responsibility of right and wrong remained. He watched William gazing endearingly at Isabelle as she passed through the gate.

'William! You're late!' Charles shouted through the window, reprimanding the boy.

'I'm sorry, sir,' William replied, a little embarrassed that he'd drawn attention to his infatuation with Isabelle.

~

She believed that God had altered the universe to a heavenly place. Her rejoicing heart faltered a little as George Hoskins approached her in the field.

'I'm not keeping an eye on you, I promise.'

'I esteem your good intention and will happily walk with you. Please take my arm while we enjoy the silence of the afternoon without chatter cluttering our treasured thoughts.'

'As you wish, my darling,' George answered. He looked seriously into Isabelle's violet blue eyes to remind her how deeply he cared. She smiled sweetly, thankful for his loyalty.

'My plan to dine alone has altered. I will join you for dinner,' Isabelle declared kindly.

'Your father informed me that Shakespeare's Hamlet is a favourite with you.'

'Oh yes, how I would love to see that play performed!'

'Then you'd better be ready within the hour. We'll dine in London before the theatre,' George informed her.

Isabelle squealed with joy and embraced him affectionately.

After a long journey by car to London followed by exquisite dining and a debut attendance at the Old Vic Theatre; George escorted Isabelle through a glamorous audience waiting in the foyer, with Mr and Mrs Harper as their chaperone. Isabelle turned a few heads as she paraded through the crowd in a fashionable evening gown. While being ushered to their seats Isabelle found herself in awe of the theatre that she'd read about in books.

As the lights faded and the orchestra played the overture, a plush velvet curtain rose slowly to expose a stage of make-believe. Being familiar with

Ophelia's dialogue and wishing she was the actress playing the part, George noticed Isabelle shedding tears of sorrow for her favourite character.

Back in Devon the next day—even after such a heavenly evening at the theatre with George—Isabelle's thoughts turned to Charles. It occurred to her that he had not been cared for as he should have been. The expression of his musical artistry needed nurturing with a delicate understanding and love. After all, two people so far removed yet entwined in each other's arms, must be living in the loneliest place on earth. Elsie interrupted her thoughts, staggering into the room with more roses.

'Your fiancé Mr Hoskins is a prince amongst men,' Elsie congratulated.

'He is indeed. I thank George with all my heart for introducing me to the theatre,' Isabelle replied.

'We've had plenty of drama downstairs with Mrs Harper ill this morning. Mr Harper blamed Lorna for the bottle of gin he found in his wife's room,' Elsie informed quietly.

Isabelle dismissed the matter from her mind. She browsed through a copy of Hamlet, inspired by the role of Ophelia and the actress who played her.

George had been so intrigued by her portrayal, and she hoped they may be acquainted. A career in the theatre may not be impossible with George. After the serving of morning tea, Elsie opened the curtains, noticing the gypsies riding bareback.

'Those gypsies are in the field,' Elsie remarked with disdain.'

Isabelle's blissful memories of life on the river had been haunting her, and she prayed that Jimmy would forgive her for staying away. To be seen on the river meant isolation from Charles; armed with the knowledge that he loved her, she couldn't take that chance.

Chapter 8

A strained atmosphere had taken command of the room as the despairing Sarah waited patiently. A carefully chosen gown that flattered her figure and complexion had not been noticed. She felt estranged from Charles; he continued to play the piano with passion, unaware of her presence.

'Charles!' Sarah announced, striving to disguise her agitated state as he continued to play.

'Shall I re-heat, ma'am?' the butler Hargraves enquired politely.

'Certainly not,' Sarah replied.

Suddenly, Charles concluded the piece and rose from the piano stool looking suave and elegant in his fashionable tails—yet, he had the look of a troubled man.

'I'm sorry. How remiss of me. I do beg your pardon,' Charles apologised as he joined Sarah at the table.

After they'd dined in silence, he prayed for the courage to speak his mind, but failed to find the words.

'Would a holiday in London appeal to you?' Charles enquired.

'Yes, my darling,' Sarah replied, pleased by his suggestion.

'My work in the parish makes a holiday impossible at this time of the year so I wouldn't be able to join you.'

Sarah tried not to show her devastation; she needed to protect her marriage.

'I'll certainly give the matter some thought. Please forgive me, I need to retire early as I have a headache.'

Charles stood courteously as she left the table.

'I'm sure you'll feel better in the morning. I won't disturb you. I'll sleep in the study.'

Charles sat in the garden, looking dishevelled after a night drinking whisky in the study. Dawn appeared over the meadow, and the butler Hargraves approached and set up coffee on the garden table. Distracted by a glimpse of Sarah watching him through the window, reminded Charles how serious the repercussions would be if he faltered on the decision that he was in two minds to make.

'I would suggest strong coffee this morning, Reverend Durn,' Hargraves remarked kindly.

'Thank you,' Charles replied, trying not to appear intoxicated.

Sarah dressed for travelling, wiped away her tears, snatched her clothes from the wardrobe and threw them into a suitcase. Charles entered, looking bedraggled, still dressed in his black tails from the night before. Shocked to see her packing, he closed the lid and placed his foot firmly onto the case. Charles had made a decision with sadness in his heart.

'Please, Sarah, everything will be all right. I promise.'

Relieved that her marriage had survived the crises she embraced Charles affectionately; after he had removed her hat and unbuttoned her coat.

Isabelle arrived early at the vicarage and noticed that the gypsy children were not playing in the garden. The front door being ajar, she entered quietly and walked down the hall to the music room.

Flushed and impatient, waiting for her beloved Charles, she prepared the music for the violin and tinkled the notes on the piano. As the clock chimed ten o'clock, she felt bewildered by Charles's late arrival. She heard a door closing upstairs, but there were no servants available to question, so she decided to investigate. Isabelle approached the closed door at the top of the stairs and peeped through the keyhole. The sight of Charles and Sarah in a state of undress, entwined in each other's arms, took her breath away. The man of her dreams had betrayed her. She ran down the stairs and out through the front door with tears spilling down her cheeks.

Isabelle collapsed under the oak tree shedding tears of despair and wondering how she would make it through the day. She had believed that Charles truly loved her; what had happened to alter his affections? The morning was long and tearful but the appearance of Jimmy slowly altered her anguished state and the loss became a little easier to endure. As they lay in the grass, Jimmy picked wildflowers and threaded them through her hair.

Drifting down river in his canoe Isabelle felt blessed to have such a wonderful friend. Intrigued by the medieval appearance of the twisted roots through the hovering mist, the black ravens swooped, making her a little nervous as Jimmy dozed in the bottom of the boat. Suddenly, George Hoskins stepped quietly through the trees. Isabelle gasped with fright; she stood in the boat and managed to maintain her balance.

'You've been sent on an errand to find me, I presume?'

'I have indeed, and I dare not return empty handed,' he replied.

'In that case I'll bid you farewell, my friend,' Isabelle announced to Jimmy as she secretly squeezed his hand. She climbed onto the riverbank where George kindly assisted her.

That evening she sat down to a formal family dinner in a glorious evening gown; a smile of pretence assisted in disguising her dark thoughts of Charles. Her affection for George, who had expressed his love and loyalty, was the only reason that she had not dined alone in her room. Mr and Mrs Harper appeared to be in good spirits and were overjoyed by the keen attention that her fiancé had displayed. George knew that he should always be prepared for the unexpected with Isabelle. He had not asked for an explanation about the gypsy boy in the canoe because he trusted her and had acknowledged that she did not discriminate. George admired her revolutionary thoughts on society. He loved Isabelle with all his heart, but knew she may be treading a dangerous path. He prayed to God that he'd be there to protect her.

Dinner concluded with the usual polite conversation, although Mr Harper had noticed Mrs Harper's altered ambiance. He realised that more than one glass of gin had been consumed for the evening.

'My dear George, can I interest you in a game of billiards?' Mr Harper asked as he signalled the butler Cummings.

'My good chap, I happily accept your offer.'

'Cummings, the ladies are a little tired so Mr Hoskins and I will be having drinks in the billiards room,' Mr Harper informed.

'Yes, sir.'

'I'll escort Mother to her room,' Isabelle offered kindly, observing her father's anxious state.

'My dearest girl, thank you.'

'Goodnight, my darling Isabelle,' George whispered.

~

Morning sunshine filled the room as Elsie puffed up Isabelle's pillows and presented a delicious breakfast in bed.

'A pot of coffee is there for the tasting, introduced by Mr Hoskins I believe.'

Isabelle relished the taste.

'In the future, my preference is coffee over tea. Thank you.'

Elsie was assisting Isabelle into a fashionable frock and grooming her hair into an elegant style when a bell rang from downstairs.

'No rest for the wicked,' Elsie exclaimed as she left the room.

Isabelle set up her easel at the open window to add the finishing touches to her painting. While she sat pondering the artwork, Elsie returned with red roses and a violin.

'The flowers are from Mr Hoskins and Reverend Durn has returned the violin that you left at the vicarage yesterday.'

'Reverend Durn is here?'

'He was, miss. But I should think that he's left by now,' Elsie advised while arranging the flowers.

Isabelle looked through the window and saw Charles in the field. She snatched her hat and hurried from the room before Elsie noticed. She sprinted across the field, following Charles into the woods. With the light barely filtering through the leaves, she approached him gasping for breath.

'Please, Charles. Talk to me. I know you love me,' Isabelle pleaded as she choked on her tears.

He embraced her warmly which had a calming effect on her emotional state.

'Yes, I love you. The sensual passion that flows through your veins and the beauty of your imaginings will bewitch me forever. But I am a vicar, and I must follow my faith. You are a young lady with your entire life before you and it is because I love you that I must set you free to be the glorious woman that I know you will be,' Charles explained, as he strove to hide his heart-felt emotion.

'No man will ever love me as you do, Charles.'

'That is true, but he will love you,' Charles reassured her. He cleared his throat and turned his head away to hide his tears.

'I'll take a walk with you if I may?' Isabelle gently took his hand.

'Mr Harper is keen for you to study in Europe, so you're to attend the master classes in Paris.'

Isabelle stood with her faculties slightly altered but felt obliged to lack the excitement that she truly felt. She had always imagined herself in Paris but to actually study there was a dream come true.

Charles had sensed the change in her ambiance that should have been a relief, but he felt disappointed; her absence would mean loneliness for him.

'I'll write every week to hear how you're progressing,' Charles told her.

'I promise to write every day. When I return, you'll be so sublimely seduced by my music that even God will be bewitched and unable to save you,' Isabelle replied with conviction.

'I don't believe he will,' Charles answered sadly.

Chapter 9

Isabelle returned to the palatial Hotel Ritz in Paris. Mr Harper had taken three suites there—one for himself, one for Isabelle, and one for her maid Elsie who had travelled with them—since November.

Filled to the brim with joy, Isabelle entered the room with a flourish. Her violin recital had been met with high esteem at the Paris Conservatorium of Music. Elsie looked up from reading her book, surprised by Isabelle's flushed pink cheeks.

'Well, young lady, I can see by the look on your gorgeous face that all has been successful. Congratulations!'

'I played like a woman possessed. I even surprised myself by the level that I aspired to,' Isabelle said rapturously. She sat at her desk to write letters to Charles and George.

'I will post Mr Hoskin's letter with Mr Harper's mail,' Elsie clarified. 'Reverend Durn must also be kept informed of my progress.'

'After the marriage you can travel to Paris whenever the fancy takes you,' Elsie remarked, enjoying every moment of the adventure but trying to distract Isabelle from thoughts of the vicar.

'My dear Elsie, you're as bad as I am. You'll be running off with a debonair Frenchman if I don't keep an eye on you!' Isabelle teased.

Mr Harper appeared in the doorway in his stylish dark suit.

'My darling girl, we're to meet Count Flaubert for lunch downstairs. It's frightfully bad form to be late.'

Isabelle and Mr Harper were escorted across the exquisite dining room. Count Flaubert stood courteously; Isabelle sat elegantly as the waiter assisted with her chair. Her stylish pink dress enhanced her feminine beauty. The count, clearly bewitched by her charm, announced an invitation to the opera that evening which Mr Harper accepted on their behalf.

'I've heard on the best authority that you gave a virtuoso performance at the recital this morning. Very few young ladies are blessed with beauty and the talent of a fine artist,' Count Flaubert said with a smile.

'Thank you. I believe you also studied at the Paris Conservatorium?'

'I did indeed, but I'm not what you'd call a gifted musician. I love music and it's been at the centre of my life, as your father would know. We played in the orchestra at Cambridge...or hasn't he mentioned his dark past?'

'I've also heard stories about your brief theatrical career.'

'My darling girl, whatever you do, please don't mention Richard III,' Mr Harper remarked.

'A promising career almost ended abruptly, when on stage halfway through a soliloquy, no familiar words of Shakespeare came to mind. The terrifying silence was disturbed by a member of the audience who shouted the next line from the dress circle,' Count Flaubert humbly confessed.

Isabelle and Mr Harper laughed heartily as the waiter served the main course. The heavenly taste of lobster silenced Isabelle, but she did manage a coquettish smile at Count Flaubert when Mr Harper was distracted by the waiter. The count's blond hair and debonair looks reminded her of Charles. Studying his sensitive green eyes, she decided that he appealed to her.

'Our last meeting at Granny Harper's funeral was a very sad occasion. I believe she'd be very proud to know that her granddaughter had blossomed into such a beautiful young lady,' the count announced.

'Your flattery is indeed too much, Count Flaubert. I'm an artist and a gypsy at heart,' Isabelle smiled.

'I'm very happy to meet a fellow traveller. My art inspires me to lift my head off the pillow every morning. My wife has keen competition. She finds it difficult to distract me from my painting,' Count Flaubert confessed.

Isabelle managed a smile but felt disappointment after hearing about the countess.

~

After morning class at the Paris Conservatorium, Isabelle decided that a walk down the boulevard would be an adventure not to be missed. She loved discovering the struggling artists with their easels set up down the narrow side street, accompanied by the musicians playing their compositions. They looked fortunate to be doing what they really loved, and their tattered clothes and well-worn shoes were of no consequence. The faces passing in the street captured Isabelle's attention; she observed an entire compilation of expressions. She was intrigued by the French people with their different customs and warm expressions. She found them forever stimulating, and thought they must have an underlying edge to their characters. After all, they went into battle for a democracy and won.

Mr Harper interrupted Isabelle's thoughts as he arrived at her favourite café, a daily ritual for morning tea. A heavily moustached waiter attended to their needs with the usual freshly baked croissants and coffee. She gladly inhaled the aroma as he poured.

In silent rapture Isabelle studied the artists, writers and musicians with such passion. She tried to appear composed while being transported to the place where they dwelled. A splendid morning ritual that she prayed would never end.

'I'm so bewitched that I'm happy to surrender my soul. If I don't wake up tomorrow, I have lived the dream today,' Isabelle announced.

Mr Harper smiled and joined Isabelle in her study of the faces in the street. When the artist in front of them completed his sketch, Mr Harper nodded his approval and sipped his coffee, deep in thought.

'When you're my age my darling, you will remember Paris with love in your heart; although Mother-England will be held in high esteem for her unwavering loyalty, and you'll be thankful for the remarkable life she bestowed upon us.'

Isabelle observed her father admiringly from under a new rose-coloured hat.

'Thank you for your wise words. I'm so blessed to have such a wonderful father,' Isabelle replied.

'Good girl. Let's have a brisk walk along the river, that should put us right,' Mr Harper suggested with a jolly laugh as he took another bite of his delicious croissant.

~

As an avid art collector, the late Granny Harper had spent a great deal of time in Paris where she became close friends with Count Flaubert's family. Isabelle expressed her joy at seeing her father's boyhood friendship rekindled. In high spirits, they arrived at the Paris Opera House to be greeted by the count and countess, a handsome couple who complimented Isabelle on her evening gown, a gift from her father. Isabelle managed to disguise her disappointment—she had not expected to see the countess. However, when the curtain rose and the overture commenced, Bizet's opera The Pearl Fishers dismissed any unhappy thoughts.

An enchanting supper at the Ritz Hotel had a calming effect on Isabelle after such a thrilling evening. The stimulating conversation with close friends of the family showed positive signs that their stay may be extended, and she had warmed to the countess after being praised for her splendid performance at the recital.

The next day she looked through the window at her beloved Paris. Her thoughts had been stirred by a letter that she'd received from her mother which lay a weighty blame on Isabelle for keeping her parents apart. Mrs Harper complimented Isabelle's good work at the Paris Conservatorium, but then explained how much joy the marriage to Mr Hoskins would bring to her. Concerned that her mother may end her stay in Paris—and that her freedom could be lost forever when Mrs Harper's wishes were granted and she married George—Isabelle knew that her wits and imagination must be applied.

Elsie entered the room with the usual red roses and a letter in her hand.

'Flowers from Mr Hoskins.'

'Thank you,' Isabelle replied, as she tied the bow of a stylish lemon hat to complete her latest Chanel outfit.

'You have a generous father indeed. I'm sure you'll turn a few heads in that dress.'

'Tell Father I'll meet him for morning tea at the usual café,' Isabelle clarified.

'You're early this morning,' Elsie said as she observed the grandfather clock in the corner of the room.

'I have an early class.'

'Very good, miss.'

The light mist began to clear as the doorman hailed a cab outside the foyer of the hotel and opened the door for Isabelle to step into the car.

'The Moulin Rouge, thank you driver,' Isabelle instructed politely. After raising his eyebrows in a surprised manner, the driver continued down the road.

When they arrived, Isabelle paid the driver and he opened the car door courteously.

'Thank you. Take care, mademoiselle. The Moulin Rouge doesn't seem the place for you,' the driver advised in English.

'I cannot leave Paris without seeing the Can-Can performed,' Isabelle insisted.

'You'll have a very long wait, mademoiselle. Would you like me to drive you back to the hotel?' the driver offered, a little concerned.

'I'm right on time, thank you driver,' Isabelle said confidently.

She stepped onto the footpath as a familiar figure appeared through the mist. Count Flaubert's appearance was certainly a surprise. He approached carrying his easel and paints. It was too late to hide, so she stood poised.

'Well, young lady, there's no doubt that you are a fellow traveller. No explanation is necessary, for we are allies.'

'Hello, Count Flaubert,' Isabelle greeted demurely.

I've been commissioned to paint the dancers at a dress rehearsal of the Can-Can. I invite you to attend as my guest.'

'Thank you, Count Flaubert. I've dreamed of this moment all my life…but please don't tell my father,' she implored.

'Your secret is safe with me. You will be introduced as a special guest from the Paris Conservatorium.'

Isabelle attempted to calm her heartfelt joy as the count escorted her to the stage door. She stood beside him in the wings. He had his easel and paints set up and a paintbrush poised—far too serious for any questions or idle chatter. The smell of grease paint appealed to her. The rehearsal pianist, an older gentleman with greying hair and a handlebar moustache, struck the first note of Offenbach's Can-Can. The dancers entered from stage left, in costume, rehearsing with an energetic flare and kicking their legs high into the air. Their perspiration dripped and glistened under the stage lights. Isabelle watched in amazement as the dancers twirled in their bright red flared skirts, showing their ruffled lace petticoats as they kicked their legs gloriously. Isabelle dared to glance in the count's direction and noticed that he had captured the spectacle on canvas.

After the ballet master waved his arms in the air, the music concluded and the dancers took a well-earned rest. Having been so engrossed in the dancing, Isabelle gasped when she looked at her watch. As the count escorted her from the stage door, she noticed that the sun-drenched buildings had emerged from the mist. Count Flaubert hailed a cab for Isabelle.

'Until we meet again, my fellow traveller,' Count Flaubert announced with affection, as he handed her the violin.

'Thank you for the best morning of my life,' she said gratefully.

Isabelle greeted her father at the café, but had to keep her once-in-a-lifetime experience a secret.

'I never dreamed that I'd love Paris so much. I can't understand why Mother won't join us.'

'I also have an affection for Paris, so I'm glad to share this precious time with you, my darling. More importantly, I want to congratulate you on your first term. You have passed with honours,' Mr Harper announced proudly.

'Oh! Such a perfect day, Father.'

She painted the faces in the street while Mr Harper lit a cigar and enjoyed a coffee poured by the waiter with the handlebar moustache. Mr Harper's thoughts were elsewhere.

'Mrs Harper has demanded our immediate return to England, but I've decided to ignore her wishes. George is more than capable of managing the firm,' Mr Harper explained.

'Thank you,' Isabelle replied, kissing her father.

An agreeable month passed, with the usual weekly bouquet of red roses from George and a letter from Charles. One morning Elsie arrived with a glorious bouquet of pink carnations decorated with pink satin bows; there was a card attached.

'Who on earth is sending you flowers? You're almost a married lady!' After opening the envelope Isabelle read the letter silently.

To my dearest fellow traveller,

Please receive my gift to you in appreciation of your delightful company and for the pleasure of assisting in your adventure. I have dedicated the painting "Dancers in Rehearsal" to you. Hoping our paths cross again one day soon.

With love,
A fellow traveller

The words brought a smile to Isabelle's face. Elsie accepted a large canvas wrapped in pink satin from the hotel porter. Isabelle impatiently removed the drape to expose a wonderfully expressive painting of *"Dancers in Rehearsal"* signed by Count Flaubert. She admired the dancers with their overdone makeup, their distorted appearance from the beads of perspiration, and red skirts that twirled into the air.

Overwhelmed by such a lovely gift, Isabelle blinked away a tear.

Chapter 10

Isabelle was diligently practising a Brahms Concerto on the violin, preparing for the next recital with the orchestra, when Elsie entered with two letters and the usual red roses. She stopped playing, a little downhearted after noticing that a bouquet of pink carnations had not been delivered.

'A letter from Mrs Harper and another from Mr Hoskins.'

Isabelle parted the lace curtains to look at her glorious Paris and placed the letters on top of the pile.

'Those letters will be full of stale news by the time you open them. It would be a good idea to read your mother's letter as she may have given you instructions,' Elsie advised.

'I already know what's in her letter.'

'You'll have a wonderful life with Mr Hoskins, I'm sure of it. Please don't upset Mrs Harper before the wedding.'

Isabelle nodded then continued practising while Elsie attended to a knock at the door. Mr Harper entered, looking elegant in his pinstripe suit.

'Can you be ready within the hour?'

'Yes, Father. Where are we going?'

'It's a surprise, but we must be on time,' Mr Harper cautioned.

They walked up an elegant path set amidst beautifully kept lawns with the occasional elm tree swaying to and fro. The setting created a tranquil mood before entering the Claude Monet Museum to begin a journey of artistic genius. Isabelle's wildest imaginings could not have prepared her for the sublime experience that awaited her. Count Flaubert and Mr Harper escorted her into the sanctuary of great art.

She thanked Count Flaubert for her gift—a painting that she'd treasure and adore for the life it represents—and inhaled his charming musk scent when he gently kissed her hand. His caring eyes charmed her as she imagined being held in his arms and gently kissed, but she took great care to be discreet in her imaginings, so as not to upset her father.

The next morning the canoes on the River Seine immediately reminded Isabelle of her dearest friend Jimmy who often appeared in her dreams. She prayed that he would forgive her because she'd left without saying goodbye. She arrived at the café, sat at the usual table and ordered, then waited for Mr Harper to arrive. She was enjoying a sense of achievement since her music studies had progressed so splendidly. Her favourite street artists, Philippe and Pierre, entered the café and greeted Isabelle with a warm smile. Recognising her as an admirer of their work, they sat down with her and helped themselves to the morning tea. Isabelle happily ordered another.

Inspired by an intriguing conversation about art and politics, Isabelle found herself endeared to the passionate ideals that Philippe and Pierre endeavoured to express on canvas. Count Flaubert had quietly pulled up a chair; he observed with absolute dismay the spirited conversation that expressed passion for a glorious France.

'What a pity the French Revolution is over as I'm sure you'd gladly march us to the guillotine,' Count Flaubert remarked.

'Meet my dear friend and great artist, Count Flaubert. Philippe and Pierre are fellow artists.'

Being uncomfortable in the count's presence, they prepared to leave.

'You must guard your generous spirit. I'm jealous of any man who seeks you out,' Count Flaubert said.

'You ask too much,' Isabelle whispered. They sat in silence, longing to touch each other's hands, but resisting.

'I've been informed of your engagement to Mr Hoskins. He's from a respectable family and will make an excellent marriage partner.'

'I'm glad you approve,' she remarked, a little disappointedly.

He embraced the chance to be alone with Isabelle, for even a few minutes would suffice.

'You must remember, my fellow traveller, that our moments together are immortal. Your charming perfume lingers in the wings of the Moulin Rouge.'

'Will you be attending my next recital?' Isabelle enquired, hoping to meet him secretly.

'I was spellbound by your music and the deep passion it stirred within my soul, well before your beauty captured my heart and held me prisoner. My paintings fall into the shadow of other great works, not yet discovered,' Count Flaubert disclosed, humbled by Isabelle's sublime musical talent.

'You are indeed an artist, Count Flaubert. Your cherished gift touched my soul deeply and forever. You have a mind so great in thought that I envy it,' Isabelle praised.

Mr Harper arrived carrying many gift-wrapped boxes and placed them onto the table in front of Isabelle. She expressed her gratitude for the gifts by kissing him on the cheek.

'Thank you, Father.'

'My dear chap, sorry I'm late.' Mr Harper greeted Count Flaubert with a firm hand shake.

'There's no need to apologise. I've been enchantingly entertained.'

Mr Harper reached for the coffee pot.

'I'm afraid you'll have to order another. My earlier guests were very thirsty,' Isabelle said politely.

'Dare I enquire as to who they were?' Mr Harper asked protectively.

'Don't worry. My introduction as Count Flaubert was deterrent enough.'

~

Isabelle woke to the rain pelting against the window. Her stomach churned at the thought of another letter arriving from her mother and prayed it wouldn't be the one to lure her father back to England.

Preparing for her next performance, Isabelle practised for many hours each day. She'd recently learned that a well-known French conductor would be leading the orchestra; her curiosity to know more about this great man persisted.

The month that followed passed quickly. Isabelle's passion grew for her recently acquainted city and a life that she had dreamed about remained hers to embrace. The constant letters from Mrs Harper were being ignored as her father had advised. A bouquet of pink carnations caught her eye amidst the red roses.

'To send an engaged young lady flowers isn't appropriate behaviour,' Elsie remarked sternly.

'Count Flaubert is a great artist and an ally who I would trust with my life,' Isabelle said with conviction, as she smelt the flowers dreamily.

'I do beg your pardon, miss, if I spoke out of turn. As Mrs Harper is not here, whatever I say is only for your own protection,' Elsie explained.

'I understand, and I appreciate your concern,' Isabelle replied.

'I heard your beautiful playing earlier. God has blessed you with a great gift that must be nurtured and looked after. It's a pity your mother hasn't arrived as she promised.'

'Father believes she will attend the concert, but I've dismissed that thought from my mind.'

'You'd pass for a famous movie star in that hat,' Elsie flattered.

'I'm in discussion with the conductor of the orchestra this morning.'

'Your music speaks volumes, miss. The words are of little consequence.'

'I always knew there was more to you than meets the eye, Elsie.'

~

Isabelle had been in awe of the level that she aspired to before her meeting with the conductor Claude Chevalier. He, too, was elated by her virtuoso playing and applauded her along with the orchestra.

'Your music has spoken well for you and I look forward to our next encounter, Mademoiselle Harper. And by the way, I like the hat.'

Mr Chevalier appeared to be a man of few words. He reminded her of Charles, in looks only, and that triggered her memory. She hadn't replied to his last letter of encouragement, but understanding the gruelling hours of practice, she knew he would forgive her.

~

Isabelle arrived early at the café to be greeted by Pierre and Philippe. They presented her with a painting of an abandoned violin in a field of wildflowers. Studying the work more closely, she noticed tears dripping from the bow.

'Payment for morning tea,' Philippe announced.

'Thank you, gentlemen. I will cherish your painting. Please join me.'

Her fashionable outfit showed quite a contrast to her guests' attire of dark threadbare clothes and well-worn shoes, but Isabelle didn't discriminate and happily ordered morning tea with the waiter.

Stirred up by a morning of stimulating conversation and, in particular, freedom of speech, Isabelle decided to broaden their minds by praising King Arthur and his Knights.

'Democracy evolved from that medieval myth,' Isabelle advised firmly.

'Yes, but a French knight, Sir Lancelot claimed the idea,' Philippe gloated.

'Banished from England forever as a friend turned foe,' Isabelle exclaimed.

'He fell in love. There's no crime in that,' Pierre replied.

'There is if the woman in question is the King's wife, the Queen of England.'

Mr Harper had arrived during the heated discussion and joined the table. He smiled proudly to see his daughter make a valid point in the argument. The waiter poured Mr Harper's coffee and introduced the guests.

'Philippe and Pierre are fellow artists, sir,' the waiter announced in English.

'Sorry, Father. I didn't notice your arrival,' Isabelle said, worried that her father's reaction to her friends may be a little harsh.

'I didn't like to interrupt such an intense discussion.'

After shaking hands with the artists, Mr Harper ordered another morning tea.

'Thank you, sir, for making us welcome,' Philippe said.

'If you are a friend of my daughter's, then you're a friend of mine, unless proven otherwise, my good chaps.'

Isabelle walked towards the hotel while Mr Harper attended to business. Amidst an afternoon of despairing, she found solace amongst the wildflowers by the river. Her memory of the beautiful painting haunted her, curious as to what triggered that image in the first place. A familiar voice became audible through the trees as Count Flaubert appeared, looking very suave in his smart suit and Panama hat.

'May I intrude on your afternoon?' He sat beside her and gently kissed her hand.

'You may, as I've missed you, and the adorable time we shared together,' Isabelle said, wishing he would take her into his arms and kiss her passionately.

'Society has made prisoners of us all, my darling, but our thoughts are free to roam the universe and take possession of our place to dream,' Count Flaubert said, gently taking hold of her hand.

They lay down in the grass and observed the clear blue sky above, their minds drifting in the splendour of the afternoon. Count Flaubert woke suddenly and reached for Isabelle's hand to discover that she had left. Understanding the dedication to her practice, he was pondering the possibility of another meeting when he noticed colourful wildflowers threaded in the lapel of his jacket. He smiled as he smelt the heavenly scent.

Isabelle practised like a woman possessed that afternoon after her chance meeting with the count. To have such a wonderful friend who understood her without explanation—she would treasure that for the rest of her life.

Elsie entered carrying a large gift-wrapped box.

'I'm sorry to interrupt, miss. Mr Harper has given instruction for you to try on your new ball gown.'

Elsie assisted her into the gown and Isabelle waltzed around the room jubilantly.

'You'll be the belle of the ball in that dress, miss.'

'More importantly, I must play music that enraptures the soul of mankind.'

'I've no doubt that you will. The usual mail has been delivered, including a letter from Mrs Harper.'

'Mr Harper attends to Mother's mail,' Isabelle said with an edge to her voice. Elsie fell silent, worried that the lack of communication with Mrs Harper may have a grave effect on her stay in Paris.

After delivering a performance she'd only dreamed was possible, Isabelle enjoyed an evening of glorious adulation. Claude Chevalier exuded such pride, as he walked Isabelle forward to thunderous applause and shouts of Bravura! Mr Chevalier presented her as a prodigy who had surpassed all expectations. Tears of joy were running down Mr Harper's face as he sat with the count and countess. They shared the remarkable experience and embraced Mr Harper warmly.

The next evening the elation continued as Isabelle had been named belle of the ball. Count Flaubert, with Mr Harper's permission, escorted her onto the dance floor and waltzed her to a heavenly place. Isabelle prayed that the music would play forever so she could continue being held in his arms superbly. She was keeping an eye on Claude Chevalier as he conversed with her father, praying that her success would extend their stay. Delighting in the last dance of the evening with Mr Chevalier, she found his suave good looks and direct manner very appealing. He believed in her ability and that meant everything to Isabelle.

Chapter 11

After a meeting with Claude Chevalier at the Paris Conservatorium, in which he encouraged a professional career in music for Isabelle, her father agreed to her completing the next term.

Celebrating the decision made, Elsie found herself twirling around the room with Isabelle, rejoicing in the splendid news. Elsie wondered what Mr Harper had said for Mrs Harper to agree—Isabelle's mother's last letter was full of venom, saying that the preparations for the wedding were in progress without a bride, and blaming Mr Harper for destroying the family. She would never agree to a career in music for her daughter and felt the marriage to George Hoskins would be affected by such an irrational decision.

Holidaying at a splendid sixteenth century chateau on a glorious estate in the Loire Valley, the count and countess welcomed Isabelle and Mr Harper to join them. After declining breakfast in bed, Isabelle happily joined Count Flaubert in the dining room. Mr Harper had taken advantage of the good weather and gone for an early morning ride with Countess Flaubert and their guests. Isabelle glanced into Count Flaubert's engaging green eyes, finding comfort in the great artist who inspired her.

'I've been possessed by a beautiful temptress,' he confessed quietly and in earnest.

Countess Flaubert, Mr Harper and the guests returned from a morning ride; their jubilant chatter and laughter interrupted Isabelle's enchanted mood.

The offer of a boat trip downriver appealed to her, but Isabelle chose to concentrate on her art and she hoped the count would follow suit. Mr Harper happily joined Countess Flaubert and her guests on a journey downriver as Isabelle and Count Flaubert painted in blissful silence with the servants quietly attending to their needs. After an elaborate lunch and fine conversation—with Mr Harper apologising for Mrs Harper's absence—Count Flaubert brought a jovial energy to the lavish sixteenth century dining room by telling delightfully outrageous stories about Granny Harper. Mr Harper smiled contentedly, amused by his good friend's humour. Isabelle found Mrs Harper's absence a relief as she had tired of her mother's precarious moods. She'd been enchanted by a life of decadence, far away from her mother's stressful letters of blame that had secretly dampened her success.

While Mr Harper enjoyed an afternoon reminiscing about his Cambridge days with Count Flaubert, Isabelle took a stroll through the magnificent gardens and wrote her letters to Charles Durn and George Hoskins. She wondered why the count had not taken her hand in secret when she'd given him many opportunities to do so. While pondering the thought, he stepped through the trees with a smile.

'A young lady should never venture through the gardens alone. The temptation is too much for me to bear, my fellow traveller.'

Count Flaubert pulled her into his manly arms, kissing her with a passion unknown to her.

'Your kiss is imprisoned within my soul,' Isabelle said blissfully.

'I've thrown away the key, my beauty,' Count Flaubert replied, observing her with a wistful smile and wishing their time together could be forever.

Elsie caught a glimpse of Isabelle walking from the gardens with Count Flaubert and became a little concerned—she hadn't noticed a chaperone. As Elsie finished the packing, Isabelle entered the room, flushed with happiness.

'You've had a good afternoon by the look of you, miss.'

'I have indeed, but music is my true love and I mustn't be distracted.'

Isabelle gazed out of the window, yearning for another glimpse of Count Flaubert.

'Mr Harper's been looking for you. The countess would like you to give a recital this evening.'

'Tell Father I'd be glad to play, but right now there's a need to gather my thoughts,' Isabelle explained as she climbed onto her bed.

As Isabelle gazed at the spectacular sunset through the window, she bathed in the rapturous knowledge that the count loved her, and she loved him. However, the thought of her father's reaction made her realise that the heavenly kiss must remain a secret in her heart forever.

~

Settling into her next term, Isabelle's music studies took priority over matters of the heart. Even though she missed her fellow traveller and loved him dearly, Isabelle happily met up with Pierre and Philippe after class while waiting for her father at the café. Philippe presented her with another painting wrapped in cloth as payment for morning tea.

'Thank you, Philippe, I'm very proud to receive your painting and will treasure it with all my heart,' Isabelle said, a little nervous of what had inspired the first one.

Many artists were gathered at the table to congratulate Isabelle on her music when Mr Harper arrived with a look of concern on his caring face. Isabelle was immediately fearful that it may be another demand to return to England. He kissed her warmly, pulled up a chair, greeted Pierre and Philippe, and started discussing the artist's work on display. Count Flaubert arrived with a smile and a little more passion than usual, but her father shook his hand with the usual fondness of their boyhood years, so Isabelle remained curious as to what had caused her father's mood.

'I will love you forever,' Count Flaubert whispered as he secretly held her hand under the table.

Isabelle smiled affectionately in response, but with her father nearby, her loving words to the count could not be expressed.

Isabelle returned to the hotel and placed the painting, still wrapped in cloth, into the bottom of her wardrobe. She noticed Elsie, who appeared to be all of a dither, busily packing a suitcase.

'What on earth are you doing?' Isabelle questioned.

'I've been instructed to return you home immediately, or I'll be dismissed,' Elsie exclaimed.

'You must ignore my mother and give the letter to my father,' Isabelle said firmly.

'Mrs Harper has had advice from a lawyer,' Elsie warned.

'I've a recital tonight, so I mustn't be late. If there'd been anything untoward, Father would have said.'

'I'm sorry, miss,' Elsie replied.

'I know you are and I understand your concern,' she answered fondly.

~

Isabelle rejoiced in the notoriety of her highly acclaimed performance and captured the admiration of Claude Chevalier.

'Your music reaches the very depths of my soul and your ravishing beauty has the power to destroy it,' Mr Chevalier remarked with a smile. As he looked into her violet blue eyes, he realised that her remarkable ability had lured him adorably; her bewitching beauty and the task of remaining distanced tested the very essence of his character.

Gazing in wonder at such a splendid and accomplished young man, and appreciating the intense interest he'd taken in her work, Isabelle thought that Mr Chevalier would certainly be a great ally if her mother continued her demands.

During the evening Mr Harper talked of England wistfully and Isabelle noticed a polite but underlying evasiveness when her father spoke to Mr Chevalier. That made her anxious but, after an invitation to ride at Mr Chevalier's Estate in Burgundy, the evening fell into a more relaxed mode.

Elsie appeared to be in a much better frame of mind since Mr Harper had advised her to ignore Mrs Harper. Isabelle read a charming letter from George and smelled the gorgeous red roses that had just arrived; she remembered him for his loyalty and his sensitive blue eyes. She thought him a true gentleman and almost convinced herself that her fiancé was her true love.

'I believe you were right about George Hoskins,' Isabelle remarked to Elsie agreeably as she folded the letter into the envelope.

'I certainly hope so, miss, as you're to be married in the spring.'

A letter from Charles also expressed his happiness about her wonderful achievement; he wrote that he thought of her with love and pride.

~

The fourteenth century chateau in Burgundy was surrounded by a picturesque landscape of fields, gardens and woods. Afternoon tea on the lawn reminded Isabelle of home. Claude Chevalier made sure his guests were entertained in style. She found meeting members of the orchestra and other talented musicians and artists stimulating. Isabelle thought adorably about spending a little precious time alone in Mr Chevalier's arms, but it appeared to be an impossible dream, especially after hearing her father mention George Hoskins as her fiancé on one or two occasions.

The thoroughbred horses provided a thrilling ride across the magnificent landscape with Mr Chevalier and her father. Isabelle revelled in the wild wind blowing through her hair, desperate to embrace a freedom that continually eluded her. The count and countess arrived at the chateau and found Isabelle and Mr Harper in good spirits. Count Flaubert adored Isabelle and looked forward to their chance meetings; he hoped their love and the warmth of their affection would be unaltered after time apart. He noticed, however, her enchanting glances towards Claude Chevalier and understood, with a little jealousy in his heart. Countess Flaubert admired Isabelle and felt relieved to see her attention towards Mr Chevalier.

Isabelle prayed that her stay—at Mr Chevalier's insistence—would be long enough to unveil the enigmatic gentleman of impeccable manners and charm. She wanted to look into his eyes with heartfelt love and unleash a kiss from the very depths of his soul that would be hers for all eternity. Although he showed her attention and praised her talent while staying at the chateau, the kiss remained a lovely daydream.

~

Isabelle entered her beloved café—a place where she felt rested and understood, where nothing else mattered apart from art. After an excellent morning of tuition at the Paris Conservatorium of Music, she looked forward to greeting Philippe and Pierre. A gypsy boy distracted her as he entered and proudly handed over his paintings at the counter for consideration. He reminded her of Jimmy and the wonderful life they'd shared on the river.

The smell of freshly baked croissants enhanced her appetite while sketching the passing faces in the street. The aroma from the coffee became too much to resist so she nodded to the waiter who poured as instructed.

'You make the best morning tea in Paris.'

'I'm flattered, mademoiselle. You're a valued customer,' the waiter replied with charm.

Philippe and Pierre made a grand entrance displaying well-worn top hats on heads of tousled hair, and threadbare suits that had been patched. After a warm greeting, Philippe proudly placed another painting onto the table.

'Thank you, Philippe, but you have paid more than your share, both of you.'

Isabelle hesitated but curiosity overrode her better judgement; she quickly glanced at the painting and saw a broken violin in a colourful field of wildflowers with swirling dark storm clouds shedding tears from above.

She quickly covered the painting with her coat, hoping that her anxious reaction had not been noticed.

Isabelle regained her composure as Mr Harper arrived with many gift-wrapped boxes, followed by Claude Chevalier. Philippe and Pierre decided to move, but Isabelle insisted they remain. Mr Chevalier had a look of surprise on his handsome face as he kissed Isabelle's hand and glanced at her friends in amazement.

'I'm very happy to see you at the café,' Isabelle said keenly.

'I celebrated my debut in music at this remarkable café,' Mr Chevalier declared with pride.

Unusual conversation followed polite introductions. Isabelle felt pleased by Claude Chevalier's eloquent discussion and understanding of the passion that drove Philippe and Pierre's art. When Mr Harper bought some of their paintings, Isabelle embraced her father for kindly supporting her friends.

'Thank you, Mr Harper,' Philippe said gratefully.

Isabelle admired Mr Chevalier's affection and kindness towards the dedicated artists but could see no opportunity to achieve the heavenly kiss that eluded her.

That afternoon, after practising a violin concerto with the orchestra, Mr Chevalier joined Isabelle in the music room. He closed the door quietly and his serious mood made her nervous.

'I'd like to discuss a letter received from Mrs Harper. She informed the Paris Conservatorium that Mr Hoskins would not approve the continuation of your music after the marriage. I'm personally saddened by the loss of your extraordinary talent. I have also found it impossible to express my feelings for you with the knowledge that you're engaged to be married, but my love for you has prevailed.'

Enraptured by the glorious words uttered to her at last, Isabelle gently held his hand.

'Thank you for the generosity of spirit that you have shown my work as a musician, a journey that would not have been possible without you.'

'I've taken your father's advice and sent a letter to Mrs Harper, deploring her decision and inviting her as our special guest to attend your next recital,' Mr Chevalier advised.

'I'm blessed to know such a fine gentleman.'

Isabelle kissed him on the lips with gratitude; he showed no resistance to the pleasure as he took her into his arms and kissed her from the very depths of his soul.

'Please forgive me for being powerless to withdraw from such a beautiful kiss,' Mr Chevalier confessed quietly.

'I forgive you because I love you,' Isabelle replied, rejoicing in such a heavenly kiss and picking up her violin.

The knowledge that Mr Chevalier was stirred to the very depths of his existence by her music, as well as his concern that Mrs Harper possessed the power to destroy Isabelle's future, brought a tear to his eye.

Chapter 12

Weeks passed without any reply from Mrs Harper to Claude Chevalier's letter. Being indifferent to the ongoing tension surrounding her mother, Isabelle paraded in a fashionable new frock, while Elsie arranged dozens of red roses throughout the room. Isabelle's thoughts were of Claude Chevalier, who adored and understood her. She felt honoured to be known as a prodigy of this great man's work. The level of music that she'd aspired to while under his direction, repeatedly brought a smile to her lovely face as they worked together in harmony.

'You can call me old-fashioned but I don't believe you should receive flowers from an admirer when your marriage is only a few months away,' Elsie remarked with a note of concern.

'I owe my success to Claude Chevalier. He's a magician who turned a dream into a glorious reality. I can play music without punishment or disapproval. If his spell lingers forever, I'll be glad of it. My dear George is a very good man, but he deserves a woman who loves him,' Isabelle declared in a distressed state. Elsie embraced her warmly, blaming the upset brought on by her mother for the outburst.

'One day you'll look back on your troubles and discover that it's not uncommon for emotions to run riot before your wedding day. I shed many tears, not wanting to make such a commitment at sixteen. But, looking back, I'm so glad that I did. Try not to let the love of your music interfere with your everyday life,' Elsie advised affectionately.

'I will despise any man who believes I should dismiss my music and pander to what they think is a better judgement,' Isabelle remarked firmly.

'Then you must stand tall and fight for what you believe is right.'

'Thank God for my Elsie,' Isabelle exclaimed with love in her heart.

~

A night at the theatre had been just what Isabelle needed to relax her mind from the ongoing pressure from her mother. The pleasure of seeing the count and countess appeared to have calmed her father who'd also been put under duress.

They ventured to a fashionable restaurant with an impressive jazz band where Isabelle danced the night away with Count Flaubert, a man she loved for his freedom of spirit.

Rejoicing in the pleasure of being in his arms, she caught a glimpse of her father looking younger than his years, spinning the countess around the dance floor.

~

The next day, Claude Chevalier entered the music room with ardour and informed Isabelle that a letter had been received from Mrs Harper, accepting the invitation to her daughter's recital. He expressed his joy that her tuition would continue. She was transported by a heavenly kiss on the lips, although a little nervous that her mother may let him down.

She worked on achieving a performance that would bewitch her mother, making her so proud that she'd consent to the next term and delay her marriage. After opening a letter from George confessing how much he loved her, and the pride he felt to hear of her wonderful success, devastated and disappointed Isabelle as she realised that her mother had lied to the Conservatorium to end her career in music. If her mother did arrive, she wondered if she'd have the energy to stand up to her after the six-hour-a-day practice regime instructed by Mr Chevalier.

Isabelle welcomed Philippe and Pierre with open arms, pleased to see they carried no painting for payment of morning tea. The aroma of the warm croissants made even the most important matters seem of no importance at all. They indulged keenly and wiped their hands clean on elegant serviettes. A serious conversation about those blessed with artistic talent followed.

'I would say we are the lucky ones,' Philippe remarked audaciously.

'My grandfather knew the Trudeau Family. They performed many great theatre productions in Paris. An extraordinary family of actors who travelled the world in the 1880s,' Pierre explained jubilantly.

'According to Granny Harper, the Trudeau Family lived in England for many years,' Isabelle announced proudly.

'Rubbish!' Philippe exclaimed arrogantly.

'Well, there's a photograph of my father as a young boy welcoming the star actress to our home.'

Mr Harper and Count Flaubert made a grand entrance, removing their Fedora hats. Isabelle welcomed them graciously as Philippe and Pierre politely shook hands to express a warm greeting.

'My fellow traveller, good news travels quickly. I'll expect you and your parents at the chateau for the weekend,' Count Flaubert remarked charmingly.

Isabelle felt disappointed that her mother's early arrival would interrupt her precious time working with Mr Chevalier, but joyous that her studies would be extended.

'Father can tell you all about the Trudeau Family,' Isabelle said to Philippe and Pierre with polite determination.

'Many theatricals were entertained at our estate during those years but the actors from the Trudeau Family were a favourite with Mother in my youth. If you ever come to England, you're welcome to visit and view their remarkable theatre history.'

'Thank you, sir,' Pierre replied sheepishly.

'I accept your humble apology, Pierre,' Isabelle remarked politely, but with a touch of sarcasm.

'I have acquired two extra seats if you gentlemen care to join us at the recital,' Mr Harper announced.

'Yes, sir!' Pierre replied with enthusiasm.

'Thank you, my good chap,' Philippe said, attempting a British accent.

'You'll both need a set of tails, but leave that to me,' Mr Harper offered.

She observed her father with pride; he demonstrated true kindness to those less fortunate than himself. Count Flaubert had been discreetly holding her hand under the table, and Isabelle returned his devotion with a loving glance.

'Does swimming in the river appeal to my fellow traveller?' the count enquired. His words brought a smile to her lips as she thought of Jimmy and their happy times spent at the river.

'My skills are poor, but I can stay afloat,' Isabelle replied demurely, aware that her father may be listening.

She caught a glimpse of Claude Chevalier in the doorway, tipping his hat in their direction.

'You're late. Mr Chevalier is waiting,' Mr Harper urged.

'How remiss of me to forget the time, Mr Chevalier is fastidious about punctuality,' Isabelle remarked as she picked up her violin and blew an affectionate kiss goodbye.

After Mr Chevalier closed the door to the music room, Isabelle accepted a polite lecture on punctuality and dedication to her work. She promised never to fail again in her duty to respect the maestro who had nurtured her talent to such remarkable extremities. However, her alluring feminine charm overrode his chastisement. Her music evoked in him a quintessential passion that flowed through his veins, moving him to another place of existence. He fought against the desire to take Isabelle into his arms. Her future in music relied on Mrs Harper's ability to see a greater vision for her daughter and let go of her preconceived ideas. Mr Chevalier believed a life without music to be impossible for Isabelle and would take steps with the Conservatorium to propagate her cause.

After many hours of practice, Isabelle sat pondering the fact that Paris had changed her forever. She remembered her first rapturous kiss with George and thought about his fine virtues of loyalty, kindness and reliability, but she didn't feel love.

Claude Chevalier had won her heart, by sharing a love of the music that embraced their souls. Mr Chevalier entered the room with a flourish and waltzed her with amazing ardour.

'My dearest Isabelle, the Paris Conservatorium has honoured you with a title,' Mr Chevalier announced with pride.

'Thank you for your perseverance. I will love you forever.'

'Hopefully Mrs Harper will be proud. I know your father will be,' Mr Chevalier remarked. He kissed her adorably then presented her with many sheets of music.

'My mother cannot refuse me now; I've earned the title of Virtuoso!'

~

Elsie fussed about the room and assisted Isabelle from her warm bath after a gruelling day of practice.

'I've informed your father that you'll be dining in your room and will be practising further. He agreed with our decision and said he admired your dedication.'

'Thank you, my dear Elsie.'

After dinner she climbed into bed and said her prayers. Her thoughts were of Claude Chevalier...why, when he had embraced her with such passion, had another loving kiss that would transcend their earthly beings to heaven not occurred? Isabelle would have taken the initiative, but without the knowledge of what took place once their passion had been unleashed to such an extreme; it remained a mystery. She'd read many books in her search for information, but none were adequate.

The next morning Isabelle woke to see Elsie setting the breakfast table.

'Sorry to wake you so early but Mrs Harper arrived unexpectedly last night after Mr Harper had gone out to dinner. You can imagine the drama that erupted when your father returned. They had a terrible argument. He showed her the many lovely gifts he'd bought to welcome her, but I'm afraid she booked her own room with that dreadful maid, Lorna.'

'I don't believe my mother is well, and unfortunately she's vulnerable to a girl like Lorna.'

Isabelle was gazing out of the window, admiring her beautiful Paris and thinking about all the happiness she'd known there, when a knock at the door alerted her attention.

Mrs Harper entered the room in an agitated state. Elsie greeted her warmly and Isabelle embraced her.

'I'm so happy to see you, Mother.'

'Isabelle is a credit to you, Mrs Harper. I believe the dedication to her music has encouraged a pleasurable outcome,' Elsie said as she fussed about the room and found a chair for Mrs Harper.

'Congratulations on acquiring a title in music, Isabelle. You can inform Reverend Durn personally when you return to England,' Mrs Harper announced.

'I love my music more than anything in the world and I'm so pleased that you understand what I wish to achieve.'

'Your father and I have not been able to reconcile our differences, but we'll do our best not to spoil your time in Paris,' Mrs Harper explained with a tear in her eye.

Isabelle wondered if her mother should have travelled at all. The mention of her return to England had been noted, but at least there'd been no protest regarding her music.

The Harpers arrived at the chateau on an unusually warm afternoon. The maid Lorna had been sent home and replaced by a French maid at Mr Harper's request. After being lured by the beauty of the river, an afternoon swim was in order. Isabelle displayed her feminine beauty in a fashionable swimming costume and Count Flaubert admired her from afar. The count and countess were joined by Mr Harper and Isabelle as they frolicked in the secluded river. Mrs Harper sat politely in silence, after her smile of approval had expanded. The arrival of Claude Chevalier made Isabelle's afternoon complete. She'd been concerned about Mrs Harper's reaction on meeting Mr Chevalier, but her mother showed admiration and respect.

A dinner of elegance and grandeur followed in a remarkable sixteenth century dining room. Isabelle paraded in her glorious rose-pink evening gown, and caught the eye of Claude Chevalier who smiled enchantingly in her direction. Mrs Harper noticed his smile as the waiter poured her first glass of gin.

'Are you married, Mr Chevalier?' Mrs Harper queried.

'No, ma'am. I fear many would say I've been married to my work.'

'I must thank you for taking such a keen interest in our daughter's ability. I'm very proud of her achievement, but I must warn you that her fiancé has not changed his mind about the continuation of her music after their marriage,' Mrs Harper said. Isabelle had received letters of encouragement from George, so she knew her mother was lying.

Mr Harper invited Mr Chevalier and Count Flaubert to join him in a game of billiards.

'Please excuse us, Mrs Harper. We can discuss the matter later in the week. Your husband has summoned me to a game of billiards,' Mr Chevalier answered charmingly.

Countess Flaubert entertained Mrs Harper and Isabelle with many amusing stories about her early marriage to the count. With Mr Harper engaged elsewhere, Mrs Harper had finished her third glass of gin and the decline in her elegance was noticeable.

'Thank you for such a splendid day, Countess Flaubert, but I have a musical engagement in the morning and Mother is tired after her journey,' Isabelle clarified, escorting Mrs Harper from the room and striving to keep her upright.

~

After a gruelling morning of practice at the Paris Conservatorium, Isabelle noticed Mr Chevalier to be unusually quiet and withdrawn. She wondered if her mother's conversation at the chateau had caused his mood. Bidding her a fond farewell, he smiled – his mood reflective – and gently caressed her cheek.

'You have surpassed all my expectations. Such beautiful playing could stir the soul of the devil himself and render him helpless to the angels in heaven,' Mr Chevalier praised.

'I love you,' Isabelle said as she embraced him affectionately, and left the music room.

His thoughts were of Mrs Harper's warning, but he'd decided to suffer her words in silence until after the recital.

Chapter 13

Arriving at the café, Isabelle found solitude in her own thoughts as she admired the paintings on display. She stared in amazement as Philippe and Pierre made a spectacular entrance dressed in black tails with well-groomed hair peeping from under their stylish top hats. Red carnations displayed in the lapel of their jackets completed the elegant ensemble.

'We've sold three paintings, so morning tea is on us,' Philippe announced.

'You look absolutely marvellous, but you're two days early!' Isabelle remarked with a twinkle in her eye.

'We are bathed and dressed as Mr Harper instructed,' Pierre exclaimed. 'I believe he meant on the day, but it's better to be early than too late.'

'We must thank Mr Harper for his kind generosity. You're lucky to have such a caring father,' Philippe remarked with gratitude.

'I thank God for him every day of my life,' Isabelle replied.

Mr Harper arrived looking pale and anxious, but his surprise at seeing Pierre and Philippe in their suits encouraged a jolly smile that seemed to alleviate his condition. He made no comment on their early readiness for the recital. Isabelle presumed her father had endured a harrowing night with Mrs Harper. The depressing state of her family made Isabelle wonder if she should continue with her music at all. But the driving force within her would not allow defeat, especially with the knowledge that her mother had lied about George.

'Your elegance is most becoming, gentlemen,' Mr Harper flattered.

'Thank you for the opportunity. We appreciate the privilege, sir,' Pierre said respectfully.

Count Flaubert entered with a cheery smile to join the festivities and Isabelle noticed Mr Harper's demeanour improving as the colour in his face returned. Her fellow traveller had a remarkable attitude to life and Isabelle felt grateful to have known such a man, believing her mother would have been different had she been blessed with an artistic gift that would enable her to express herself more eloquently.

The next day passed with little fuss, Isabelle completed another regimented regime with the orchestra under Claude Chevalier's instruction. He praised her work, quietly confident that her success would silence the objections from those who were concerned.

The count and countess joined the Harper family for an elegant dinner at the hotel. Whatever her husband had said, Mrs Harper felt it was within her best interest to attend dinner. Isabelle would have loved Mr Chevalier to accompany them but thought it wise for him to avoid contact with her mother until after the recital.

The next day Mr and Mrs Harper joined Isabelle for breakfast; her father took great pleasure in presenting a gift.

'I've kept Granny Harper's necklace for a fitting occasion, and that day has arrived,' he declared proudly.

'My darling girl, all the luck in the world for tonight, not that you'll need any. I heard your magnificent playing yesterday when I visited the Conservatorium and introduced myself personally,' Mrs Harper kindly advised with a smile.

Mr Harper strove to disguise his annoyance in front of Isabelle.

Elsie answered a knock at the door and re-entered with a spectacular display of red roses.

'From George Hoskins, miss,' she announced to Isabelle as Mrs Harper took the card to read.

'You'll always be able to rely on Mr Hoskins. He'll be a loyal and devoted husband.'

'I'm sure of it, Mother,' Isabelle said as she kissed her on the cheek and took the card from her hand.

'Good luck, my darling,' Mr Harper announced, taking Mrs Harper's arm and escorting her from the room.

~

Mr Harper, looking very suave in his black tails, had been knocking on Mrs Harper's door to no avail. The French maid opened the door and expressed Mrs Harper's apology—she was not well enough to attend. Mr Harper entered the bedroom and saw Mrs Harper, still in her dressing gown, staring out of the window into oblivion. He bristled with anger and assisted her to stand.

'Madam, you have twenty minutes to get dressed in your evening gown or you'll attend the recital as you are. I can promise you, either way, you're going,' Mr Harper said sternly.

He waited patiently on a chair in the hall. After hearing movement in the bedroom, he knew the maid had attended to Mrs Harper. A short time later, Mr Harper nodded his approval as his wife appeared in her glamorous evening gown looking elegant and enchanting. He politely escorted her out the door.

After giving the performance of her life, the full house applauded Isabelle thunderously, shouting 'Bravura!' and 'La Stupendous!' as they stamped their feet, hoping for an encore to be performed. Mr and Mrs Harper stood proudly beside the count and countess, all shedding tears of joy for such a triumphant performance. The roar of applause had overwhelmed an emotional Philippe and Pierre as Isabelle bowed graciously to the splendour of their ovation. Claude Chevalier tapped his baton for the attention of the orchestra; the audience sat in their seats and silence prevailed. Isabelle then played a solo that sent the audience into a frenzied state of applause and adoration, her music stirring them to the very brim of ecstasy.

Closing the door to Isabelle's dressing room firmly, Claude Chevalier passed the glorious display of flowers and took Isabelle into his arms, unleashing a desire from the very depths of his soul. He kissed her with the love of a man possessed, and Isabelle reached a captivating place of existence, previously unknown to her.

'I played for you, my beautiful man. May all our dreams come true,' Isabelle said with heartfelt feelings of sublime love.

Caught up in the enjoyment of the evening, Mr Harper had dismissed his wife's earlier behaviour and danced with her pleasurably at an elegant restaurant. Isabelle's radiance in Mr Chevalier's arms alarmed Mrs Harper; she observed them waltzing gracefully, portraying a lover's dance. Mr Harper had noticed the attraction some time ago but didn't wish to intervene. He applauded the great maestro's elegance and refinement, and appreciated that he had a history of aristocratic blood flowing through his veins. The agreeable influence Mr Chevalier imposed upon Isabelle had matured her noticeably. The count and countess had joined in the celebration and Mrs Harper showed her relief to see Isabelle dancing with Count Flaubert. As the count looked into Isabelle's violet blue eyes adoringly, he smiled. He had been a little worried about what he'd observed with Mr Chevalier.

'A word of advice from a fellow traveller, and I make no judgement as you well know. As an engaged young lady, soon to be married, your true love can never be known or shown,' Count Flaubert cautioned.

Later, while Elsie busily tidied the room, Isabelle opened a letter from her fiancé and let forth a squeal of delight.

'George has consented to a delay of two months, so we can stay in Paris.'

'I don't mean to dampen your spirits, miss, but I don't know how your poor dear father will cope. The maid resigned after Mrs Harper's recent behaviour. The doctors had to be called and Mrs Harper's refusal to attend the sanatorium has only escalated the problem.'

'I have a class this morning, but Father's meeting me afterwards at the café. I'll discuss the matter with him then.'

~

Admiring Philippe and Pierre's ability to blend into society at any level, Isabelle stood on a crowded corner observing the street where they lived and created their art. She noticed that their elegant tails and top hats were causing quite a sensation. Two of their paintings sold while she stood watching.

After being greeted with adulation at the café, she sat down to morning tea and relived the previous evening all over again. Her wish that George would meet a wonderful woman and be the one to break the engagement had not come to fruition—even though there must be many gorgeous women who would be happy with such a handsome and loyal gentleman. Mr Chevalier's devotion and love for her had been made clear but, being a gentleman of honour, he demanded that their love be silenced until the breaking of the engagement had been made official.

Jovial laughter disturbed her thoughts as Pierre and Philippe joined Isabelle; adorned in their evening tails from the night before.

'Here is the star! Pierre announced, as he politely stepped forward, assisted Isabelle from her chair, and waltzed her divinely. Mr Harper and Count Flaubert arrived and sat quietly, enjoying the celebration for Isabelle. However, a dark cloud hung over them. Mrs Harper had been taken to the sanatorium against her will at the doctor's insistence after she'd collapsed from alcohol poisoning.

Mr Harper was distressed by the traumatic event; Mrs Harper's screams of objection were still echoing in his ears. Isabelle had been reminded of Pierre's painting—dark clouds gathering and tears falling onto a broken violin—when her father informed her of the situation.

Mr Chevalier greeted Isabelle with love in his heart. The passionate plans for her music and the engaging talk of their stay in Paris assisted in lifting her spirits.

Mr Harper and Count Flaubert had recovered from the trauma of the morning and the day continued agreeably. It pleased Isabelle that her father showed admiration for Mr Chevalier and she believed that—once her mother had learned a little more about his family—she too would welcome him. Being an aristocrat would alter the image of Claude Chevalier in her mother's mind forever. Maybe then Isabelle could break her engagement to dear George Hoskins. Importantly, she'd need her mother to regain her health to be able to understand her beloved Mr Chevalier's history.

When they closed the door to the music room, all other cares and woes diminished. Only their love for each other and the extraordinary passion for their music mattered. They were driven by the fear of a loss that remained unimaginable.

'Dearest Isabelle, my late father's wise words come to mind as we endure this fearful and anxious time. He used to say don't dance until the music plays. He felt those words saved his life in wartime,' Mr Chevalier remarked, saddened by their situation.

A month passed and Isabelle embraced each day as if it were the last. Her love for Mr Chevalier blossomed in secret, although she wished her man of honour would falter and take her to a faraway place where she could be entwined in his arms forever.

'I hear your mother is much improved. Mr Harper has instructed the staff to begin packing by the end of the month,' Elsie informed.

Isabelle could hardly breathe after hearing such news.

'I'm sure Father would have mentioned the matter if that were the case,' Isabelle replied. The trauma felt, caused her to sit down and gather her thoughts, fighting to suppress her tears.

'You look as if you've seen a ghost, miss. I'm sorry to have startled you. I thought you knew.'

'I'm in the wilderness, Elsie. A day without Mr Chevalier and my music is more than my heart could endure.'

Elsie noticed the tears running down Isabelle's face and dearly wished she'd never mentioned the matter. Realising that Mr Chevalier had won Isabelle's heart, Elsie embraced her warmly and hoped the passage of time, the return to England, and the excitement of her wedding would mend her great loss.

Chapter 14

Waking in England to find the rooftops of Paris had disappeared, Isabelle gazed through the window with a heavy heart and longed for her lessons with Claude Chevalier to resume.

Elsie entered with breakfast in bed as Mrs Harper had instructed. Isabelle's mother was very happy to have her daughter back in England with wedding preparations in progress.

'You're to wear the new evening gown tonight as George Hoskins and Count Flaubert will be guests at dinner.'

The prospect of seeing Count Flaubert lifted Isabelle's spirits. Her fellow traveller, being an ally, could possibly organise a holiday in Paris before the wedding—that way she could secretly meet Mr Chevalier and resume her music. After returning to the same ordered life under her mother's rule, the feeling of suffocation had driven her to put on a hat and venture into the field.

'Your mother has given strict orders for a quiet day, miss.'

'I won't be long, I promise,' Isabelle said, collecting her easel and paints.

After wandering aimlessly through the daffodils, she found solace under the oak tree, not knowing how she would make it through the day let alone a lifetime. Jimmy appeared, smiled affectionately, hesitated, then dried her tears with his shirtsleeve.

'To cry that many tears means your love will never die and you'll wake one day and there he'll be, standing before you.'

Jimmy wished that the tears were for him, but he was still very happy to see her. He had missed Isabelle more than he'd believed possible, but he knew he must love alone.

'I've missed you, Jimmy, and thought about you often. Please forgive me for not saying goodbye when I left.'

'I could offer you a journey downriver if that would help,' Jimmy said, attempting to brighten her day.

As they drifted down the secluded river, Isabelle closed her eyes while daydreaming of her beloved Paris, and the wonderful people she had grown to love would be held in her heart forever. Isabelle had worked so hard to achieve a level in music aspired to by very few musicians, and yet the glory of her achievement would vanish into the wilderness the day she married George Hoskins. Even with George as her ally, it would never be the same. She knew her father would have agreed to her staying in Paris, but he felt so disturbed by her mother's illness that he'd been held at ransom to avoid a repeat occurrence.

Isabelle opened her eyes and saw Jimmy swimming in the river catching fish with his hands. She removed her glamorous lemon frock, folded it carefully, and dived into the water in her petticoat.

'Welcome home!' Jimmy announced, happy to be able to raise her spirits. Isabelle floated through the reeds, enjoying the sun on her face.

'You've always been able to save me from the wilderness, my dearest friend,' Isabelle said.

Enjoying the tranquil afternoon, drifting with the current, Jimmy was alerted to a crunching sound in the undergrowth. He signalled for Isabelle to get dressed speedily.

'I'm not keeping an eye on you, I promise,' George said, after he'd appeared through the trees.

'It's not quite the greeting I expected after being apart so long, but all is forgiven. I'm sure you've been sent on an errand,' Isabelle remarked, attempting to tidy her wet hair.

'I have indeed. Your father is anxious not to upset your mother.'

'Meet my friend, Jimmy Williams, who taught me to swim.'

'I'm Isabelle's fiancé, George Hoskins. Delighted to meet you, and I must thank you for your assistance. Swimming lessons are a must for adventurous young ladies.'

'I'm pleased to meet you, sir,' Jimmy replied courteously.

'We have a pressing engagement, so I hope you will excuse us. I'm sure we'll meet again sometime,' George said as he assisted Isabelle from the canoe and helped fasten the buckles on her elegant shoes.

As they walked through the field in silence, George took her by the hand and stepped behind a tree. His lovely kiss, enchanted her.

Transported by the adorable kiss, Isabelle stood with her eyes closed, waiting for another. George smiled, believing his love would be enough for both of them, and kissed her again.

'I'm very proud of your wonderful success, my darling. If need be, we can move to London or Paris if you wish to continue your music studies.'

'Thank you for the offer, it means a great deal to me.' George's offer had been a nagging reminder of her mother's attempt to sabotage her music.

Later that evening, Isabelle entered the grand Edwardian dining room in a magnificent gown. Mr Harper, George Hoskins and Count Flaubert stood courteously for her to be seated, and Mrs Harper smiled approvingly.

'I'm so happy to be home in England for the preparation of my marriage to George,' Isabelle announced charmingly, disguising her heavy heart.

Her fellow traveller nodded his approval, and Mr Harper smiled proudly— he knew how much Paris meant to her. Isabelle's ability to override such a loss and present herself with graciousness pleased her father immensely. Mrs Harper looked at Isabelle and George, glad that she'd persisted with the marriage.

'I'm so thankful that you've made such an elegant transition and recognised your place in society. A secure and loving gentleman such as Mr Hoskins is exactly what you need. He may appreciate fine music and art but I doubt if he'll allow a life of decadence for his partner in marriage,' Mrs Harper said.

'Countess Flaubert would gladly agree with you, Mrs Harper. Early in our marriage my dear wife believed the artist to be a strange but lovable creature. She attempted to lure me from my work by appearing naked in the field before me. I unashamedly confess that I placed the next brush stroke onto the canvas regardless of the distraction,' Count Flaubert remarked.

Amused by Count Flaubert's charming response, Isabelle had noticed her mother chuckling, and a glimpse of Lorna leaving the dining room alerted her to the glass of gin that had been served to Mrs Harper. Her father signalled the butler Cummings to the table, and the glass in question, was discreetly removed. Mrs Harper flashed a steely glance in her husband's direction; the count noticed the exchange and stood swiftly to make an announcement.

'All stand and raise your glasses to the engaged couple, Isabelle and George,' the count announced grandly, disguising a little sadness. Mr Harper assisted his wife to stand and they sipped champagne for the toast.

George embraced Isabelle with a noticeable love and understanding. The night ended well as the gentlemen made their exit to the billiards room.

After reading a letter from Mr Chevalier begging her not to enter into a marriage without love, and pleading for her to end the engagement, Isabelle closed her eyes and daydreamed of Paris with her beloved Claude Chevalier kissing her passionately. Elsie entered in a state of anguish.

'There's been terrible trouble downstairs over Lorna disobeying the rules. Mr Harper's threat of a sanatorium in London quietened Mrs Harper considerably,' Elsie exclaimed as she placed a splendid sheath of red roses onto the table.

Isabelle read the card and smiled blissfully after noticing the flowers were from Mr Chevalier. Elsie's silence pleased her—she knew that her maid disagreed but understood.

'I miss your beautiful playing,' Elsie remarked as she prepared the bath.

'Paris has haunted me every day of my life. Now that I've lived such an amazing dream, the privilege is mine and will remain so for all eternity.'

'Your words are as unforgettable as the music you play. I pray every night for the good Lord to put your world back together. I hope you find the strength to withstand the onslaught and embrace the dream that is yours.'

'Thank you for your words of wisdom. I very much needed to hear them today,' Isabelle replied as she sank down into a warm bath, hoping her cares and woes would drift away.

Dressed in a fashionable frock and relishing in a delicious morning tea, Isabelle's thoughts were of the café in Paris and her dear friends Pierre and Philippe. She was reminded of the painting still wrapped in cloth in the bottom of the wardrobe. Pierre's other paintings had disturbed her—seeming accurate like a prediction—but she didn't believe he meant to be malicious. He had simply painted a vision that he saw in his mind.

Isabelle felt the painting in the wardrobe should remain a mystery until her wellbeing had improved.

Under the oak tree, her thoughts were still of Paris. Count Flaubert appeared and sat beside her.

'You found me.'

'I'm your fellow traveller, my darling. Wherever you are, I will seek you out. I'm returning to Paris this afternoon.'

'Please take me with you,' Isabelle pleaded.

'You know I would if it were possible. I have urged your father to delay the matrimonial proceedings until Mrs Harper's health improves.'

'You are an angel from heaven.'

'We'll have you back in Paris one day soon, I promise,' Count Flaubert replied, keenly.

Isabelle resumed her practice that very afternoon, encouraging a generous smile from Elsie who believed music would assist with her recovery.

Elsie had found the painting wrapped in cloth at the bottom of Isabelle's wardrobe and placed the package onto the table. Mrs Harper entered the room and waited patiently; enchanted by the music being played.

'Your father has kindly been to see Reverend Durn. Your music lessons will resume until your marriage, when George will make those decisions for you,' Mrs Harper informed Isabelle.

'Thank you, Mother,' Isabelle rejoiced, kissing her mother affectionately.

'I'm happy to have you home and your behaviour is pleasing indeed, but I must warn you not to be seen at the river. There would be severe consequences.' Mrs Harper left the room with a noticeable unsteadiness in her walk.

Isabelle had been distracted by the painting and removed the package nervously from the table.

'One has to be in a confident state of mind when viewing Pierre's artistic endeavours,' Isabelle said as she placed the painting into a cabinet and turned the key in the lock.

'Understood,' Elsie replied as a magnificent bouquet of pink carnations arrived.

'Thank God for Count Flaubert. I don't know how your father will manage without him,' Elsie remarked fondly.

'He's a prince amongst men,' Isabelle replied, realising Elsie had warmed to him.

Isabelle saw Charles walking through the field and wondered why he hadn't sent flowers to welcome her home. His letters were conversations about music— not a mention of Sarah or the vicarage—in which he praised Isabelle proudly for her extraordinary achievements. To wait another week before her lesson seemed an impossible task, so she swiftly changed into her riding outfit and made a quiet exit without being noticed.

Isabelle galloped across the meadow and a feeling of exhilaration embraced her. She rode past the vicarage and slowed down as she noticed young Lola swinging on the gate.

'Hello,' Lola greeted cheerfully.

'You've grown since I've been away,' Isabelle remarked joyfully.

'I'll have my own pony by Christmas,' Lola announced with a cheeky smile.

'I look forward to that day,' Isabelle replied as she rode away.

'Reverend Durn is out and Jimmy is swimming at the river,' Lola advised in a raised voice as Isabelle waved goodbye.

Galloping at speed across the field—the sound of thunderous hooves spurring her on—Isabelle had found the medicine needed to endure the days ahead. She longed to join her friend Jimmy on the river, a place she felt protected and understood, but refrained. Her mother had made the consequences very clear.

Isabelle had arrived home to find Elsie all of a dither. She revealed the remarkable news that both Mr Chevalier and the Reverend Charles Durn would be guests at dinner. After Isabelle stepped into a warm bath, daydreaming of her glorious kiss with Claude Chevalier, Elsie dressed her into an exquisite rose pink evening gown, threaded her hair delicately with wildflowers and wore Granny Harper's ruby necklace. She hoped that her grandmother's spirit would encourage a splendid evening.

As Mr Chevalier—the suave and elegant gentleman she remembered—greeted her, she was desperate to kiss him passionately and fall in love all over again. Her man of honour had successfully arranged lessons for Isabelle at the London Academy of Music, supported by Mr Harper and the Reverend Charles Durn who would supervise in Mr Chevalier's absence. Charles showed his pleasure at seeing Isabelle; Sarah smiled fondly, although her marriage to George Hoskins would be a relief. Mrs Harper remained quiet during dinner, pleased to see the situation under control; she recognised Mr Chevalier as a powerful influence who had been good for Isabelle. Mrs Harper had been making every effort to improve her health so that her daughter's marriage to Mr Hoskins would be sooner rather than later as Mr Harper had instructed.

Isabelle knew her father loved Paris almost as much as she did, but more than anything he desired to see his family harmonious.

'How is my beautiful Paris surviving in my absence?' Isabelle enquired of Mr Chevalier.

'You're sadly missed. Pierre and Philippe send their love,' Mr Chevalier informed her.

He looked at Isabelle with sadness in his eyes; he'd hoped her lessons would continue in Paris. However, he recognised Mrs Harper's power and wondered if his love for Isabelle would ever be possible.

'Our love may be silenced but one last kiss to take with me would suffice for now,' Mr Chevalier whispered to Isabelle later.

'I'll show you the adorable gardens in the morning and direct you to a secluded place,' Isabelle whispered in response.

~

The rain pelting against the window woke Isabelle from a glorious sleep and she remembered her romantic arrangement with Mr Chevalier.

'I'll breakfast in the dining room this morning as I have business to discuss with my father and Claude Chevalier.'

'The gentlemen left for London at least an hour ago, miss,' Elsie announced as she placed a breakfast tray onto Isabelle's bed.

'On the table please, Elsie. Breakfast in bed is not a privilege for married women because they have no privileges. They have no rights at all.'

Elsie fell silent, realising Isabelle's upset after the man of her dreams had left without saying goodbye. Isabelle dressed speedily and picked up her easel and paints.

'Please, miss,' Elsie pleaded.

'The rain has stopped and I'm sure you'll think of a good excuse. I love you,' Isabelle answered as she left.

After walking through the field—cautious of venturing near the tall trees where prying eyes may be observing her—Isabelle set up her easel under the oak tree. Creating art would ease her pain; a feeling of tranquillity would override her disappointment.

Jimmy distracted her, approaching with a charming smile.

'I don't wish to interrupt your art but I'd hoped a journey down river would appeal?'

'The secret river would be advisable.'

'At your service, ma'am.'

Drifting on the secret river Isabelle wondered if this sanctuary of beauty with its never-ending sounds from the waterfall had bewitched her forever. Visions of this place had appeared repeatedly in her dreams. She did not acknowledge young William and Peter when she caught sight of them fishing upriver. Isabelle respected Jimmy's wishes for his glorious haven to remain unknown.

After a delicious lunch of freshly caught fish cooked over the campfire, Jimmy climbed a tree. Suddenly, bees swarmed around Isabelle and she screamed.

Jimmy slid down the tree trunk clutching the honeycomb and laid it safely onto the easel. Grabbing Isabelle by the hand they ran to the river and jumped in. After being rescued from the bees, they sat by the waterfall relishing in the honeycomb.

'King George's favourite,' Isabelle announced.

'How do you know?'

'I've been to London to see the Queen,' Isabelle teased.

Rejoicing in their happy time together, Jimmy had managed to cure Isabelle of her woes.

Chapter 15

When she entered the vicarage, Isabelle felt as though her venture to Paris had been a dream. Charles embraced her with keen affection and Isabelle – enchanted by such an exuberant welcome – kissed his cheek.

'Your talent has not surpassed your beauty, but now they are evenly matched,' Charles said.

'I apologise for being stand-offish. I had no forewarning of Mr Chevalier being a guest that evening,' she explained.

'Forgive me, but I only noticed the most beautiful young lady I had ever seen,' Charles replied charmingly.

Isabelle talked about her great passion for Paris joyously and explained her attendance at the Moulin Rouge, trusting Charles implicitly with her secret. She played music from the depth of her soul that brought tears to his eyes.

'Selfishly, I welcome you home, but I realise that Claude Chevalier has taken you to another level in music, beyond the reach of us mere mortals. My pride in your success makes every day worthwhile,' he confessed.

'Thank you, dearest Charles, for your inspiring letters of encouragement and your kindness of thought.'

'I believe the next lesson will be with Claude Chevalier at the London Academy. According to his instructions, I will tutor at the vicarage the following week.'

Elated by the news, she forgave Mr Chevalier for leaving without saying goodbye. Her disappointment had subsided. Her thoughts were of Mr Chevalier as she packed her violin into its case and kissed Charles fondly.

After he closed the door, Charles felt confused. Loneliness overwhelmed him; he still longed for the girl who had loved him unconditionally, but understood that Paris had altered her, possibly forever.

Isabelle delighted in seeing young William sitting waiting for his lesson. He stood grandly when he saw her; he looked distinguished in a stylish suit with his curly red hair well-groomed.

'William! You look so grown up. How lovely to see you,' Isabelle greeted, joyfully.

'Paris has been very good to you. I think you always knew it would be. You're even more beautiful than I remember,' William confessed.

'Thank you for the compliment, I will treasure it.'

'I saw you on the river yesterday,' William said hesitantly.

'I will love you forever if you keep my secret.'

'I promise I will. Did you see the Can-Can in Paris?'

'Oh William, the most extraordinary two hours of my life were spent at the Moulin Rouge. The Can-Can surpassed all my expectations. A secret never to be disclosed.'

'Cross my heart and hope to die.' he said passionately. Charles appeared in the garden with a smile.

'William, you're late,' he chastised in a jovial manner.

'I'm sorry, sir,' William replied, hurrying through the garden.

~

The anticipation of seeing Mr Chevalier alone had filled her to the brim with happiness. Isabelle dearly wished to discuss the man she loved with her father, but the risk of Mrs Harper intervening made it impossible.

Isabelle arrived at the manor to find silence—only disturbed by the occasional servant carrying out their duty. She'd visited many grand homes with chatter and laughter echoing throughout and, even though she loved her parents dearly, she sometimes wished that her family had been different.

As Isabelle practised diligently in readiness for the arrival of her maestro, Elsie entered with two sheaths of red roses.

'From Mr Chevalier, miss.'

Inhaling the perfume from the roses, Isabelle took Elsie by the hand and twirled her around the room.

'I love him,' Isabelle confessed.

'I know you do. I'm praying for your wish to come true,' Elsie answered.

'Oh, thank you,' Isabelle said, appreciating her dear maid's love and understanding.

A week seemed like an eternity. Isabelle strove to curb her spirited ways in fear of her mother overriding Mr Harper's instructions for her music tuition. Lorna had also been a concern; she continued to perform duties despite the fact that Mr Harper had dismissed her.

Isabelle concluded a strict practice regime, finishing an arduous piece and then flopping into a comfortable chair. Mrs Harper entered the room.

'Your father has given permission for an afternoon ride with Mr Hoskins, who will also be your guest at dinner. We're very pleased to see such responsible behaviour, and the dedication to your music is impressive.'

'Thank you, Mother.'

Galloping across the moors, Isabelle's cares and woes vanished momentarily. George showed such happiness in her company. Dismounting by the river, they sat in peaceful silence.

'A honeymoon in Paris should put us right,' George commented.

'You have no idea how much that means to me,' Isabelle replied.

'I think I do. I love you all the more for such devotion to your music.' George held her in his arms and kissed her with heartfelt passion.

As they galloped back across the moors Isabelle thought about the passionate kiss and what may follow. She'd been to the library again to look for books on the topic, to no avail.

Jimmy and the gypsy boys appeared on the river in their canoes, paddling to the rhythmic beat of the Celtic drum. Isabelle gave a hearty wave as they galloped past the river. George observed her smiling at Jimmy and struggled to subdue a feeling of jealousy.

~

Isabelle's flushed cheeks distracted Elsie as she entered her room with a flourish.

'I know I've mentioned this matter before, but I'll never agree with the modern ways of not being chaperoned before the wedding. I realise Mr Hoskins is a well-bred gentleman, but I've known of many fine gentlemen whose breeding has eluded them in a moment of passion.'

'Thank you for your concern, but I would trust Mr Hoskins with my life.'

'I'm sorry, miss. I know it's not my place to comment.'

'I'm pleased that you care, Elsie,' Isabelle answered fondly.

~

After Isabelle and George had rejoiced in their afternoon ride, a strained atmosphere hovered over the manor at dinner. Mr Harper discussed the morning's events in the courtroom and congratulated George on the strategy and skill that had won them the case. Isabelle observed her mother; she was wearing a plain black evening gown and her hair portrayed a woman devoid of her usual elegance.

Mr Harper's eyes expressed his annoyance at his wife for showing her personal tragedy at dinner. George had noticed her disturbed demeanour but kindly ignored her silence. Isabelle attempted to make light of her mother's behaviour by telling George about her dearest friends, Pierre and Philippe.

'Amongst the street artists of Paris, my father's generous spirit will be remembered forever. According to Pierre, many of the artists are selling their paintings in order to buy top hats and tails.'

Her parents gave their permission for Isabelle to retire early; she needed to prepare for Mr Chevalier's arrival. She'd happily climbed into her bed with a good book when Elsie entered carrying many gift-wrapped boxes.

'Your father is a very generous man. I don't believe anyone needs to put up with such abuse. Poor Mr Hoskins had to assist Mr Harper in helping your mother up the stairs.'

'I have no comment on the matter. Mr Chevalier will arrive any day now, and I can't have anything interfering with my music,' Isabelle explained, a little tired of her mother's drama.

Isabelle wrote a letter to George apologising for her mother's state of health and thanking him for his kindness.

~

Isabelle arrived at the Royal Academy of Music in London with her father. She had dressed fashionably and waited for what seemed like an eternity in eager anticipation. Claude Chevalier finally appeared in the hall to greet Isabelle and Mr Harper graciously. His elegance and suave good looks were as she'd remembered, but his elusive manner disturbed her. She tried to override his mood by reaching out and embracing him with her music.

After Isabelle's lesson, Mr Chevalier gazed through the window deep in thought and looked into her eyes with a little sadness.

'I've received another letter from your mother, reminding me that your lessons will cease after your marriage. This contradiction is disturbing as everything has been arranged with your father. I've already organised your lessons at the academy.'

'Mother has not been herself of late and I apologise. My father will attend to her. I can assure you, my music is everything to me and no matter what happens I will continue playing forever,' Isabelle declared. She would not allow her mother to intervene.

'Thank you for your reassurance, my darling. I worship the ground you walk on. The thought of losing the girl who I love so dearly is unbearable.'

After returning to the Dorchester Hotel, where Mr Harper had booked three suites, Isabelle was unusually silent. Elsie did not mention Claude Chevalier and went about her usual duties. Isabelle gazed out of the window at the exciting London streets and wished her life could be different. She believed Pierre and Philippe had found freedom by living for the passion of their art.

'Apparently, we're returning early in the morning, miss, so I'll pack everything except the outfit for tomorrow,' Elsie advised.

'Did running away ever cross your mind when you were young?' Isabelle enquired.

'Many times, miss. But of course I never put the plan into action because the next day everything always appeared to be different,' Elsie replied with a chuckle, making light of Isabelle's dark thoughts.

As she arrived for an evening of elegant dining, it was clear that Mr Chevalier had been in discussion with her father at his club that afternoon. Everything appeared to be in order and Mr Chevalier seemed a much happier gentleman. Isabelle's evening gown caught many an eye, but Mr Chevalier remained spellbound by the enchanting young lady he'd fallen in love with. He longed for the day he could hold her hand and stand beside her, with their hopes and dreams together as one.

'Isabelle could be one of the finest young violinists in the country. As we discussed, I'm hoping that we can facilitate her journey and allow her great gift to be explored with no boundaries,' Mr Chevalier said.

'I'm flattered by such words and I pray that my ability surpasses your expectation. I am indeed in your debt for such attention to detail in teaching me the technique to allow the violin to sing so beautifully.'

Mr Harper smiled proudly at his daughter's eloquence and realised the deep regard she had for Mr Chevalier. He wondered if he'd made the right decision, leaving Paris and pandering to Mrs Harper's difficult behaviour, when Isabelle seemed so happy and content within herself.

~

Isabelle woke to sunshine beaming through the window. She caught a glimpse of Jimmy and the gypsy boys in their canoes on the river. After slipping into her dressing gown she noticed that Elsie had arranged her breakfast on the table.

'Thank you for respecting my wishes,' Isabelle remarked as she sat down to read the London Times.

'My pleasure, miss. Mrs Harper has given instruction for a quiet day. You're to decide on a design for the wedding gown. And a bridal high tea is in preparation for next week.' Elsie realised this news would not be well received.

As Elsie prepared a very warm bath for Isabelle, she was surprised to see Lorna arrive with the linen.

'I'm carrying out Mrs Harper's orders,' Lorna announced as she left the room. Elsie closed the door firmly behind her.

~

She needed a little adventure before enduring an afternoon of wedding talk with her mother. Isabelle put on her hat and picked up the easel and paints.

'An enjoyable wander through the fields is a must after experiencing such a stressful few days. If Mother Nature inspires me, I will strive to do her justice.'

'Please, miss! Don't upset your mother before the wedding,' Elsie cautioned.

Isabelle was willing to walk forever had she not met Jimmy in the field. He carried her easel and paints and joined her on the venture.

'I had a feeling you'd pass this way today,' Jimmy said.

'I'm so glad that I did,' Isabelle replied.

'When I first met you, I knew we'd be friends,' he remarked proudly.

'You'd love the artists Pierre and Philippe. They are in touch with what really matters in life. Not unlike Granny Harper. I recognised a connection with her very young,' she confessed.

Isabelle and Jimmy drifted peacefully down the overgrown river in a canoe, enjoying their precious time together. Jimmy alerted Isabelle to Lorna paddling by in a boat, but they were secluded by the bushes.

~

Elsie was arranging a magnificent display of red roses as Isabelle entered.

'From George Hoskins,' Elsie announced, cautious of mentioning the wedding.

'Thank you. The flowers are lovely. Are there any letters from Mr Chevalier?'

'No, miss, but I promise to hide the mail in a safe place away from prying eyes,' she reassured.

Overpowered by a feeling of hopelessness, and fearing that Mr Chevalier may not continue with her music, Isabelle tried to hold back the tears.

Mrs Harper's relentless interference with the academy had become a fatiguing exercise for all those involved. The timely appearance of Count Flaubert would be very welcome to give her father the support he needed. The situation seemed unimaginable when, just a few months ago, such happiness prevailed in Paris.

~

A week passed and the only topic of conversation was Isabelle's marriage. After she'd viewed and approved all the wedding invitations, Mrs Harper and Elsie entered with more dress designs from the bridal selections. No letter had arrived from her beloved Mr Chevalier.

'The decision to resume your music once you are married has been agreed upon and George will communicate with the Royal Academy in London. There will be no further contact with Claude Chevalier. You are too young to realise the importance of such decisions. A marriage to George Hoskins will bring you a wonderful life, allowing for your rightful position in society,' Mrs Harper clarified calmly.

'Did you have a choice of husband, Mother?' Isabelle enquired, struggling to suppress her distraught state.

'No, I did not,' Mrs Harper confessed after a long silence.

'And have you experienced a lifetime of bliss following your parents' choice?' Isabelle retorted.

'Such insolence and bad manners will not be tolerated. You will be confined to your room for a week!'

Elsie looked up from her sewing, devastated for Isabelle who fell onto the bed crying tears of shattered pain for her loss. Elsie knew she could offer no words of comfort.

~

A long and tedious week followed. With Mr Harper and George Hoskins in London on legal matters, Elsie was Isabelle's only ally. There had been no reply to her letters from Mr Chevalier or Count Flaubert. Isabelle couldn't find the inspiration to pick up the violin. She tried not to think of tomorrow and the emptiness that followed in her life. She had already been privileged to live her dream, but that had diminished into dust.

Chapter 16

With her punishment over, Isabelle painted by the river. The question on her mind being, how to put her shattered life back together. She hoped to see Jimmy that afternoon, but—to her delight and surprise—it was Count Flaubert who appeared on the river in a canoe. A jubilant squeal escaped her lips as he paddled to the riverbank. After stepping onto the grass and admiring her art, he kissed her hand courteously.

'I prayed for your arrival and here you are,' Isabelle greeted, expressing her joy at seeing him.

'My fellow traveller, I'm happy that I can be here for you. Your letter painted a tragic picture. I know you need comfort, not confinement.'

'Thank you, my dearest friend. I have your painting hanging on my wall. The Moulin Rouge saves me in those dark days when I believe I will never see the light.'

The count gently held her in his arms, as the tears flowed.

'I've seen Mr Chevalier and there is no doubt that he's in love with you, but you must understand that he's in an impossible position. The rules of our society do not allow him any claim on you unless the engagement to George is broken,' Count Flaubert explained.

'After finding such a glorious place of existence, how can I possibly dismiss it?' Isabelle asked with determination.

'Always remember that your parents will not be here forever, and a solid secure marriage is of the utmost importance to your future. At sixteen, I realise that is not how you perceive romance, but it's the reality of life and we must respect it. Your father worships the ground you walk on and he is your ally, but his task is to keep the family together. That has been extremely difficult due to your mother's illness. I'm sure you realise that, but sometimes it helps to hear it said by a fellow traveller. Allow me to assist you. Stepping into a canoe can be a tricky business.'

'I'll be the navigator. I know these rivers well, and we don't wish to get lost in the wilderness,' Isabelle said.

'We all wish for the intangible that lures us into the unknown. My love for you is unconditional,' Count Flaubert replied.

Isabelle found comfort as the count embraced her affectionately while they drifted down river. She felt blessed to have known such a fine gentleman.

An abandoned canoe could be seen on the riverbank that afternoon as the sun filtered through the leaves. The count had entwined Isabelle in his arms as they lay in the grass, well secluded. After being enchanted by her kiss and the warmth of her closeness, he would have loved to throw caution to the wind and make love to the most beautiful temptress he'd ever known, but—being her father's best friend and respecting her trust in him—he found contentment by enjoying her company.

'Do you know of any books that explain marriage?' Isabelle enquired.

'If I come across such a book, I will send it to you in haste,' Count Flaubert replied, loving her all the more for such adorable innocence.

Isabelle arrived at the manor in a much happier frame of mind.

'I noticed you through the window with Count Flaubert and felt he'd be the one to cheer you up,' Elsie said fondly.

'I've had such a lovely afternoon with my dearest friend. He has gently unscrambled my thoughts and, as if by a miracle, they have all found their rightful place.'

'Dare I ask if you were chaperoned?'

'He appeared on the river like an angel from heaven, a gift from God arriving just in time to save me from a terrible fate.'

'Mr Harper and Mr Hoskins are involved in a court trial in London, so your wedding is postponed for a month,' Elsie informed her.

'You've made my day complete.'

Wedding arrangements were hardly what Isabelle had in mind during such pleasurable weeks of sunshine. With her mother's stern rule being disruptive to her time spent on the river, she struggled to dream gloriously about her beloved Mr Chevalier. Her father's arrival home would be most welcome.

~

Isabelle's fellow traveller looked across the table and smiled encouragingly as he strove to comfort her role in society that he had displayed so superbly. She could never dislike George, no matter how hard she'd tried; he'd been a gentleman of his word—attentive, kind and loving—and his enchanting kisses had not been forgotten. But, despite the great effort made, she couldn't feel the love like she did with Claude Chevalier. Mr Harper congratulated his future son-in-law for his remarkable work for the firm and George responded graciously, drawing attention to the extraordinary success that Isabelle had also achieved with her music.

'Thank you, George, for your kind words. I sincerely appreciate the acknowledgement of my ability,' she remarked agreeably and glimpsed coldly in her mother's direction to remind her that she'd lied about George.

~

Isabelle hurried through the field, worshipping a heavenly freedom from wedding conversation. She'd missed Jimmy's company. He had seemed to live without complications since his father had mended his ways.

Jimmy appeared and Isabelle approached the riverbank. 'I knew you'd be here,' Jimmy said.

'How could you know when I didn't know myself?'

'Call it magic if you will,' Jimmy remarked with a cheeky grin as he assisted her into the boat.

Jimmy caught a glimpse of Lorna through the trees and signalled for Isabelle to lie low in the canoe. He feared—even though he'd taken great care—that Lorna may have followed him and taken the opportunity to perform a curse on Isabelle. Paddling at speed, he knew they were safe once they'd entered the secret river.

The morning sunshine made the river a heavenly place to be. Isabelle felt such love for her friend Jimmy but knew the impossibility of such a romance. Jimmy was amused by her wet petticoat as she hung her dripping wet dress on a tree branch to dry.

'I have feelings for you, but I realise how difficult that would be,' Jimmy remarked quietly.

'I know,' Isabelle answered and held his hand in response.

Jimmy encouraged her to join him in the grass and daydream the morning into the afternoon. She enjoyed warm comfort in his arms.

The surprise of Mrs Harper's appearance was alarming. She snatched the frock hanging on a tree branch and threw it at Isabelle with all her might.

'Get dressed this instant!'

'Please, I can explain,' Jimmy exclaimed, as he leaped to his feet and pleaded for a hearing.

'I've seen enough! Your father will be informed, Master Williams.'

Jimmy glared at Lorna, who'd been hiding amongst the trees. He ran across the field to the vicarage, worried about what may happen to Isabelle. Lorna paddled the canoe back to the manor as Mrs Harper had instructed while Isabelle sat silently with her mother.

Reverend Durn had asked for tea to be served in the library to calm Jimmy's distressed state.

'Why were you with Isabelle at all?' Charles enquired, trying to make sense of the situation.

'Adventures on the river give her comfort from an engagement she feels powerless to break, sir,' Jimmy explained as best he could.

'You did nothing wrong in the eyes of God?' Charles questioned.

'No, sir. We enjoyed each other's company and love to swim in the river.'

'Were you fully clothed?'

'Almost. Isabelle always wore her petticoat.'

Charles looked out of the window at the gypsy children at play.

'I'll call on you once I've discussed the situation with Isabelle and her parents. Please, finish your tea and scones. The butler will look after you.'

Stepping into the Bentley sports car, Charles drove across to the Harper Estate. He knew Mrs Harper to be of the old school, intolerant of any irrational ideas or new thoughts, but found Mr Harper to be in tune with change. After the First World War, ideals had altered, but for some—like Mrs Harper—the comfort of the old ways remained.

The butler Cummings presented an afternoon tea to the Reverend Durn, Isabelle and her parents. The knowledge that Charles would be an ally boosted Isabelle's confidence.

'That will be all, Cummings,' Mr Harper announced.

'Thank you, sir,' Cummings replied.

'I've spoken to Jimmy and nothing has happened to be alarmed about. In the name of God, they've done no wrong.'

'I will not tolerate such disgraceful behaviour. Isabelle is engaged to be married into a very fine family indeed,' Mrs Harper said.

'I realise that swimming in the river is not considered ladylike for a young lady of noble birth, but times are changing. I'm hoping you will consider that carefully in your judgement of Isabelle,' Charles advised.

'Jimmy's father has been informed of the situation,' Mrs Harper warned.

'I'm sorry to hear that. I'd better attend to the Williams family before church,' Charles replied.

After Reverend Durn had left, the atmosphere altered and a mood of sternness took command as Mrs Harper moved nearer to Isabelle.

'You selfish, wretched and ungrateful girl. Who will marry you now!' Mrs Harper screeched hysterically.

'I need to hear what Isabelle has to say. Please be silent, madam, and allow her the right to speak,' Mr Harper insisted.

'You've pandered to her every whim! All the expensive gifts, music lessons in Paris, encouraging her to believe she is a great musician,' Mrs Harper scoffed.

Mr Harper thumped his fist onto the table so hard that the crockery smashed onto the floor.

'My darling girl, please go to your room. I need to discuss this particular matter with your mother.'

He closed the door and turned sharply in Mrs Harper's direction.

'It would have been better for Isabelle if we'd stayed away in Paris,' Mr Harper announced.

'With your women!' Mrs Harper replied bitterly.

'How sad you are. I came back because I loved you,' Mr Harper replied before excusing himself and leaving the room.

Mrs Harper looked up to see the door closing, poured herself a glass of gin and sat alone.

~

Charles felt great concern for Jimmy and knew he must deal with the situation immediately. He picked Reverend Harris up along the way and informed him of what had happened. When the vicars arrived amongst the tall trees, there was a scuffle happening between Jimmy and his father Sam Williams. Charles stopped the car and tried to intervene as Sam raised a stick and belted Jimmy. Children screamed and scattered as elders observed the violent beating. Sam belted him with a vicious blow to the head, but Jimmy tried to fight back. Charles stepped in, hitting the stick out of Sam's hand as Rosa screamed hysterically.

'You have shamed me!' Sam shouted as he hit his son again with his fist.

'We did nothing wrong!' Jimmy screamed.

'Sam, he's your son,' Martin yelled to bring him to his senses.

Charles shoved Sam with all his might to try and keep them apart. Sam stumbled backwards, grabbed the stick and hit Jimmy so hard that the boy fell to the ground unconscious. Rosa ran to Jimmy and Lorna approached cautiously.

'Stay away from my Jimmy!' Rosa screamed hysterically at Lorna who ran away into the woods.

Martin attended to Jimmy's wounds while Charles grabbed Sam and snatched the stick, throwing it far away.

The elders began to chant a pagan ritual. Jimmy glimpsed the pagan "White Girl". He'd heard about the girl with the beauty and whiteness of the mist at dawn, and knew he'd been cursed. As she vanished through the trees, he stumbled to his feet and made his way through the woods with swollen eyes and a bloodied face. He discovered Lorna holding a voodoo doll, performing a ceremony in a frenzied state. He snatched the doll and threw it into the river, grabbing Lorna when she tried to retrieve it.

'Jimmy, please forgive me,' Lorna screamed.

He shoved her to the ground and walked away, the doll swirling downriver with the strong current.

Young William and Peter were peering through the leaves at Jimmy as he climbed into his canoe and pushed it away from the riverbank.

'Please don't send my Jimmy away!' Rosa screamed hysterically.

Jimmy looked back at his people fading into the distance, very sad to have lost his family.

Lorna was staggering along the riverbank, but Jimmy showed no interest as he drifted by.

'Jimmy, please help me!'

Lorna stumbled forward and fell. The swirling current swept her away as she disappeared under the water.

Chapter 17

Isabelle felt deeply concerned for Jimmy as Elsie filled her in on what she knew of the situation.

'I wonder where we'll all be ten years from now,' Isabelle pondered.

'God knows, miss,' Elsie replied.

'I'll be twenty-six years old with the occasional theatre engagement and a little travel, entertaining a society that I have no interest in at all,' Isabelle remarked unhappily.

'I do have some good news for you. I found a bundle of Mr Chevalier's letters hidden in the sideboard drawer downstairs,' Elsie informed her.

'There is a God after all. I was beginning to believe it must all be a myth and I'm so pleased to be proven wrong.'

Isabelle had been allowed to meet Reverend Durn in the library. He'd been disturbed by the extent of her punishment for what he believed to be innocent in the eyes of God. With Mr Harper being away in London and Mrs Harper unresponsive, it made a meeting with Isabelle very difficult.

'Devonshire tea is my very favourite,' Isabelle announced, putting on a brave face for Charles.

'Mine to. I must say you're looking very well indeed considering such a long period of isolation,' Charles remarked.

'I think about you every day. I wonder what you're doing. I imagine what Jimmy is up to. Have you seen Jimmy?' Isabelle whispered.

'He's been cursed and sent away. I desperately tried to stop the ritual, to no avail. I'm sorry to bring you bad tidings but I felt that the responsibility to inform you of such a tragedy was mine,' Charles answered. Tears spilled down Isabelle's desperately unhappy face.

'I don't think I have the strength to persevere and display the pretence of love. In the eyes of God, that must be hypocritical.'

'I'll pray to God for your great strength of mind to find the outcome and the happiness that you're in search of,' Charles replied with care. He felt sorrow for the beautiful girl who had bewitched him.

Charles bid her a fond farewell, and Isabelle waved to him through the window as young William joined him for a ride in the Bentley sports car.

Her days were spent reading all the romantic letters from Claude Chevalier which Elsie returned to their rightful drawer downstairs each afternoon. Isabelle replied to her beloved explaining the circumstances and Elsie took the mail to the post office herself, giving the return address of her sister so that Mrs Harper could not interfere with the mail.

Isabelle decided to try and find Jimmy on the river the day her punishment ended. She knew Charles would assist and that God would have the power to reverse the terrible curse.

William and Peter observed Jimmy drifting in his canoe through the overgrown trees; they were shocked by his pale and lifeless face.

'I miss Isabelle,' William said.

'Do you think we'll ever see her again?' Peter asked.

'No, I don't believe we will,' William replied unhappily.

'Jimmy needs food,' Peter urged.

'It's forbidden. Mother told me that the pagans practice witchcraft.'

'Nobody would know,' Peter exclaimed.

William lay back in the rowboat looking up to the sky. 'I'll marry Isabelle one day,' he announced.

'In your dreams,' Peter scoffed. He looked around, very uneasy at the heavy mist rolling in, with the horror of witchcraft curses fresh in his mind.

~

Mr Harper had returned and Isabelle dined at his insistence. She'd written to her father regarding her feelings for Mr Chevalier and, so far, he'd been silent on the matter. His delight at seeing her showed a glimmer of promise.

'How is George?' Isabelle enquired, knowing her father would be pleased that she'd asked that question, even after revealing her love for Mr Chevalier. He didn't answer straightaway; he pondered the question while sipping French wine from a crystal glass.

'He's very well indeed and looking forward to seeing you. His clever legal manoeuvring won the firm a very difficult case. I've sent him on holiday to the south of France to show my gratitude for his excellent work,' Mr Harper said proudly.

'Give him my hearty congratulations,' Isabelle replied, relieved that time would be on her side.

'You can give him your best wishes personally. I thought we may join him for a family holiday. The count and countess have happily agreed to host us,' Mr Harper announced.

'Oh Father, how I would love such a holiday. Maybe Philippe and Pierre could join us?' Isabelle suggested passionately.

'I don't see any reason why they shouldn't. They must be due another set of tails and top hats by now,' Mr Harper replied, laughing heartily.

Mrs Harper appeared a little detached but managed a smile.

'Your endurance to harsh punishment has served you well. As a reward you will resume your lessons until your marriage. The French Riviera will be most enjoyable for us all,' Mrs Harper remarked.

Isabelle found it difficult to smile, but forced her face muscles to do so. 'Thank you, Mother.'

~

Isabelle woke to a spectacular sunrise, opened the windows and looked down to the river, wondering if Jimmy may pass by. She hoped Charles had been wrong about the curse. Her dearest friend had been punished for no reason. Surely such a wrong could be put right; if that was not possible, Isabelle thought, there can't be a God at all.

Elsie put a letter from Mr Chevalier into her hand, and Isabelle squealed excitedly. She sat immediately and read in earnest. Elsie knew that the letter contained good news on seeing Isabelle's smile.

Distracted by William throwing a pebble up at the window, she looked out and noticed that he held a pretty bunch of wildflowers in his hand.

'Wait for me,' she instructed in a raised voice, flattered by his gesture.

After tying a sun hat under her chin, Isabelle picked up her easel and paints.

'Enjoy the heavenly morning,' Elsie remarked, with a joyful note of celebration in her voice.

'Oh, I will, believe me. God has blessed me with glorious freedom. Nobody has the right to meddle with my day and pass harsh judgement,' Isabelle replied, rapturous to be leaving her room after two months of confinement.

After thanking William for the flowers Isabelle walked through the fields with him. Meeting Charles at the vicarage gate as planned, the three of them set off to explore the river in the hope of finding Jimmy. Charles welcomed Isabelle, with the same affection of days gone by, which made William a little jealous as he walked behind carrying her easel and paints.

'Happy birthday, William,' Charles said with a smile.

'Thank you, sir. I've turned thirteen today.'

'How remiss of me! Have a wonderful birthday,' Isabelle said, giving him a gentle kiss on the cheek.

A tiring morning of searching followed—paddling upriver in a canoe, exploring amongst the trees on the water's edge—but they didn't find Jimmy. William, with his friend Peter, was the only one of the search party who had seen Jimmy since the curse; he knew that Jimmy believed he had no choice in his destiny and showed no desire to return. As exhaustion prevailed, they gave up their search for the day and returned to the vicarage.

William showed surprise and joy as the vicarage butler entered with a birthday cake and thirteen lit candles. Isabelle encouraged a wish to be made before he blew out the flames. She kissed him on the cheek fondly and he blushed boyishly.

'Your secret is safe with me,' Isabelle declared.

'Never let your birthday wish be known or shown,' Charles said, with the wink of an eye in William's direction.

'Understood, sir.'

Isabelle informed Charles that her search for Jimmy would continue each day until all avenues had been exhausted.

'Promise me that you'll study the Bible and find the answer to dismissing the powers of pagan witchcraft,' Isabelle pleaded.

'I will continue to do everything I can,' Charles replied, feeling helpless against such evil.

Isabelle sat at the piano and played the enchanting song that Jimmy had composed for her on the flute. Tears spilled down her face and Charles embraced her tenderly. As a trio, they played an afternoon of treasured music for Jimmy, in the hope it would bring him home. After the sunset appeared through the window Charles decided to drive Isabelle to the manor in case of more trouble with Mrs Harper.

Isabelle woke very early the next morning and practised for an hour before breakfast.

'You and that violin are made for each other,' Elsie remarked, pleasurably.

'I think you're right. It's a love affair for all time,' Isabelle replied, gently stroking her instrument.

Elsie answered a knock at the door and returned with an enormous display of red roses.

'George Hoskins.'

'Thank you,' Isabelle replied, laughing as she read the card.

'I'm glad he can make you laugh,' Elsie commented.

'George has been to the Moulin Rouge and confesses to being both shocked and enraptured by his experience,' Isabelle said, laughing heartily and remembering her own sublime visit.

~

Charles kept his word, joining Isabelle and William every morning in search of Jimmy. Isabelle mentioned her dear friend Jimmy in a letter to Claude Chevalier and he sympathised about the terrible wrong that had been committed. He also urged her to break the engagement to George Hoskins so that they could marry and live blissfully in their own heavenly world. Isabelle knew her father liked Mr Chevalier and approved of his family history of aristocracy and wealth—even if he had not dreamed of his daughter marrying a maestro of music. Mr Harper had not mentioned Isabelle's letter in which she revealed her feelings for Mr Chevalier.

After a morning walk across the fields, Isabelle approached the vicarage with William. Lola wasn't in her usual spot, swinging on the gate, and it seemed as though the gypsy children had vanished. During Isabelle's lesson, they received the news that Jimmy's body had been found by a fisherman in a faraway place; the body remained unclaimed by his family.

Isabelle believed that her tears would fall forever as she kneeled beside Jimmy's grave. He had been buried near Granny Harper on the Estate with Mr Harper's permission. Isabelle's father insisted on a service for Jimmy at the chapel, also insisting on Mrs Harper's attendance. Charles and Sarah stayed close to Isabelle to comfort the loss of her dearest friend who understood the very essence of her soul. He'd vanished from her life without reason or warning, and she knew in her heart that he'd be irreplaceable for all time.

Later, Isabelle stood on a chair, removing Jimmy's paintings and sculptures from the suitcase hidden on top of the wardrobe. She jumped down, spread his work on the table, and admired his art that she would treasure forever. Elsie arrived with three bouquets of flowers.

'George Hoskins, Claude Chevalier and Count Flaubert, miss,' Elsie announced as she reached for the letters in her pocket.

Isabelle read the letter from Mr Chevalier and strove to suppress her tears of joy.

'Can you keep a secret, Elsie?'

'I've been doing so from the day you began to talk,' she smiled.

'Father has organised another term at the Paris Conservatorium of Music under the command of Claude Chevalier,' Isabelle whispered.

'You're a very lucky young lady to have such a loving father,' Elsie replied, very pleased for her.

She read the letter from George, glad to hear his kind thoughts about Jimmy. He explained how lucky she'd been to have known such a free spirit with a likeness to herself. George wrote that the privileges of life's simplicities go unnoticed for most as their vision is minimal. Isabelle was deeply moved and surprised by George's observation; she had perceived him in a different light— a man of the law with plain thoughts. Count Flaubert also touched her heart as a fellow traveller who understood the devastation of losing her gypsy soulmate.

She woke the next morning to see Elsie fussing about the room. A warm bath had been prepared and her favourite dress was hanging over the back of the chair. She heard a car pulling up on the driveway.

'Your mother has given instructions, miss,' Elsie clarified.

'Good Lord! George Hoskins has arrived. We were supposed to join him on the French Riviera,' Isabelle exclaimed disappointedly.

'He's returned early, miss. Your parents wish for you to spend some time together, before your father escorts you to Paris to resume your studies. Mr Hoskins will be running the firm while Mr Harper is away. I must say, your mother's health is much improved since Lorna's dismissal.'

'According to Reverend Durn, she drowned in the river after performing the terrible curse on Jimmy,' Isabelle disclosed, void of emotion.

'Well, I can't say that I'm sorry after the trouble that girl incited,' Elsie replied.

The picturesque gardens were a perfect setting for Isabelle and George to enjoy each other's company before her departure. Mr and Mrs Harper were charmed by Isabelle's elegant beauty and George smiled, showing his love for her. He understood the devastation and anguish that she had endured during her long confinement and respected her great will. He agreed with Mr Harper and felt that the continuation of her music in Paris would be just the right medicine for her to recover from the loss of her friend before the wedding.

~

Jimmy was foremost on Isabelle's mind as she crossed the field on the way to her lesson at the vicarage. She sensed Jimmy's presence while passing her favourite oak tree, then found a sculpture of herself in a petticoat protruding from the hollow of the tree. She picked up the beautifully carved art and held it close to her heart, knowing Jimmy had returned with her gift. The knowledge that she could have saved him had she not been confined broke her heart and she cried tears of despair.

Charles tried to comfort Isabelle and she strove to embrace her lesson with passion. They played a magnificent duet, realising it may be the last time they would do so.

'I will always love you, Charles, but I believe you were right in your choice,' Isabelle said with a smile as she packed her violin next to Jimmy's sculpture.

A Rolls Royce pulled up at the vicarage; George Hoskins and William stepped from the motor.

'I've been sent on an errand and a happy traveller joined me along the way,' George said with a smile. William greeted Isabelle with a bunch of flowers.

'Thank you, William. They're lovely. Reverend Durn has been waiting for you,' Isabelle exclaimed.

She enjoyed a captivating drive and a riveting conversation about the Moulin Rouge with George. Isabelle adored their intimate kiss as they parked by the roadside wondering if she may have felt differently if they'd spent more time alone. George had never spoken much about his family but he mentioned for the first time the pressure he'd endured from his parents. He said he never wanted to repeat the process with their children. Isabelle felt so moved that she kissed him again.

'I will treasure your heavenly kiss and hold it close to my heart always. But we'd better drive home or they may never see us again,' George said with a wry smile.

As they approached the ancient oak trees, reminding her of Granny Harper, a smile appeared on her happy face.

'I played with Granny under those trees and just loved the intriguing stories she had to tell. I believe she influenced and changed my life forever.'

'Being less fortunate in that regard, I inherited a granny with a stern authority, totally void of any storytelling. The Bible was the only book allowed in the house.'

George took Isabelle into his arms and kissed her tenderly before they arrived back at the manor.

'Time to make our entrance, my lovely temptress. Your father will be waiting and I've no desire to explain the reason for being late.'

Elsie observed Isabelle arriving in a blissful mood and remained silent on the subject of a chaperone.

'We've half an hour to be ready and downstairs,' Elsie announced.

'I've had a wonderful afternoon. In doing so, I've realised that I didn't really know George at all,' Isabelle confessed with not a care for being late.

'Therefore, Paris will give you time to relax and make up your mind without any pressure from the family,' Elsie commented.

Enraptured by his bride-to-be as she entered the room in an exquisite evening gown; her beauty bewitched him and he wished for their marriage to be sooner rather than later. Surprised by how many guests had been invited, Isabelle felt a little disappointed, wishing she could spend more time with George. He looked so handsome in his smart new tails. Reverend Durn and Sarah embraced her warmly, along with Reverend Harris and his wife.

A captivating evening of diverse conversation was enjoyed by all. After such splendid dining and fine wine, George escorted Isabelle onto the dance floor as the London Quartet played her favourite Strauss Waltz. George danced her around the room with grace and charm as Mr and Mrs Harper showed their pleasure.

Chapter 18

Isabelle smiled blissfully as they disembarked at the palatial Hotel Ritz in Paris. She felt at home in the plush elegant suite as she opened the curtains and delightedly viewed the rooftops of Paris. Elsie had unpacked her violin in readiness as a gruelling morning of practice followed. The rapture at the thought of seeing Mr Chevalier and the possibilities of all their dreams coming to fruition overwhelmed her.

Arriving at the café for morning tea, she was welcomed like royalty by her dear friends Philippe and Pierre.

'How I've missed you!' Isabelle said, embracing them.

She acknowledged the waiter with the handlebar moustache who smiled in return.

'Welcome home, mademoiselle,' the waiter said as he presented a large plate of warm croissants.

'It's so lovely to see you, and don't worry about payment,' Isabelle said to Phillipe and Pierre, noticing a painting on the table.

'This work is sold,' Pierre exclaimed proudly. 'Many sales are required before we can visit your glorious England, but one fine day we will arrive on your doorstep.'

Mr Harper and Count Flaubert made a grand entrance in their Panama hats carrying many gift-wrapped boxes. Isabelle welcomed her father affectionately, knowing that he'd been to a meeting with Mr Chevalier. She greeted him with the knowledge that he alone had made all this possible. The count kissed her hand courteously; her fellow traveller had always displayed unrelenting support for her.

The happiness Isabelle felt being back in Paris surprised even her. She hadn't encountered the man of her dreams as yet but believed her tutoring would commence in the morning. Count Flaubert smiled keenly at Isabelle's childlike curiosity as she peered into the boxes, delighting in the exquisite gifts from her father. Philippe and Pierre were joyous after Mr Harper presented them with gift boxes containing new suits. Mr Harper was glad to be able to afford such generosity. He ordered more croissants and coffee for the table and they all indulged agreeably. An expressive conversation about art followed.

Claude Chevalier, looking suave and elegant in a stylish suit, removed his Fedora hat upon entering and smiled adoringly at Isabelle as he kissed her hand. She tried to control her flushed cheeks and remain poised.

'I'm sorry to interrupt your colourful morning, but I was passing and had a feeling you may be here.'

'Please join us,' Mr Harper insisted, pleasurably.

'Unfortunately, I have a rehearsal, but I very much look forward to seeing you both, tomorrow,' Mr Chevalier said charmingly, smiling in Isabelle's direction.

Isabelle spent time with Count Flaubert that afternoon as her father had business to attend to. The count gladly showed her around his captivating Paris. After being introduced to many well-known artists at a restaurant of the count's choice, Isabelle felt in her element visiting places that she'd read about in books. There had been stimulating chatter amongst the artists, including an offer to paint Isabelle's portrait, which Count Flaubert declined respectfully on Mr Harper's behalf. After spending such an engaging time socialising and being presented to Parisian Society, neither Isabelle nor her fellow traveller wanted the remarkable afternoon to come to an end.

Elsie opened the door, as enthralled as Isabelle to be back in Paris. 'Your violin awaits you, miss.'

'I've had the most extraordinary afternoon with Count Flaubert.'

'No chaperone I suppose,' Elsie remarked.

'I feel as though I've just stepped off the merry-go-round and all has fallen silent,' Isabelle announced, ignoring Elsie's comment.

After three hours of gruelling practice, Isabelle stepped into a warm bath of rose petals in front of the roaring fire and dreamed the day all over again.

~

As Isabelle had retired early, she woke excitedly at dawn and practised for many hours before breakfast. Her rose-coloured dress complimented the red hair that fell gracefully to her shoulders from under a stylish hat.

'I can't believe the day has arrived and I'm actually going to spend time with him,' Isabelle said wistfully, approving her look in the full-length mirror.

'All the luck in the world, miss. I pray to God that all your dreams come true,' Elsie said kindly.

Mr Harper waited with Isabelle until the door opened and Mr Chevalier appeared. He greeted them with ardour, showing great style and panache. Once the formalities had been discussed, the moment Isabelle had been patiently waiting for arrived. She entered the room alone with Claude Chevalier and removed her violin from the case in readiness. Not knowing what her father had discussed with Mr Chevalier, Isabelle felt the best approach would be to stay calm and poised, allowing her music to speak for itself. As she concluded, he smiled and praised her brilliance. Then he took her into his arms, kissing her with a love so fine that she recognised Mr Chevalier to be her man.

'I love you,' Isabelle said, blissful in his arms.

'You will never know how much I have longed for this day,' Mr Chevalier replied quietly, with love in his heart.

Isabelle tried to cool her flushed cheeks as she left the Conservatorium. Philippe and Pierre joined her on the way to the café, looking smart and elegant in their new suits and top hats.

'We have made one sale today so far, but we have paintings for you for payment,' Pierre said.

'Sell your art. I can assure you that Father doesn't mind buying morning tea,' Isabelle replied, always a little nervous of what vision she may encounter.

Isabelle was in her element at the café, sketching the faces in the street. She looked forward to the day she could make her own decisions and not have to wait patiently for her father's instructions. But, appreciating the opportunity he had already given her to be with the man of her dreams, she decided to remain patient.

A very handsome young man introduced himself as being one of the students at the Paris Conservatorium and said that he'd heard a great deal about Isabelle Harper and her brilliance. She'd been quite surprised by his forwardness.

'I'm Antoine Aubrey. You don't know me, but I've heard a great deal about your genius.'

'I'm Isabelle Harper and I'm delighted to meet you. May I enquire as to which instrument you play?' Isabelle asked, admiring his dark brown eyes and unruly fair hair.

'The cello is my forte, a difficult instrument if you don't have a natural ear for music. Since my lessons commenced at the Conservatorium, my work is much improved and that has made my father a happier man.'

Isabelle introduced Philippe and Pierre, and—after Mr Aubrey initially showed surprise that the street artists were her friends—they entered into a controversial but stimulating conversation about French and British politics. Count Flaubert made his entrance and pulled up a chair.

'I'm just in time to save you from the guillotine, my darling Isabelle,' Count Flaubert announced, staring inquisitively at Antoine Aubrey.

'I do beg your pardon, sir. I'm a pupil at the Conservatorium and it is bold of me to make Miss Harper's acquaintance without a chaperone.'

'You're forgiven if you have acquired the title of artist,' the count exclaimed.

'I'm striving to, sir. I do know your fine work as an artist,' Mr Aubrey replied enthusiastically.

'Like my fellow traveller, Miss Harper, I try to make some sense of life,' the count replied.

'Please do join us for morning tea, Mr Aubrey. My father will be arriving shortly, and I know he will approve,' Isabelle said.

Mr Harper certainly warmed to Antoine Aubrey after discovering he'd studied with his father at Cambridge. Count Flaubert was happily reminiscing about those wonderful years as Mr Aubrey senior appeared through the crowded café.

Isabelle spent another splendid afternoon with the count; she found him irresistible and felt blessed in his company knowing her father held him in high esteem. After a delicious seafood lunch, Count Flaubert joined Isabelle lying on the riverbank. Her thoughts were of Claude Chevalier and when they would be able to marry. Mr Harper had not discussed the situation with her at all, but she realised the trouble he'd gone to so that she could be with him.

'The importance of making your love known is essential,' Isabelle said, as she spoke her thoughts out loud.

'It is, indeed, my beauty. But, more importantly, the rules of our society must be in place in order to live your dream,' Count Flaubert remarked, understanding the frustration of being so near and yet so far.

~

After an inspiring lesson, Claude Chevalier sat Isabelle down to make plans for their future.

'I have a meeting with your father next week. I need to know where we stand in this arrangement.'

Isabelle dismissed the slight impatience shown by her beloved, but managed to cheer him with a loving smile.

'May I suggest a walk in the gardens to dream our cares away,' she kindly advised.

'You may, but firstly, I'm inviting you to perform in concert at the end of the month.'

'I'm privileged, and I thank you,' Isabelle replied.

'In the meantime, there's nothing better than the country air and green fields to clear your thoughts, and I look forward to welcoming you and your father to the chateau.'

~

A crowd of entertaining guests mingled at Mr Chevalier's grand chateau in Burgundy. Isabelle, who arrived with Mr Harper, joined the count and countess; embracing the light-heartedness of the occasion after a very serious week. Isabelle received a warm greeting from Mr Chevalier and noticed many of the pupils from the Conservatorium were in attendance, including Antoine Aubrey.

Isabelle had been lured by the fairy-tale views of the chateau; they inspired such romantic thoughts, of her handsome Mr Chevalier. A familiar voice interrupted her daydream.

'Do you ride, Miss Harper?' Mr Aubrey enquired.

'Of course. But, as I'm in concert, the rules are no sport.'

'This may surprise you, but my greatest ambition is to be the fastest runner in the world.'

'Good heavens! I would have thought that a difficult task to achieve.' Isabelle said, surprised by his choice.

'Not if you train as the great athletes do. My father disapproves, of course, as he has great ambitions for me to be a fine musician. Maybe one day I will achieve that brilliance, but I'd still like to be a sportsman.'

'You certainly have acres of land here to try your skills.'

'I'm a sprinter and I need someone to time my run.'

'I don't see any complication. Just hand me the stopwatch when you wish to run and I'll press stop when you finish the race.'

'Thank you, Miss Harper. I appreciate your kindness.'

Isabelle had warmed to his direct manner; he reminded her of Jimmy.

~

Mr Aubrey senior, Mr Harper and Count Flaubert had formed a Cambridge reunion, recalling fond memories of times gone by. A cosy atmosphere from a roaring fire enhanced the magnificent room. Isabelle smiled in Mr Chevalier's direction; she dreamed of being in his arms and wished all the guests would leave the room so they could be alone at last.

The next day, Isabelle gazed through a romantic sixteenth century window to see the beauty of a canal lined with poplar trees in the early morning sun. Elsie fussed to have her ready for breakfast in the dining room where Isabelle hoped to have a moment alone with her beloved. As she hurried down the hall, Mr Chevalier reached out from a doorway, pulled her into his arms and kissed her with a love so divine she never wanted to leave such a heavenly place.

The mood at breakfast was an enjoyable one as the guests planned their day. Unable to join Mr Chevalier, Mr Harper and Count Flaubert on a morning ride, Isabelle ventured along the picturesque canal on foot to be met by Mr Aubrey.

'I have a stopwatch if you could spare a moment of your time.'

'Sorry…my thoughts were far away,' Isabelle confessed.

'I'll signal you to start, and when I pass the tree, press stop.'

'All too easy.'

Isabelle carried out his instructions, the sprint finished and Mr Aubrey observed the result with surprise.

'You have inspired me,' he said as he put the stopwatch into his pocket.

A ball in the evening took place in a room of grandeur. Mr Chevalier waltzed Isabelle who wore an evening gown of exquisite elegance. As they swept blissfully past Mr Harper, he smiled, recognising how much they meant to each other. Wishing that the evening would never end, and the music would play forever, Mr Chevalier looked into Isabelle's violet blue eyes and prayed they'd be together for all time.

'Thank you for sharing the most beautiful night of my life,' he said.

'An evening that will live in my heart forever,' Isabelle replied as the last note of a Strauss waltz played. The room took on a feeling of emptiness with just idle chatter lingering within the walls.

Chapter 19

Arriving back in Paris, Isabelle browsed the bookshops looking to find an informative read about marriage. The lady behind the counter appeared friendly enough but, looking more closely, Isabelle made the decision against such an awkward question.

'You look troubled,' Mr Aubrey remarked.

'Oh! You startled me,' Isabelle replied, surprised to encounter Mr Aubrey in one of Paris's many bookshops on such a delicate matter of enquiry.

'Can I be of assistance, mademoiselle?' Mr Aubrey asked eagerly.

'I don't think so, certainly not on the fragile subject that I need to research, but thank you for your solicitude,' Isabelle answered.

~

A week of rigorous tutoring followed, and Isabelle adored the treasured time spent with Mr Chevalier. She was surprised to see Mr Aubrey practising with the orchestra. She waited for the appropriate moment and welcomed him.

'I can't believe that I've been selected and wonder if my father had an influence,' Mr Aubrey exclaimed in a bewildered state.

'After hearing your magnificent playing I know that Mr Chevalier has chosen you on merit. He's not a man who can be easily persuaded. One day we should arrive early and see how our instruments converse,' Isabelle suggested kindly.

'I'm humbled by the offer, mademoiselle, and will happily accept,' Mr Aubrey replied.

That morning in the café a delectable air of splendour seemed to accompany morning tea as Philippe and Pierre handed out the invitations for a grand showing of their art and welcomed Isabelle with ardour. Mr Harper and Count Flaubert joined in the festivities after a late arrival. A book—still in its fancy wrapping paper—caught the count's eye.

'You found that book you were in search of?' Count Flaubert asked Isabelle with a grin.

'I'm afraid not, but I found an interesting novel, recommended by a very good friend,' Isabelle informed him.

'Antoine Aubrey appears to be a very nice young man,' Mr Harper commented.

'He is indeed, and Mr Aubrey has had recent success with his music.'

Gazing at the faces in the street, Isabelle sat pondering as to what the future may bring. There had been a meeting with her father and Mr Chevalier but not a word had been mentioned to her. She would dearly like to take control of the conversation but knew that would result in silence. Her father hadn't mentioned George but the red roses were arriving as usual. Isabelle reminded herself time and time again of the trouble her father had taken to enable her relationship with Mr Chevalier. It was a relief not to have received a letter from her mother; Isabelle had found no room in her heart for forgiveness. Mrs Harper had shown no remorse for the horrific wrong she had committed as Jimmy had lost the most precious and blessed wonder on earth, his life.

~

Philippe and Pierre looked quite spectacular in their top hats and tails with red carnations elegantly placed in the lapel of their jackets. They proudly escorted Isabelle into their grand exhibition. Astounded by the quality of artistic presentation, Count Flaubert had invited the notoriety of Paris. The crowd mingled, impressed and inspired by the work. Isabelle was proud that her father had organised a greater part of the event and watched him congratulate Philippe and Pierre on their remarkable success.

Mr Chevalier made an elegant entrance, showing deep affection as he kissed Isabelle's hand. It became clear to Mr Harper that a decision would soon have to be reached—possibly the most difficult one he would ever have to make.

The thrill of the morning escalated and many more paintings were sold. Mr Harper and Count Flaubert had certainly guided the business side of the venture, which proved very lucrative for the young artists. Pierre embraced Isabelle in tears of bewilderment, realising his life as a street artist was changing.

'You're overwhelmed, and so you should be. Embrace the day as there'll be many more to follow,' Isabelle urged passionately.

'We'll be on your doorstep in England sooner rather than later,' Philippe said eagerly.

'My mother may not be very agreeable,' Isabelle informed them, with a note of hilarity in her voice.

'Oh yes! Mrs Harper. Thank you for the warning, my good friend,' Philippe remarked.

~

The morning practice at the Conservatorium proved to be successful. Mr Aubrey joined Isabelle and their instruments conversed beautifully. Mr Chevalier stood spellbound as he listened to such sublime music being played. The overwhelming joy of being appointed star soloist in concert made Isabelle realise her divine destiny. Mr Aubrey would partner her for the duet.

'I so look forward to working with you,' Isabelle said keenly.

'I'm humbled by your brilliance and I pray that I can do you justice.'

~

Isabelle took a romantic walk by the river with Mr Chevalier. They remained secluded amongst the trees to allow a little more expression of love.

'I intend to thank your father for his generosity of spirit and advise a suitable date for our wedding, my darling,' Mr Chevalier said with an urgent tone in his voice. Isabelle sensed his underlying impatience, but felt a calm approach would be more effective. She had noticed that her father did not respond well to matters of urgency.

'I believe a weekend by the seaside would have an encouraging outcome,' Isabelle suggested, with a note of contentment in her voice.

'There's something to be said for early man and his simple idea of two people falling in love,' Mr Chevalier remarked, finding a little humour in the situation.

'Father can see how much we mean to each other and he quietly altered the situation. I'm so glad that he did,' Isabelle replied.

'One day we'll look back on these troubles and be amused. We'll be an old married couple with at least six children to comfort us beside a cosy fireplace and be full of wonder at our splendid life,' Mr Chevalier daydreamed, gently taking Isabelle into his arms.

~

Elsie opened the door and noticed Isabelle's flushed cheeks.

'I can see that you've had an enjoyable afternoon, young lady.'

'I have indeed. I'm the happiest girl in the universe,' Isabelle confessed as she glanced through the mail on the mantelpiece. She noticed a letter from George and filed it with some other unopened letters. Opening the cabinet to return her books, Isabelle noticed the painting wrapped in cloth. Throwing caution to the wind she removed the cloth to be astounded by what she saw—the painting showed Jimmy's lifeless body. Even more bewildering was the fact that Pierre had no idea of Jimmy's existence.

'I would put the painting back in its rightful place for now. You're to dine with your father and Mr Chevalier,' Elsie announced, a little concerned by Isabelle's anxious state.

That evening they dined in the kind of restaurant you would expect royalty to frequent if the French Revolution had not occurred. A sea of charming faces in search of a splendid life filled the room. Isabelle felt a little anxious due to her father's reserved manner, so she encouraged a conversation about music and art to make Mr Chevalier feel at ease. She was worried that Mr Harper may have already made the decision on who she would marry—and decided on George. She smiled generously, relieved by the arrival of the count and countess, but not even her fellow traveller could alter Mr Harper's serious mood.

'After much consideration, a decision on my daughter's future has been made. I will allow the current engagement to be broken and a marriage to Claude Chevalier made official,' Mr Harper announced.

Isabelle felt elated; her dreams and prayers had been answered. Overwhelmed, she strove to suppress her tears of joy.

'There are no words to express the extraordinary happiness you have bestowed upon me, Father,' Isabelle announced with deep affection.

'I'm honoured by your decision, sir, and look forward to a life of love and true contentment with your beautiful daughter,' Mr Chevalier said, direct from his heart.

Even though she was overjoyed that her dream had come true, Isabelle realised how difficult it would be for her father to explain the upsetting news to George Hoskins. Isabelle felt that she should write to George at once and explain truthfully what had happened. She liked and respected him and hoped they could remain friends.

~

After a very inspiring morning playing with the orchestra under the direction of Mr Chevalier, Isabelle skipped down the street and found herself in a secluded bookshop still searching for the information that had eluded her. She imagined with wonder her wedding night with a lover so dear to her heart.

Isabelle gasped at the sight of her mother, looking unusually glamorous. She made a quick decision to remain hidden from view and would be seeing Mrs Harper soon enough now that the broken engagement had been made official.

Mr Aubrey appeared with several books tucked under his arm. 'Gracious!' Isabelle remarked, surprised by their chance meeting.

'I've had trouble finding someone to time my run, so I'm appealing to your generous spirit,' Mr Aubrey explained.

'Tomorrow would be a better option. Choose a park nearby and remind me after rehearsal. By the way, your playing has moved me sublimely. I believe the cello may be your greatest skill after all,' Isabelle remarked encouragingly.

~

Elsie greeted Isabelle with a magnificent new Chanel evening gown.

'Your parents have invited the count and countess to dine. Claude Chevalier will accompany you as your engagement has been made official. I must say Mrs Harper looks very well indeed and seems to have accepted the change of fiancé graciously. This new gown is a generous gift from her,' Elsie remarked, cheerfully.

'I would say Mother has delved into the impressive line of aristocrats that Mr Chevalier has emerged from. That alone should pacify her and encourage Mother to embrace her future son-in-law,' Isabelle remarked coldly.

'Your father is a prince amongst men, Isabelle. He has made what appeared to be an impossible dream come true.'

'My journey with Claude Chevalier will be a sublime and heavenly existence, my darling Elsie.'

'I'm proud of you, miss. Your great strength of mind has carried you through the dark days and into the light.'

~

Mrs Harper displayed a pleasurable response to the engaged couple at dinner and that seemed to please Mr Harper. Isabelle looked radiant as she smiled adoringly at Mr Chevalier. Count Flaubert felt such joy for her and smiled reassuringly in Isabelle's direction. After dancing the night away in Mr Chevalier's arms, she woke the next day in a blissful frame of mind ready for the strenuous practice regime which awaited her. Elsie had prepared breakfast at the table and Isabelle sat in wonder of such happiness.

'We dreamed a beautiful dream and here we are, my dear Elsie.'

~

Isabelle hurried down the stairs of the Conservatorium with Mr Aubrey close on her heels.

'Mr Chevalier said much the same as you and advised for the cello to be the first consideration. So, I've retired early as a sprinter and will put all effort into my music. Can I escort you to the bookshop as I know you were in search of information?'

'Not today but I'll find the answer to the question one day soon. I can feel it in my bones,' Isabelle said nonchalantly.

Chapter 20

Isabelle sat down at the café and was surprised by the early arrival of Count Flaubert. He immediately took advantage of a little time alone with Isabelle, kissing her hand endearingly as he admired her exquisite ruby and diamond engagement ring.

'My adorable fellow traveller, we rarely spend a moment alone. I would like to express my happiness and wish you a blissful marriage. I know how much Claude Chevalier means to you. I will never forget the wonder of your presence at the Moulin Rouge and the extraordinary hours spent with you that will remain locked in my heart forever.' Count Flaubert reminisced such a lovely memory, and smiled.

'We'll share those splendid hours for the rest of our lives. No matter where we are, we'll recall the magic,' Isabelle replied.

Pierre and Philippe ambled into the café with an air of grandeur wearing smart tweed jackets and fashionable Panama hats. Isabelle and Count Flaubert found their transformation highly amusing.

'You must allow me to take you for a spin in our new sports car,' Pierre offered with pride.

'Father will be arriving any minute and I know he'd be very upset to find he wasn't the first passenger,' she said cheerily.

Isabelle greeted her father with treasured affection while the waiter attended to their table with an air of professionalism. Mrs Harper surprised Isabelle by making an appearance at the café and presenting her with a stylish hatbox.

'Thank you, Mother,' she said appreciatively, kissing her on the cheek.

'The hat attracted my attention. Only a beautiful young lady could wear such a charming piece.'

Mr Harper showed such joy as his wife made the effort to win her daughter back. Pierre escorted him to the new sports car where he proudly became their first passenger.

A remarkable afternoon had been enjoyed by all. Any previous woes were forgotten on such a colourful day. After seeing her parents driving in the smart red sports car, Isabelle laughed heartily. Many customers joined in the frivolity and Mr Chevalier arrived in time to appreciate the eccentricity of the afternoon.

~

Isabelle removed the lid from the glamorous box and found herself in raptures. She tried the hat on in front of an elegant mirror.

'What do you think?'

'It's the most gorgeous hat I've ever seen,' Elsie remarked admiringly.

'My mother endowed me with this glorious gift. I'm overwhelmed by her gesture to be forgiven.'

'You'll be blissfully married very soon, and your husband will protect you from any upset. Mrs Harper will realise that her future with you will always be at the advice of your husband,' Elsie reassured her.

'As we met in France, I'm more than happy to be married here.'

Surprised by the decision, Elsie realised that Isabelle had not completely forgiven her mother. She knew Mrs Harper would be very disappointed if the wedding was not in England.

~

Waking to the rain pelting against the window, Isabelle faced an early morning practice. Her ambition to be a great violinist had met with the maestro's approval; he could see the determination in her eyes.

'I must say, you're playing like a woman possessed,' Elsie remarked.

'I hope so. Amidst all the excitement and glamour of the wedding, I must remain focused on giving the performance of my life. Being a great violinist is still my priority,' Isabelle said passionately.

~

Mr Aubrey caught Isabelle's eye after rehearsal.

'I'm so pleased you have retired as a sprinter. Your love affair with the cello is very special indeed,' Isabelle praised keenly.

'I must say that you are my sole inspiration. While you accompany me, I will blissfully play on.'

'Can I entice you to join us at the café?'

'I've often noticed you all at play and have been tempted many times but haven't found the courage to make a bold entrance since I had stiff competition with the artists,' Mr Aubrey confessed.

'I'm inviting you to join our table as a permanent guest,' Isabelle said, taking him by the arm and escorting him to the café.

After the first plate of croissants, Mr Aubrey warmed to the experience.

'I must admit to being very disappointed when I discovered that you were engaged to Claude Chevalier. I recognised you as the girl for me, but I have faced the reality squarely. I appreciate our wonderful friendship,' he said with a smile.

'So do I, Mr Aubrey,' Isabelle replied.

While admiring the art for sale, Mr Aubrey became distracted by Philippe and Pierre as they sat at the table.

'We've met before, I believe,' Pierre said, shaking his hand courteously.

'Are we competitors?' Philippe asked jokingly.

'I am an artist, but I create music on the cello,' Mr Aubrey replied, amused by their colourful smart suits and the flowers protruding from their top hats.

Pierre and Philippe were distracted by a pretty young girl entering the café and approaching Isabelle.

'You must be my brother's fiancé. Mr Chevalier sent me on an errand to say he'd be a little late. He thought it would be acceptable for me to join you. My name is Mary Chevalier,' she said cheerfully.

'Please meet my friends, Mr Aubrey, Philippe and Pierre,' Isabelle greeted with enthusiasm.

Isabelle thought that Miss Chevalier could be a lovely friend for Mr Aubrey. Philippe and Pierre were hovering like bees to the honey pot, so Isabelle took control and sat Mary next to Mr Aubrey.

'And what would your creative expression in life be?' Antoine Aubrey enquired with a smile.

'I'm committed to being a concert pianist, but my passion is writing,' Miss Chevalier replied.

'May I be so bold as to enquire how old you are?'

'I'm sixteen years old and very wise for my years,' Mary Chevalier declared as her brother entered the café.

Mr Chevalier kissed Isabelle's hand with love in his heart. He acknowledged his sister and smiled, when he noticed Mr Aubrey showing her attention.

'We have an afternoon to ourselves and I wondered if a romantic paddle down the river in a canoe would appeal to you. We could discuss our special day while we drift into oblivion and wonder what the rest of the world is doing with their time.'

'How could I resist such a sublime invitation?'

~

Isabelle drifted blissfully down the picturesque river in Mr Chevalier's arms. She knew the man of her dreams would always be there for her, just as their love of music would embrace them forever. Their pleasurable silence was disrupted by Mr Aubrey and Miss Chevalier appearing on the riverbank.

'I can see you're in need of a chaperone, so we'd like to oblige,' Mr Aubrey offered.

'Please join us and delight in this heavenly afternoon,' Isabelle greeted.

Mr Aubrey assisted Mary Chevalier into the canoe while Mr Chevalier gazed into Isabelle's violet blue eyes adorably. As they drifted with the current, Isabelle couldn't imagine being happier.

'I wish you both a splendid marriage,' Miss Chevalier said as she embraced her brother with such affection the canoe almost overturned.

'Allow me,' Mr Aubrey announced as he quickly came to the rescue and settled the canoe.

'May I be your bridesmaid?' Mary asked in earnest.

'I'd be thrilled if you'd join the bridal party,' Isabelle encouraged, full to the brim with joy.

~

After hurrying up the stairs, Isabelle entered the hotel room with a flourish.

'Where on earth have you been? Count Flaubert and Claude Chevalier are to join you at dinner,' Elsie urged.

'I've had the dreamiest afternoon with my beloved and his sister.'

'You need to calm down as your cheeks are very flushed, miss.'

'I'm so thrilled about the concert. I must play beyond my capabilities and reach for the stars.'

'I'm sure you will, miss. There are very few born with such a gift from God.'

'I do hope so as nothing can interfere with my performance,' Isabelle said in earnest.

Elsie attended to a knock at the door and returned with Mrs Harper.

'I won't hold you up as the table is booked for eight o'clock, but I wanted to tell you about our meeting at the bridal salon tomorrow.'

'Mary Chevalier will be my bridesmaid,' Isabelle announced joyfully.

Mrs Harper tried not to show her disappointment, wishing Isabelle had chosen her cousin to play a part in the bridal party.

~

Isabelle treasured the evening spent with her fiancé; they found such pleasure in each other's company. The wedding discussions met with Mr Harper's approval, but Mrs Harper had not been as agreeable. Count Flaubert—quite aware of such a power struggle—held Isabelle's hand discreetly, to support her stand on such matters.

Looking a picture of elegance in her crimson lace evening gown, Isabelle danced the night away in Mr Chevalier's arms. As she climbed into bed that night, thoughts of her beloved overtook any objections made by Mrs Harper. Her prayers had been answered by her father's authority.

After Isabelle finished rehearsing the next morning, Mr Aubrey joined her and they observed the activity of the street artists with fascination.

'How quickly life changes with opportunity. I can't imagine Pierre and Philippe back in their old lives,' Isabelle commented as she admired the great work presented on the street.

'The past will always colour the present, hopefully to create a greater vision for the future,' he said commendably.

'Wise words, Mr Aubrey. I do hope we can still have our enjoyable discussions.'

'I'm pleased to hear you say that as I thought you may have passed me by to Miss Chevalier and I'm very glad to hear that is not the case.' Mr Aubrey remarked with a great deal more ardour.

~

Much talk on the style of Isabelle's gown had taken place before the appointment at the bridal salon. Isabelle knew what she wanted, and the designer would create the gown to her instruction. Amazingly, Mrs Harper smiled generously at Isabelle's choices. An easy afternoon followed, deciding on a long veil of feminine elegance. Surprisingly, many tears were shed that afternoon. Mrs Harper realised that her little girl had grown up and would live far away from Mother-England. Mr Harper entered the salon, deeply moved by Isabelle's need to comfort her mother's tears.

The café was a lovely escape from wedding conversation. Isabelle sat alone with her treasured thoughts when, to her surprise, Pierre and Philippe arrived with Mr Chevalier forming an unlikely trio. She smiled blissfully to see her beloved; their rehearsal that morning had resembled perfection, so she felt assured that his mood would be agreeable.

'I've been daydreaming of Paris and the remarkable life we've had the chance of starting together,' Isabelle announced joyfully to Mr Chevalier.

'I'm privileged, my darling.'

Mr Harper and Count Flaubert made a flamboyant entrance carrying many gifts for Isabelle.

'Thank you, Father.'

'I'm pleased to have been able to join you and enjoy your very fine company, sir,' Mr Chevalier said as he welcomed Mr Harper warmly.

'The pleasure is mine I can assure you. I know my daughter's happiness will always be with you,' Mr Harper replied.

~

Isabelle sat staring at the rooftops of Paris, pondering over a letter to George Hoskins that she'd meant to write a while ago. She had thanked him for her introduction to the theatre—an experience that she would never forget—but more importantly, for her first kiss which would remain in her heart forever.

'I do hope George is not too upset.'

'I may be old-fashioned but I believe he will appreciate that you have made the effort to make contact,' Elsie said kindly as she removed an exquisite evening gown from the wardrobe and noticed the painting of Jimmy's body.

'Do you wish to keep this art, miss?'

'I do indeed. Are you familiar with people who can foresee the future?'

'I've known one or two with such a gift. My great aunt had an amazing vision of her brother being shot on a beach. Six months later, war was declared, and it happened exactly as she'd envisaged in her mind. I'll take your letter with the post this afternoon.'

'Thank you. Mother is very emotional at the moment. I find her behaviour out of character.'

'I think you'll find your mother has many regrets about her past behaviour and she's fighting hard to make amends,' Elsie replied.

'I pray to God that you're right. I'll find forgiveness a little easier if that is indeed the reason,' Isabelle replied with a sadness in her eyes as she thought about Jimmy.

'Your parents loved each other very much in those early years. I find it difficult to pinpoint exactly when her behaviour started to change, but we all adjusted quietly, including your wonderful father.'

'I can't imagine Granny Harper's scandalous behaviour being tolerated by my mother.'

'No, but surprisingly I never heard a cross word between them in all my years of service. In fact, I would say they enjoyed each other's company.'

Isabelle smiled wistfully. She dearly wished to remember her parents' happy years. Her love for Mr Chevalier would make up for the loss; she looked forward to sharing everything with him and living gloriously. Her curiosity about the wedding night remained a mystery, but no longer seemed to matter. She assured herself that it would be an experience of beauty with the man of her dreams.

Observing Elsie through the window on her venture to the post office, Isabelle realised how blessed she'd been to have Elsie to herself. She rejoiced in the news that her maid would continue in Paris after the wedding and not return to England. Isabelle suddenly realised that a day without her would be unimaginable.

~

Mr Aubrey escorted Isabelle and Miss Chevalier to the café, a new Panama hat showing off his unusually groomed fair hair.

'I must say you're looking very smart in your new ensemble,' Isabelle flattered, noticing that her mother had arrived.

Pierre presented Mrs Harper with a charming portrait of herself.

'I thank you for your very fine work. I will cherish it always. More importantly, I thank you for all the pleasurable time you have spent with my daughter, Isabelle,' Mrs Harper remarked warmly.

'When we visit Mother-England, I expect to see the painting hanging in its rightful place,' Pierre said with a cheeky grin, hoping for an invitation.

'You are welcome to visit our home any time. I hope you will excuse us. The girls have an appointment.'

'The privilege is ours. We'll drive you to the salon,' Pierre said.

'Thank you, Pierre. We'll accept your offer,' Isabelle announced boldly.

'I've always dreamed of driving in a sports car,' Miss Chevalier confessed.

'A safe journey to the beauties of Paris!' Mr Aubrey declared with ardour.

Isabelle had chosen a fashionable rose-coloured gown for Mary Chevalier. She noticed how the design pleased her mother as her future sister-in-law paraded enchantingly. When Isabelle appeared, looking breathtakingly beautiful in her delicate white lace gown and veil, Mrs Harper's eyes filled with tears. She realised how right Isabelle had been in her choices and lived for the day that all would be forgiven by her daughter.

Chapter 21

An elegant weekend at the chateau in the Loire Valley with the count and countess had been just what Isabelle needed. Her fellow traveller always adored her visits and made a delightful fuss that her beloved Mr Chevalier reacted to charmingly. One of Pierre's paintings was hanging in the majestic hall, which met with his approval as he and Philippe entered. They were overjoyed that an invitation had arrived at last and amazed at the beauty of the elaborate chateau. Count Flaubert welcomed the young artists with great enthusiasm.

Stealing a heavenly kiss amongst the shrubbery, Mr Chevalier took Isabelle into his arms and they daydreamed of their splendid future. Miss Chevalier and Mr Aubrey paddled by in a canoe, enjoying the pleasure of each other's company. Pierre and Philippe were rejoicing in their newly found freedom and running naked through the trees as they'd found the river too enticing to resist. To their dismay, the count and countess, appeared around the river-bend. Panicking, the two artists jumped into the water with a loud splash. The count and countess strove to suppress their hilarity after seeing such a spectacle.

'Your secret is safe with us!' the count shouted in jest.

'Thank you, sir, for being such a good sport. I'm afraid our swimwear was left behind in Paris,' Pierre said graciously.

Dinner that evening was an extraordinary experience, particularly for Pierre and Philippe. The grandeur of the room overwhelmed them and Count Flaubert welcomed their novice experience. The gentlemen enjoyed a night of billiards; Count Flaubert patiently encouraged Pierre, Phillipe and Mr Aubrey to learn the skills and participate in society with the best of them.

The next morning, Isabelle woke early. Elsie dressed her to dine downstairs as she dearly wished to have breakfast with her beloved. The count gazed at her effortless beauty as he escorted her into the majestic room where Mr Chevalier looked a touch jaded. Mr Harper, Pierre, Philippe, and Mr Aubrey all looked surprisingly subdued too.

'My darling, allow me,' Mr Chevalier said as all the men stood for Isabelle to be seated.

'I gather the gentlemen had an adventurous evening,' Isabelle remarked, with a mischievous smile.

'Our marvellous host showed us a lovely evening that I enjoyed a little too much,' Mr Chevalier confessed as Mr Harper nodded in agreement.

'My darling father, coffee should put you right in no time at all.'

Isabelle stared at the splendour of the chateau, realising she would be married by her next visit and wondered how different her life would be. She loved Mr Chevalier with all her heart and felt so happy that her music could continue.

~

She spent the afternoon browsing in the bookshops of Paris with Mary Chevalier, and found it extremely relaxing. Isabelle had hoped Mr Aubrey would join them as she found his company pleasurable. Apart from Jimmy, she had not been able to connect with the thoughts and ideas of boys her own age.

Philippe and Pierre were reminiscing about a remarkable weekend, recalling the count with great fondness, as they indulged in morning tea and prepared new paintings ready for the next exhibition. Isabelle greeted her dear friends admirably. Mr Aubrey appeared, looking very smart in a stylish suit, with many books still wrapped in fancy paper.

'One day I'll surprise you and present you with the book you were in search of,' Mr Aubrey declared.

'I would be astounded, there's no doubt in my mind about that!' Isabelle exclaimed.

She had a discussion with Mary Chevalier about the modern-day woman and was surprised when her future sister-in-law stated that modern young women still have to agree with their husbands. Claude Chevalier appeared through the crowded café and heard his sister's comment.

'In marriage, the wife must be entitled to make her own decision,' Mr Chevalier announced flamboyantly.

'You fill my heart with pride every day,' she said, with a generous smile.

Isabelle enjoyed walking to the hotel in her own time; digesting the happiness she felt after hearing Mr Chevalier's modern approach to women. Noticing a letter from George Hoskins on the sideboard upon her return, she was full of curiosity about how he'd react. After reading the long letter, and feeling blessed to have been forgiven, he expressed his wish to remain friends throughout their lives. Isabelle held the letter close to her heart and smiled.

~

The concert being only a few weeks away meant a tough practice regime for Isabelle. She met Mr Aubrey at the Conservatorium for a rehearsal of their duet, an enchanting experience indeed as the artistic work showed great promise. Mr Chevalier listened intently, greatly moved by the emotional music.

Lost in her own thoughts and dreams of the future with her beloved Mr Chevalier, Isabelle was surprised when her dear friend Mr Aubrey caught up with her.

'I'm very glad that I chose music as a career,' he confessed.

'You'd have been sadly missed, especially by me. Please join me for afternoon tea, Mr Aubrey,' Isabelle said.

'The pleasure is mine; I can assure you. I realise you're to be married soon but friendship between musicians is acceptable.'

'I'm sure Mr Chevalier would agree with you.'

'I don't speak French at home as a rule because my mother is English. Her family come from Norfolk,' Mr Aubrey explained.

'Is she in England?'

'I'm afraid so, but I'll be happy to see her at the concert.'

'I look forward to meeting her.'

'Mr Chevalier expressed his idea of the modern young woman very well and I noticed that you agreed,' Mr Aubrey remarked.

'Indeed, but my mother would not. For most, the old ways are very hard to change,' Isabelle replied.

Miss Chevalier arrived with Pierre and Philippe holding a painting she'd secured at the exhibition. Mr and Mrs Harper arrived in good spirits along with Count Flaubert. After Mr Chevalier's arrival, many plans were discussed for the preparation of the wedding including Isabelle's desire for the Reverend Charles Durn to marry them.

She attended the final fitting of the delicately embroidered bridal gown, made from fine white lace and enhanced by a lengthy train of elegance. Isabelle's beauty took Mrs Harper's breath away; she smiled with deep pride for her daughter as the bridal salon put on a splendid afternoon tea.

~

A letter arrived for Isabelle from Reverend Charles Durn amongst the afternoon mail.

'He has agreed to marry us, Elsie. My wedding day will be perfect!'

'Your father will be pleased. He has made a great effort to ensure your happiness.'

'Such wonderful news about Charles! The man is the very reason for my music and I adore him. He recognised my ability and nurtured me through the hard times.'

'You have always spoken so well of him. I'm glad to know your vicar will marry you and do you justice. You're a very special girl and it's been a privilege to rear you,' Elsie said with great warmth.

'Thank you. I couldn't imagine a day without you.'

'A marriage at sixteen can be a confusing experience. You're stepping into a bewildering adult society. Very different to my day of course. Change is imminent.'

'Mr Chevalier agrees with women's freedom of speech,' Isabelle announced proudly.

'Then you're a very lucky girl to have chosen a modern-day man!'

'Music is the very existence of both our souls, so we are bonded together forever, without a conscious thought for tomorrow or thereafter.'

~

A visit to the bookshops on such a cloudy wet day appealed to Isabelle; she enjoyed time alone browsing unknown novels. After purchasing one that appealed, she noticed a book entitled Marriage. Seizing the opportunity, she enquired whether it would be suitable for a young bride. At that moment Mr Harper and Mr Aubrey entered the shop and Isabelle let forth a short gasp, startling the shop assistant.

'I thought you'd given up on that book,' Mr Aubrey said.

'What book is this?' Mr Harper queried.

'I have given the entire venture away and gladly found a romantic novel that will suffice,' Isabelle reassured. The girl behind the counter looked at her curiously.

Mrs Harper joined them and they went to the café to shelter from the weather, where the logs on the fire radiated a comforting warmth.

Later in the day, Count Flaubert arrived with a noticeable spring in his step.

'My fellow traveller, your art has just sold at a lucrative price. I came directly with the news.'

'Oh, my heaven! I can't believe it,' Isabelle uttered in joyful disbelief.

'Your wonderful father stared in absolute shock as the sale was executed in grand style. We were disappointed that you weren't present.'

'I had no idea the painting would be anything special,' she confessed.

'Great art is in the eye of the beholder, my beauty.'

Mr Harper entered the café and embraced Isabelle, with loving affection.

'Congratulations to the elusive artist,' Mr Harper remarked proudly.

Mr Aubrey stood at the café door as Isabelle said her fond farewells. They left in very good spirits for rehearsal with Mr Chevalier.

An excited tension filled the room as Isabelle concluded her practice. 'I'm humbled by your magnificence,' Mr Chevalier confessed.

'I hope to surpass all your expectations and give you an evening of surprises,' Isabelle said, with a twinkle in her eye.

'Mr Aubrey, you also played very well indeed,' Mr Chevalier praised.

'I believe I did, sir. Thank you,' Mr Aubrey replied, mopping his brow with a handkerchief.

'We have a grand audience awaiting us, so make sure their expectations are fulfilled,' Mr Chevalier announced to the orchestra.

Chapter 22

Isabelle arrived at her elegant hotel suite looking for peace and quiet to prepare for the grand recital. Many great musicians of note would be in attendance from Europe and England. She had received a divine new evening gown as a gift from Mrs Harper.

'Mother has chosen well,' Isabelle praised as she admired her gown in the full-length mirror.

'I've never seen an equal, miss, and possibly never will. May all good wishes be yours tonight,' she said caringly.

Elsie made sure there were no interruptions—apart from a surprise visit from Reverend Charles Durn who'd arrived in time for the performance. The Reverend was aware of the great pressure upon her in regard to her music, and knew he'd remind her of sad thoughts of Jimmy that were very close to her heart.

Mr and Mrs Harper joined the count and countess as they awaited the grand performance with ardour. A stylish Philippe and Pierre had been greeted keenly by Mr Harper. No expense had been spared; they wore fashionable top hats and tails, with haircuts of the latest Paris fashion.

Reverend Durn shed tears of pride as Isabelle transcended the audience to a glorious place. Her music captured the full house and held them prisoner—a performance that surpassed all greatness. Claude Chevalier proudly escorted Miss Harper forward after her solo. She took a bow gracefully, appreciating the amazing applause that arose to a crescendo with the audience shouting Bravura! After an astounding fifteen curtain calls, Mr Chevalier tapped his baton in readiness for the duet to be played as an encore. Miss Harper and Mr Aubrey aroused the full house, inspiring thunderous applause.

After a night of celebration with Claude Chevalier—including meeting with high praise from the great European maestros—Isabelle realised how lucky she'd been to have a father who quietly shared her vision and allowed reality to shine.

Isabelle embraced Reverend Charles Durn and his wife Sarah to show her love and appreciation for their attendance. She rejoiced in hearing all the news from the vicarage and conversing about her dearest friend Jimmy.

Her love for Charles had altered to a deep friendship, for which Sarah was thankful.

~

She woke from a pleasurable sleep and daydreamed about the success of the night before. Elsie entered in a fluster with breakfast on a tray.

'Don't get up, miss. I've been instructed to serve breakfast in bed to the star violinist.'

'On the table, please. Unless women's rights have been introduced overnight.'

'Yes, miss,' Elsie replied, happy to see Isabelle standing her ground.

'Did my mother ever mention her rights as a woman?'

'Not that I recall. But, in those days, you never spoke of such matters.'

'I guess it's easier to remain silent, and a great deal more effort to fight for what you believe is right. I could never imagine myself remaining silent,' Isabelle replied.

'I would certainly agree on that point,' Elsie remarked with a smile.

'I've been educated on the modern woman in a relatively short time and I thank Paris for that.'

~

Isabelle's family had been invited to Mr Chevalier's chateau in Burgundy for a weekend, and she looked forward to some quality time with her beloved. They were joined by the count and countess and Isabelle delighted in Mr Aubrey's presence and the appearance of his mother.

'Do forgive my lack of contact, but I wasn't well after the journey from England. I wish to express my hearty congratulations for your glorious music. It healed my soul and has given me a new beginning,' Mrs Aubrey said, holding her son close.

'I'm overwhelmed by the compliment, thank you, and I'm pleased that your health has improved. The news that we'll be seeing more of you is very gratifying. Mr Aubrey is one of the finest musicians I've heard. You must be very impressed indeed with his accomplishment.'

'I couldn't be more proud of my beautiful son,' Mrs Aubrey replied.

Discreetly looking for Mr Chevalier in the majestic gardens, Isabelle noticed his jacket hanging from a tree branch. He appeared suddenly, pulled her into his manly arms, and kissed her with such sublime passion that if she should die and go to heaven, such a kiss would suffice for all time.

As they rested blissfully in the field amongst the wildflowers, hidden from the world and very much in love, Isabelle caught a glimpse of a sad but stylish Mr Aubrey through the trees. She prayed he would find the love of his life and be the debonair gentleman she knew he would be.

The joy of riding the thoroughbred horses through the field with Mr Chevalier had been just what Isabelle needed. She released the tensions of the arduous practice regime of months gone by. Joined by Mr Aubrey and Mary Chevalier, they galloped at speed across the wild fields, revelling in the blood pumping through their veins. As the sun glistened on the splendid river, her thoughts were of Devon. Mr Chevalier noticed her altered mood as she slowed her horse, so he slowed and joined her.

'I've been reminded of Mother-England and my deep love for her, although France has embraced me equally and so beautifully.'

'The choices are ours, my darling, and we'll make them together. I'm the happiest man alive, I'm sure of it.'

Mary Chevalier and Antoine Aubrey laughed heartily as they galloped along the shallows of the river splashing each other playfully. Isabelle delighted in seeing Mr Aubrey enjoying Miss Chevalier's devilish behaviour as she galloped hard, waving as she passed him by. Mr Chevalier laughed at the shocked look on Mr Aubrey's face.

'We men had better stick together. The women seem to be taking the upper hand,' Claude Chevalier announced.

'I believe they are, sir,' Mr Aubrey replied.

'I'll race you home,' Isabelle challenged, flashing a mischievous glance in Mr Chevalier's direction.

She galloped at a devilish pace and reached the majestic gates ahead of him.

'I surrender and will accept defeat gracefully, I promise. As long as you keep it our secret,' Mr Chevalier said, assisting Isabelle from her horse and kissing her passionately.

The late arrival of Reverend Durn and his wife Sarah pleased Isabelle tremendously as there were important matters to discuss regarding the wedding. She also longed to sit with Charles and talk about Jimmy, their mutual and glorious friend; Charles understood the tragedy that she held in her heart. But it wasn't to be. Sarah and Charles walked by the river, taking in the beauty of the gardens, before a delectable afternoon tea had been served. The scones with jam and cream were blissfully devoured.

'A match for Mother-England, don't you think?' Mr Chevalier enquired boldly.

'Not quite, but almost,' Isabelle replied with a twinkle in her eye.

Charmingly haunted by his memory of the girl who once loved him so passionately, Reverend Durn gazed in wonder at such a splendid young woman and knew she'd chosen well.

'I'm pleased to spend quality time with you both and look forward to your marriage in the name of God,' Reverend Durn said with deep respect and affection.

The grand sixteenth century chandeliers sparkled above the guests. The count danced the countess with such panache that Mr Aubrey became inspired by the idea. He twirled Mary Chevalier with such enthusiasm that he almost lost his footing; he seemed enchanted by her. Isabelle waltzed splendidly with Mr Chevalier, looking into his expressive eyes and surrendering to a love so fine. The romance of the room inspired Mr Harper to entice his wife onto the dance floor. Isabelle noticed a rare display of affection from her parents which pleased her enormously.

Mrs Aubrey, a handsome woman, joined Isabelle to announce that she was returning to her husband in France.

'I'm glad for you, Mrs Aubrey, and I believe your decision to be the right one, especially for your son,' Isabelle remarked kindly.

~

A week of hectic wedding preparation followed before the big day. On the eve of the marriage, Mrs Harper wanted to have a bridal high tea, but Isabelle politely declined and rested in a sublime bath of rose petals. She drifted blissfully and very much in love while Elsie rinsed the soapsuds from her hair.

As she woke up on the best day of her life, Isabelle found the time to read a letter from George Hoskins. He wished her all the happiness in the world. Isabelle was grateful for his fine friendship.

She noticed another painting wrapped in cloth laying on the table, and Elsie observed her anxious state.

'Don't open it, miss! Don't spoil your day,' Elsie advised.

Shrouded in curiosity, Isabelle threw caution to the wind and hastily removed the cloth. To her amazement she saw a remarkable painting of a bridal bouquet with fancy ribbons and bows tied to a horse-drawn carriage galloping high into the heavens. Isabelle smiled divinely while Elsie muttered a prayer of thanks.

'Come on, miss. You can't be late on your wedding day.'

Elsie assisted as Isabelle dressed herself in the most enchanting wedding gown ever imagined.

'I'll be seventeen years old by Christmas and a married lady. I never thought I would see the day,' Isabelle confessed as she picked up her bridal bouquet.

'To be honest, miss, neither did I,' Elsie replied.

The architecture of the romantic fifteenth century church enhanced the noble occasion. A spectacular crowd gathered as Isabelle and her proud father arrived at the church in a horse-drawn carriage.

The early snowflakes floated in perfect harmony as the radiant couple descended the church steps. The crowd cheered as they greeted the newlyweds. Keeping with tradition Isabelle tossed her bridal bouquet high into the air, smiling joyously as Miss Chevalier made a secured catch.

As a glorious sun rose on the splendour of the morning after, Isabelle sat in awe of her beautiful husband and daydreamed about her wedding night all over again.

Chapter 23

A seventeenth century chateau, which had been home to Granny Harper but damaged during the First World War, had been given as a wedding present, therefore finding its rightful owners. Granny Harper would have agreed with such decadence. As the last of the restoration builders vacated the grand estate, Mr Harper waited patiently for Isabelle and Claude Chevalier to return from their honeymoon in the south of France.

After stepping from a chauffeur-driven limousine, Isabelle gasped delightedly at the splendour of the chateau.

'Thank you, Father, for such a treasured gift,' she said, in absolute awe of his generosity.

'Sir, from the very depths of my soul I thank you,' Mr Chevalier said with a warm handshake.

~

Isabelle's dedication to her music never faltered, which pleased her loving husband. He happily devoted his life to her brilliance and accompanied her on tour. After completing two years of international tours, they joyously returned to their home.

The chateau was running like clockwork with full staff engaged under the command of the butler Mr James and the housekeeper Mrs Wilson. Elsie remained as Isabelle's maid and Mr Edwards, her husband, had gladly joined the staff as Mr Chevalier's valet.

~

Mr Aubrey joined Isabelle in the café after rehearsal, wearing suave black tails in readiness for a special engagement at the Chevaliers that evening. He was pleased to see Isabelle for a moment on his own.

'Am I correct in ordering a strong black coffee for Mr Chevalier? Your beauty has distracted my thoughts,' Mr Aubrey said.

'That is his usual,' Isabelle confirmed.

The waiter with the handlebar moustache approached with a smile. 'Welcome home, mademoiselle.'

'I found it hard to stay away,' she remarked with sincerity as Mr Aubrey assisted with her chair.

'My family send their love and were impressed by your performance in London,' Mr Aubrey said.

'How is your mother?' she enquired, a little concerned.

'My parents are still together,' he replied, with a noticeable confidence in his voice.

'I'm pleased for you,' Isabelle said, smiling affectionately.

'I'd like to marry Mary Chevalier, but my father believes that I'm too immature for marriage,' he remarked disappointedly.

'Mr Chevalier would be supportive,' she reassured him.

Philippe and Pierre made a flamboyant appearance in their top hats and tails.

'Good afternoon, mademoiselle,' Pierre announced with good cheer.

'We were beginning to sulk as there'd been no invitation to the chateau,' Philippe remarked in a jovial manner.

'I'm the happiest girl in the world to welcome you to our home. We've been on tour for an eternity,' Isabelle declared.

Her face filled with girlish joyfulness as Mr Chevalier arrived and kissed her with beautiful tenderness. Mr Aubrey felt a little jealous but had to admire a love so fine. He was quickly distracted by Mary Chevalier's bewitching smile, encouraged by Mr Chevalier. The limousines arrived at the entrance to take them to the chateau for the weekend.

The enchanting chateau was a surprise to all. The count and countess were early and had already taken a walk through the fields of wildflowers in bloom. Elsie found a mood of contentment and happiness in Isabelle's new home. Among a great art collection, Count Flaubert's Dancers in Rehearsal was displayed—a painting she held close to her heart. Following Isabelle's instructions, Jimmy's paintings had been framed and displayed in the main hall. Mr Harper and Count Flaubert believed his art to be exceptional.

'Shall I prepare the new gown from Mr Chevalier for this evening?' Elsie enquired.

'Thank you, my darling Elsie. I'm so pleased to be home.'

'We all need to catch our breath. As you're planning to start a family, touring for another year may not be wise, miss,' Elsie advised.

'Music is as important to me as the air I breathe. I couldn't imagine a year without playing.'

In the grand dining room, full staff were in attendance.

'My lovely wife and I welcome you to our home,' Mr Chevalier announced, with an enchanting glance to Isabelle.

Count Flaubert had not lost the art of holding Isabelle's hand discreetly, and the habit brought a smile to her face. Friends from New York—musicians they'd met while on tour in America—had arrived in time to dine. An evening of fine food, stimulating conversation and dancing made for an unforgettable evening. Pierre and Philippe enjoyed themselves a little too much, but their French charm encouraged good cheer. Another grand art exhibition, inspired by Count Flaubert, had come to fruition. Mr Aubrey and Mary Chevalier joined the American guests and attempted to emulate the Charleston, a new dance from America, while much laughter and gaiety prevailed. The butler Mr James had been busily preparing rooms for the guests and he realised this would not be the only evening of social splendour that would occur.

Delightfully exhausted, Isabelle and Mr Chevalier danced the last waltz of the evening along with their guests, then her beloved swept her out of the door while kissing her superbly.

~

Rejoicing in the news of her first pregnancy, all tours were cancelled for the year. The happy couple adored their home and had a lifestyle that suited them so perfectly; they had no desire to leave the estate. A remarkable collection of toys cluttered the nursery, creating a room of make believe, and Mr and Mrs Harper eagerly awaited the arrival of their first grandchild.

Just after Isabelle's nineteenth birthday, the most important event in her life happened without complication. All her dreams became a glorious reality. Elsie smiled in wonder at Isabelle who looked radiantly beautiful after the birth of her twin babies.

'A great artist or a poet could not have envisaged what I have seen today, miss,' Elsie said with a tear in her eye.

Claude Chevalier was in absolute awe of his adorable wife and babies. 'What little treasures they are, my darling.'

'Both nannies have agreed to an American tour next year,' Isabelle declared rapturously.

Mr Chevalier loved her even more, realising her determination to continue her career.

'Our little angels will be playing Beethoven before they can talk,' he bragged.

'Wherever we tour, our children will be with us,' Isabelle declared.

~

Elsie strove to pull the corset tight enough for Isabelle to fit into her favourite evening gown. Slumping into a chair, exhausted from the effort, Elsie admired Isabelle's figure as she twirled proudly.

'Thank you, darling Elsie.'

Reverend Charles Durn and young William were to be guests at dinner, so Isabelle wanted to look her very best.

William presented well in his smart black tails. Isabelle smiled endearingly as he tried to settle himself and find the confidence to make a good impression. He had heard what a hard taskmaster Mr Chevalier could be, but he prayed for a scholarship to further his music studies. Reverend Durn showed his usual caring ways and adored seeing Isabelle.

'Sarah sends her love and will arrive for the Christening,' he advised.

'We look forward to the day,' she replied.

'You have a charming home. I felt welcome as soon as we arrived,' William remarked cheerfully.

'Having babies agrees with you. Your beauty has surpassed the expectation,' Reverend Durn said graciously.

'I'm a very lucky man,' Mr Chevalier said with a smile.

'I must know...have you fallen in love with Paris?' Isabelle enquired mischievously.

'Absolutely and irrevocably,' William replied.

Mr Chevalier and William shared a passion for thoroughbred horses and would avoid a discussion about music until the official audition at the

Conservatorium. The butler, Mr James, made sure the waiters attended to their every need; they enjoyed the best food and wine imaginable.

'The people of our parish are very proud to claim an international violinist as one of their very own,' Reverend Durn said with admiration.

'How lovely to hear they take an interest,' Isabelle replied gratefully.

After practice the next day at the Conservatorium, Isabelle and Mr Aubrey passed the bookshops on the way to the café.

'I shopped here yesterday and found you a gift that may come in handy.'

'Thank you, I will treasure it,' she replied, a little worried as to what he had found.

As Isabelle rejoiced in a jubilant welcome from the café staff, Mr Aubrey placed a book in fancy wrapping paper on the table. As the waiter served morning tea, she removed the paper to expose a book entitled, Bringing up Baby with two pair of booties inside the cover.

'For Priscilla and Edward, in case their feet are cold,' he advised. 'Thank you, my dearest friend. Mary Chevalier is a very lucky girl.'

'By the way, my father has approved the engagement. Whatever Mr Chevalier said, it worked,' Mr Aubrey remarked thankfully.

'I'm thrilled for you. I know you'll be very happy.'

'Our tour next year is a pleasurable prospect,' Mr Aubrey declared with ardour.

'How blessed we are to have such opportunity,' Isabelle replied. 'It is indeed a privilege,' he said with conviction.

Mr Aubrey senior waited patiently at the door as he strove to attract his son's attention.

'Excuse me, Mr Aubrey. Your father's waiting,' she urged. He blew her an affectionate kiss as he hurried to the door. 'Say hello to Priscilla and Edward for me.'

Isabelle enjoyed her time alone, blissfully content with her dear friend's choice of book and his caring interest in her babies. While relishing croissants and coffee, she was surprised by William's early arrival. His smile told a happy story.

'I start my music studies next term. I wanted you to be the first to know,' he announced.

'Congratulations, my dear William. Your work is impressive, so I'm not surprised by such an achievement.'

'The Moulin Rouge is secretly on my wish list,' he said in a whisper.

'Remind me on your eighteenth birthday and I'll have a word with my fellow traveller,' she replied with a smile.

'I long for the day when I'm married. I thought it was going to be to you,' he said, a little sad that his wishes had not come true.

'You'll find the right girl when you least expect to. Cherish that moment when you do,' Isabelle advised.

Reverend Durn appeared a little anxious as he approached through the crowded café.

'We have a meeting with Mr Chevalier in five minutes,' he said.

'I'm sorry, sir,' William replied, picking up his violin.

Reverend Durn kissed Isabelle's hand fondly, which seemed to have a calming effect on his distressed state.

'I'm pleased to hear of your tour next year. A life without music is not for you.'

'I knew you'd understand,' Isabelle said with a warm smile.

William hesitated then kissed her on the cheek as he hurried to the door. 'Thank you for your encouragement,' he said cheerfully.

'Goodbye my dear friend,' she replied affectionately.

Isabelle noticed her father who had quietly made his way through the crowd; he had not wanted to interrupt her precious time with Reverend Durn and William.

'Our vicar will be disappointed that he missed you.'

'I'll catch up with him at the Christening. Your mother is shopping for the twins, but she'll join us in due course,' Mr Harper said as he sipped his coffee.

'You both look very well. Being grandparents agrees with you.'

'The happiest we've been in years, my darling girl. I understand and admire how hard you've worked to achieve a splendid career in music, and it's certainly a modern-day way of thinking for a young woman to have a career and a family. More importantly, you have a husband who supports your ideals. Your mother is slowly warming to the idea so give her time and understanding.'

'Thank you for your wise words,' Isabelle replied.

'George sends his best wishes. He's engaged to a charming young lady,' Mr Harper said.

'I'm pleased for him, Father. We'll always be friends.'

'He said the same,' Mr Harper replied.

Mr Chevalier arrived, looking very handsome in his stylish dark suit. He removed his Fedora hat and made his way through the crowded café.

'Bless you for being early, my darling,' Isabelle greeted with a loving smile.

'Priscilla and Edward are waiting so we dare not be late, my beauty.'

Mr Harper laughed heartily, realising the twins were already ruling the household.

Chapter 24

The next few summers passed in perfect harmony. The twins adapted to a life of touring and displayed a keen interest in music at an early age.

Returning to their splendid home was always a relief after arduous practice regimes and touring, but the love for her music drove Isabelle to aspiring heights of achievement. Mr Chevalier—in awe of his wife's ability—supported her proudly. The Chevaliers never failed to spend the afternoon with their children and adored the frivolity of the games played. Pierre and Philippe presented the twins with a hand-carved rocking horse as a gift; a favourite with Priscilla and Edward, they passionately emulated their parents riding across the field.

Isabelle welcomed a night out at the opera with the count and countess. The music of Madame Butterfly engaged Isabelle emotionally and tears trickled down her cheeks. Mr Chevalier handed her his handkerchief and kissed away a tear. A night of social decadence followed, inspired by the music of the Charleston.

Count Flaubert longed for a waltz with Isabelle but, alas, that wasn't to be as Mr Chevalier swept her around the dance floor all evening. When silence prevailed and the musicians took a well-earned break, her fellow traveller managed to hold her hand and charm her discreetly.

A late lobster supper at a remarkable restaurant of Mr Chevalier's choice made the evening complete. Isabelle realised how lucky she'd been in marriage and the treasured life he'd bestowed upon her. She felt he'd read her thoughts as he smiled in her direction. She found herself wishing he'd lure her into his arms as she longed for the haven of their home.

~

Elsie stoked the logs on the fire as Isabelle relaxed in her bath.

'I had the most adorable evening a girl could ever imagine,' she declared.

'Mr Chevalier said much the same, miss. He's out riding and will see you at breakfast downstairs.'

'I promised to read a story to Priscilla and Edward this morning. I dare not dishonour our agreement,' Isabelle announced with a smile while Elsie wrapped her in a towel.

'I don't wish to spoil your day, miss, but your mother arrived last night with that maid we were told had drowned in the river. Mr Chevalier rang your father very early this morning. He should arrive by lunchtime. Mr James has prepared a room for your mother, and Lorna is in the maid's room. As far as I know they're still sleeping.'

'My babies are waiting. I'll discuss the best plan for Mother with Mr Chevalier. She seemed so happy with Father,' Isabelle said sadly.

'I'm sorry but you had to know,' Elsie advised caringly.

'Please let Mr James know so he can prepare a room for Mr Harper.'

'I believe Mr Chevalier has already addressed the matter,' Elsie said as she tied Isabelle's hair up under a riding hat.

'Thank God for my beloved,' she said, striving to be cheerful for her children.

Elsie could hear laughter from the nursery and felt the love of Priscilla and Edward would ease a difficult road ahead.

Mr Chevalier held Isabelle in his arms and kissed her tenderly before they sat down to a very fine breakfast.

'On a lighter note, my darling, our children loved the story. We played all the parts. They were ready for a morning sleep when I left. The nannies were absolutely thrilled.'

Very little conversation took place until coffee was served.

'Mr Harper has experienced your mother's illness first-hand, so I believe we should allow him the right to make decisions for the best. Count Flaubert will join us this afternoon,' Mr Chevalier said in a quiet voice.

'Thank you, my dearest husband. It's the unexpectedness of it that has disturbed me.'

The sound of horses' hooves galloping across the field felt like the best medicine after such stressful news. A rightful decision needed to be made without blame or vindictiveness. Isabelle couldn't bear to think about Lorna, but knew her father would return her to England immediately and seek the best medical attention available for her mother.

'There's nothing more exhilarating than a strong breeze blowing through your hair to calm the soul and dismiss all cares and woes,' Isabelle said.

'Such a sport could cure the devil himself, I'm sure of it,' Mr Chevalier announced.

Count Flaubert rode hard in their direction; by the look on his face, they realised he was not the bearer of good tidings. He pulled up, a little short of breath.

'Mr Harper has arrived early, thank goodness. The doctor has attended to Mrs Harper, recommending hospital without delay, but she's refused his advice,' Count Flaubert declared with a deep concern.

'Mother overslept this morning and that's unusual for her,' Isabelle exclaimed fretfully.

They rode back and met Mr Harper at the chateau. Her father assisted her to dismount and she embraced him with heartfelt love. The noble gentleman who had made all her dreams come true had tears of despair spilling down his face.

Count Flaubert and Mr Chevalier gave their enduring support as Isabelle sat in silence, praying for her mother to survive the illness. The doctor returned with a nurse and did everything possible to save her life. Isabelle felt the need to be alone with her mother and give her father a well-earned rest. She gently held her hand and whispered words of forgiveness. A glimmer of a smile and the slight squeeze of her hand meant everything to Isabelle.

'I love you, Mother,' she whispered as Mrs Harper squeezed her hand a little tighter. Isabelle realised that her mother needed to be forgiven for the wrong she'd done.

Elsie woke the Chevaliers in the early hours of the morning.

'Isabelle! I'm sorry to wake you but your mother is asking for you,' she urged as she handed her a dressing gown.

The solemnity of the room and the chill she felt upon entering was hauntingly disturbing. Isabelle gazed upon her mother's face, so altered. Her pale, drawn appearance and tousled hair told a tragic story. Isabelle kissed her father affectionately on the cheek and held Mrs Harper's hand.

'There is a slim chance if she makes it through the night,' Mr Harper whispered.

'I'm here, Mother,' Isabelle said softly.

When Doctor Raymond approached to take her pulse, he did so with concern. As the nurse: busily prepared the medication, the doctor paused.

'I'm sorry, sir.'

The doctor closed Mrs Harper's eyes.

'Your wife has passed away.'

~

The death of her mother affected Isabelle more than she'd ever imagined, but with the love of her beautiful husband and children, Isabelle regained the strength of mind to make it through each day.

They returned to England, where preparation for Mrs Harper's funeral was in progress. The gypsies were not allowed to attend. Mr Harper had taken a strong stand and banished Lorna from the estate for life. Isabelle and Mr Chevalier were extremely supportive of Mr Harper at such a heart-wrenching time. Count Flaubert remained at his friend's side, assisting where he could. Reverend Durn welcomed them at church on Sunday and Isabelle believed the Reverend's sermon would assist in their grief. William expressed his sympathy at morning tea as the large congregation welcomed them home.

~

The magnificent Edwardian dining room remained unchanged. The evening brought back many good memories as Isabelle strove to forget the bad. She had dressed herself in an elegant pink lace evening gown, a favourite of her mother's. The servants were attentive under the command of the butler, Mr Cummings, and presented a splendid dinner. Isabelle's mind harked back to the many grand evenings when she was growing up. Her parents displayed such style and expressed an eloquence in conversation that she'd admired as a child when first allowed to participate in the aristocrats' domain. Mr Chevalier touched her hand tenderly.

'A penny for your thoughts, my darling.'

'I do beg your pardon. I must admit to being miles away,' Isabelle replied.

'I'm happy to hear of your world tour my dearest daughter. The dedication to your work will be a saviour,' Mr Harper advised.

Count Flaubert kept an eye on the proceedings; he knew the upset of the funeral arrangements would be distressing for both Isabelle and her father.

'We have an art exhibition in New York so hopefully our dates will connect,' Count Flaubert said.

'Philippe and Pierre will be quite a surprise package for the New Yorkers. We're expecting the top hats and tails to turn a few heads,' Mr Harper declared.

~

On the morning of the funeral, Isabelle had been in two minds about whether to practice, but the dedication to her work made the decision for her. Mr Chevalier woke to her glorious sounds and smiled; he knew the music would inspire a strength of mind to endure a day of sadness and loss.

Elsie assisted Isabelle with her fashionable black dress and hat, grooming the shiny red hair that fell elegantly to Isabelle's shoulders.

'You look lovely, miss. Your mother would be proud.'

'I still can't accept the finality,' Isabelle replied.

'In time you will. The good Lord will see to it,' Elsie reassured her.

Reverend Durn gave a moving sermon to farewell Mrs Harper. Mr Harper stood proudly, speaking well of his wife and explaining the illness that took her life. Isabelle played an enchanting lullaby on the violin, in memory of her mother. George Hoskins and his fiancé were amongst the mourners.

Surrounded by family and friends in the spectacular gardens of the estate, Isabelle and her father welcomed the mourners and were thankful for their enduring support. A splendid lunch had been served outdoors at a grand dining table set under the oak trees—Granny Harper's favourite place for entertaining. Isabelle sat with her husband while Priscilla and Edward insisted that they sit with their grandfather.

Dinner in the evening displayed a grand affair to honour Mrs Harper's wishes.

'Your mother would have been proud of such a delicate lullaby. The sound you created was sheer beauty to the ear,' William praised.

'Love the violin and it will sing for you,' Isabelle replied.

'I've tried but it doesn't wish to converse with me,' William complained.

'Then you don't love it enough,' she responded with a smile.

'You must forgive my dear wife's directness, but I believe she'd like you to think about the reason for her comment,' Mr Chevalier clarified.

'I look forward to working with you in Paris, sir,' William said eagerly.

'I believe it's my privilege to take your talent to its extremities,' Mr Chevalier said with a firm handshake.

Isabelle approached George Hoskins and looked into his kind blue eyes. He kissed her hand with sadness in his heart.

'My condolences. I pray that the good Lord will care for you and protect you.'

'Thank you, George. I'm very pleased to see you.'

'Allow me to introduce my fiancé Miss Jennifer Harrington,' he announced.

'I'm delighted to meet you, Miss Harrington, and I wish you every happiness for your wedding next June.'

Mr Chevalier arranged billiards for the evening, knowing the game to be a favourite of Mr Harper's and wanting to bring a little cheer to his sadness.

'We buried your mother and somehow made it through the day, my darling girl.'

'I love you, Father, and I believe you should live with us in France.'

'Your mother and I had already bought a chateau in the Loire Valley to surprise you. Count Flaubert kindly found the property for us. We're almost neighbours,' he said, managing a smile.

'I'm so pleased. I'd have been worried about you, all alone in this big house.'

'I've made George a full partner, so he can run the firm when I'm in France,' he clarified with conviction.

Chapter 25

Curious as to what had occurred with Lorna, Isabelle called into the vicarage to unravel why they were led to believe she had drowned.

'I've made sure your favourite morning tea will be served,' Charles Durn said caringly.

'Thank you for remembering,' she said with a smile.

'I do have information from Sam Williams that Lorna was picked up by fishermen way downriver after the gypsies had seen the swirling current carry her away. Lorna did not return to the estate so how she reconnected with Mrs Harper remains a mystery. I can understand why you need to know. If I can find her, I will certainly ask her the question.'

'How is Sarah?' Isabelle enquired.

'After all these years, she's pregnant and we're looking forward to becoming parents,' Reverend Durn announced proudly.

'I'm very happy for you both. There's no greater gift from God than your children,' Isabelle replied.

'As you become focused on the tour, with the love of your husband and children to comfort you, the sadness will gradually subside. My grandfather would be very proud to know his violin will be in concert in America.'

'Every day I strive to surpass yesterday and play the best music possible.'

'That's the difference between a good violinist and a virtuoso,' Reverend Durn said, remembering the gorgeous young girl who had once loved him.

'My husband is a great comfort to my father, but I had better return before lunch.'

'May I drive you home? I'll be meeting Sarah in the village.'

'I'm going to take a walk by the river and pick some wildflowers. Hopefully, I'll remember the good times,' she replied.

'Try not to delve too deeply. Grief is a powerful emotion. Allow for time to pass and all will settle in its rightful place,' he said as he walked her to the gate.

She sat under her favourite oak tree enjoying the gentle breeze through her hair. The sudden appearance of Mr Chevalier surprised her; he approached with a loving smile and kissed her. Isabelle knew the man of her dreams would save her and guide a pathway to a blissful happiness. Harking back to resurrect a mother who could never be revived, she decided to stay in the present and let go of the past to a greater degree.

~

Isabelle, Claude Chevalier and their children spent the months of June and July in England. The passage of time made her loss a little easier to endure and she enjoyed daily rides with Tiger, galloping across the moors. The sound of the Celtic drum alerted her to the gypsies paddling their canoes downriver; it reminded Isabelle of the heavenly times spent with Jimmy. Mr Chevalier, Mr Harper and Count Flaubert appeared, riding at speed.

'I'll race you all home!' Isabelle shouted.

Galloping hard and jumping the fences with ease Isabelle arrived safely at the stables. Mr Chevalier was a close contender with Mr Harper and Count Flaubert half a length behind. Much laughter prevailed, and she felt the joy of a new beginning blossoming.

Mr Aubrey and Miss Chevalier were welcomed graciously to the estate, with Mrs Aubrey acting as chaperone. They had just returned from a holiday in America.

'Mr Chevalier informed us of your sad news. I hope you received our card of condolences,' Mr Aubrey advised, with a warm smile to Isabelle.

'I did indeed. Thank you for your kind thoughts. They were much appreciated.'

A delectable lunch had been served in the gardens. The butler Mr Cummings attended to their every need, appreciating the sound of happiness and laughter in the home.

'You fell in love with France. Do you feel the same way about America?' Mr Aubrey enquired.

'Not the same way. Granny Harper influenced me as a child and started my love affair with France. But, don't mistake me, Mother, England is always in my heart,' she reassured.

'I'm pleased to hear of your loyalty,' Mrs Aubrey acknowledged.

'America is certainly leading the way for women and their rights,' Mary Chevalier proudly informed them as she lit a lady's cigar to Mrs Aubrey's surprise.

'My dear husband has influenced my father in this regard,' Isabelle remarked.

'Will my brother be joining us?' Miss Chevalier enquired.

'He kindly accompanied my father on an errand. I'm expecting them shortly,' she announced pleasurably.

Mr Aubrey stood unexpectantly, flicking his serviette to dismiss a bee.

'Sorry if I startled you, but I'm allergic to bee stings,' he announced with concern.

'We can move if you wish,' Isabelle suggested.

'I'll bravely fight the battle. When the delicious apple pie and cream is served, our friend will rapidly lose interest,' Mr Aubrey replied.

'Did you choose a career in music or writing?' Isabelle queried, curious of Mary's decision.

'A concert pianist, I'm afraid, but when I'm of an age with life's experiences behind me, I may put pen to paper and create my own world on the page,' she declared boldly.

'I look forward to the day,' Isabelle remarked encouragingly.

Isabelle's husband and father arrived at lunch, and the nannies introduced an excited Priscilla and Edward who joined their parents.

'I'm sorry we're late, my darling,' Mr Chevalier exclaimed, greeting her affectionately and kissing the twins.

'It's all my fault, my dearest girl,' Mr Harper explained.

'You're forgiven, Father. Please relax as Cummings has the matter in hand.'

Introductions to Mrs Aubrey were made, the engaged couple were welcomed warmly by Mr Harper, and Mary Chevalier greeted her brother with love.

~

Being back in France—where rehearsals had begun for the American tour—caused a feeling of blissful contentment. Mr Aubrey noticed Isabelle enter the café with a spring in her step and followed her. They received a charming welcome from the staff.

'Welcome home, Mrs Chevalier! Morning tea is yours for the taking,' the waiter with the handlebar moustache announced.

Isabelle glanced at a painting on the counter and saw a woman who resembled her mother standing alone in a field of wildflowers; there were dark clouds shedding tears from the heavens above. She sat quickly as Mr Aubrey assisted with her chair.

'Are you all right, Isabelle?' Mr Aubrey enquired with concern.

'Thank you for asking, but I'm feeling much better,' she replied.

'Allow me to order a special morning tea for the girl who will always remain a glorious dream.'

'That's iniquitous, my dearest friend. Your fiancé loves you and I know you love her. My darling maid, Elsie, has always warned that romantic ideals let you down.'

'Point taken, my beauty.'

Isabelle gave a girlish squeal of delight when she noticed Phillipe and Pierre approaching through the crowd. The well-worn top hats and tails with tousled hair was a surprise after such a success, but the joy of their company far outweighed the expectation. Amongst many welcoming kisses and handshakes, Count Flaubert arrived and joined in an inspired afternoon of conversation.

'All our paintings are sold, so afternoon tea is our pleasure,' Pierre announced proudly.

'How's the car travelling? 'Count Flaubert asked.

'Very well indeed but in sad need of an oil change and petrol,' Philippe replied, devouring a croissant.

'Father described you as wealthy artists of Paris,' she declared with a cheeky smile.

'We were, but wealth took us by surprise I'm afraid. The excitement of the adventure encouraged extravagance,' Pierre replied.

'But America awaits our genius and who knows what the future may bring,' Philippe announced boldly.

'I think I'll take charge of the finances at the New York exhibition,' Count Flaubert cautioned.

Laughter prevailed as Mr Harper arrived with new top hats and tails.

'Every picture tells a story,' Mr Harper announced as he handed the gifts to Pierre and Philippe to rapturous applause.

~

Elsie tidied the children's toys after the nannies had put them to bed in the nursery. Isabelle admired her new gown as she removed it from the box.

'Mr Chevalier has excellent taste,' Elsie praised.

'I'm so happy to be home and my darling husband agrees. He believes we should hibernate from the rest of the world.'

'It would be a crying shame not to be seen in that gown, miss. Your Mr Chevalier is a true prince. You couldn't have married a better man.'

'He's my king,' Isabelle said with a girlish smile.

Elsie dusted the photograph of Mrs Harper and Isabelle sat at the dressing table to look more closely at it.

'My mother's alcoholism had the respectable title of an illness. I've often wondered if the truth had been expressed, being an aristocrat from the old school, the shame may have urged her to abstain. The question of Lorna may never be answered, so we must move on as Mr Chevalier advised, and our children must take priority. I thank God that I experienced very happy parents, even though it was only for a short time.'

'I know you'll move on, miss. Always remember that time is your best friend,' Elsie replied.

'Who are the guests at dinner this evening?'

'Mr Harper, Count Flaubert, Countess, Flaubert, Mary Chevalier and Mr Aubrey,' Elsie explained.

'How charming. Prepare my new gown,' she said with ardour.

Chapter 26

Her mother's original French paintings from the manor in Devon created a grandness in the Chevaliers' elegant dining room. The gentlemen stood for Isabelle to be seated. Her father's good cheer pleased Isabelle.

Preparations for the art exhibition were underway and Count Flaubert had encouraged Mr Harper to travel to America. Isabelle had thought of a constructive idea in memory of her mother. Mary Chevalier and Countess Flaubert would be the right people to discuss such a proposal with. After the gentlemen had adjourned to the billiards room, the opportunity arose.

'Thank you for such a splendid dinner. I'm pleased to see that you and Mr Harper are recovering from your loss,' the countess said as Miss Chevalier joined them.

'I believe Mother's problem should not have been dealt with in silence just because she was a woman and, in particular, an aristocrat of wealth. The seriousness of the illness slipped under the radar because alcoholism had never been mentioned. One fine day I intend to create a beautiful place that women can attend and seek treatment for this condition. Rich or poor, all will be accepted and respected. A place where the problem can be recognised for what it is, and doctors are available,' Isabelle announced.

'Bravo! My dearest sister-in-law, how right you are. Not only are you one of the great violinists but this idea is inspiring,' Miss Chevalier declared.

'Not a word until after the tour. I'll discuss it with Father upon our return.'

'Your gypsy soul is a great gift from God. I envy it,' the countess confessed with a warm smile.

'I don't believe you'll ever stop playing music,' Miss Chevalier said in earnest.

'Only when the blood ceases to flow through my veins and all existence is denounced.'

'I would love to write plays for the theatre, but first I must master the Greig Concerto and travel to Germany. I'm in concert next month,' Miss Chevalier disclosed.

'Congratulations. Your hard work has been rewarded,' Isabelle replied.

'I'm feeling a little left out, having neglected my music studies to become an artist. My work eventuates in my mind, but not on the canvas. One day both may happily marry,' Countess Flaubert remarked cheerfully.

~

The clouds lifted and a day of sunshine cheered the mood. Isabelle was putting the finishing touches to a piece of art, after being humbled by a glance at Count Flaubert's work. Mr Harper stared at a blank canvas for what seemed like an endless time, then suddenly began to mix the oils. He painted—to Isabelle's surprise—an oak tree which had an uncanny resemblance to her favourite tree on the estate in Devon.

'Well done, Father,' she remarked encouragingly.

'I didn't do too badly for a first attempt,' Mr Harper said, with a note of contentment.

'I've never heard of a lawyer becoming an artist, but there's a first time for everything,' Count Flaubert goaded.

Isabelle became discreetly distracted from her art as she'd glimpsed the shadow of a girl vanishing through the trees nearby; her long hair flowing in harmony with the wind. Isabelle stood quickly for closer viewing, but only the moving shadows of the tree branches were visible. She blamed her vivid imagination for the distraction. Count Flaubert and her father were enchanted by the next brush stroke but noticed Isabelle had returned to the easel.

'You look a little pale my darling girl,' Mr Harper remarked with a concern.

'I've never felt better,' Isabelle reassured, with a loving smile.

Count Flaubert glanced at Isabelle's portrait of Granny Harper with a keen eye. Impressed by the depth of character she'd expressed; he took the opportunity to praise her work. He prayed that one day the passion felt for her music would be evenly matched with her art.

'A masterpiece in progress,' the count said with ardour. 'Thank you for your inspiration,' she replied graciously.

Mr Aubrey called in that afternoon and, while the ride across the fields seemed to calm his agitated state, he was clearly not his usual charming self. Isabelle wondered if Miss Chevalier's tour may have interfered with their wedding plans. For afternoon tea the butler Mr James served them delectable cream cakes.

'My fiancé has suggested I forego my career and follow her to Germany. I'm not happy, but your company has mellowed my thoughts. I thank you for your kindness,' Mr Aubrey said.

'Art is a great release from any cares and woes that may intrude on our lives,' she advised with a warm smile.

'I'm intrigued. The lady in the portrait is displaying a smile as if she knows me. It's uncanny,' he exclaimed with admiration.

'The gentlemen are in the billiards room if you care to join them. Tell my husband that I won't be long,' she said, concentrating intensely on the next brushstroke.

'That breeze is very chilly, so please take my jacket.'

'Mr James is arriving with more coffee if you would like,' Isabelle offered without taking her eyes off the painting.

'How do you know?' he enquired, scanning the field.

'Passing through the wildflowers at four o'clock is his usual practice if we're painting in the field.'

'Amazing! Here he is, right on time,' Mr Aubrey remarked as he observed his watch.

'Mr Chevalier has been honoured internationally for his great work in Paris,' she disclosed proudly.

'A world class conductor such as your husband is the making of a fine orchestra. Excuse me, but I can see that Mr James is carrying a coat, so I will leave you in his capable hands. May your creative powers be unleashed onto the canvas,' he replied fondly.

'Mr Chevalier has urged for your kind attention, sir. If you'd escort Mrs Chevalier back to the manor, he'd be grateful. A very cold night is expected. All fires are lit, ma'am.'

'Many guests will be arriving,' Isabelle advised. 'Miss Chevalier?' Mr Aubrey queried hesitantly.

'Yes. Promise me that you'll enjoy the evening in a nonchalant manner,' she cautioned politely.

'I promise,' Mr Aubrey replied.

~

Pierre and Philippe caused great amusement that evening. Mr Chevalier was notified by telephone that their car had run out of petrol, so he sent a chauffeur driven Rolls Royce to rescue the artists. They arrived wearing full-length mink coats. Count Flaubert and Mr Harper winked in Isabelle's direction, adoring the artists' eccentricities. The butler Mr James raised his eyebrows in disbelief and signalled the staff to await further instructions.

'I'll assist you with your coats if I may. The fires will keep you warm enough, I can assure you,' Mr James said.

Pleased to see Miss Chevalier and Mr Aubrey smiling together, Isabelle signalled for dinner to commence.

'As you are the accountant for the next exhibition, Count Flaubert, you need to be advised that zero will be our starting figure,' Pierre announced.

'Viva La France!' Philippe exclaimed, indulging in a glass of fine wine from a crystal glass.

Isabelle had always held her friends in high esteem, feeling she'd learned the true meaning of dedication from Pierre and Philippe. Mr Chevalier had grown to admire a great passion for their art. Gazing in Miss Chevalier and Mr Aubrey's direction, Isabelle prayed for their ambitions to be agreed upon and a fine marriage to be the outcome. Mr Aubrey's smile indicated a chance for an understanding between them. She hoped the happiness of her own marriage would be an inspiration.

~

The exhausting practice regime left little time for troubled thoughts. Morning tea at the café was a blissful routine. She enticed her beloved husband to join her in sketching the faces passing in the street. Mary Chevalier and Mr Aubrey also joined in the creative art.

Mr Chevalier bestowed high praise on Isabelle and Mr Aubrey for their extraordinary musical ability and dedication. Mr Aubrey had decided that Germany would not be a possibility for him as the orchestra must take priority. However, the outcome had been positive and a future wedding date settled upon.

Being a soloist Isabelle rejoiced in a little freedom. She ventured along the riverbank, looking at the canoes and remembering the part they'd played in her young life. While relaxing under a tree and enjoying her cherished imaginings, Count Flaubert appeared.

'I'd hate to intrude on your daydreaming,' he said, kissing her hand.

'I'm amazed you found me. I didn't mention my venture to anyone.'

'Who knows what that is? If you need to give it a name, call it instinct.'

'Father is very partial to his new home,' she remarked.

'We're neighbours. At least something good came out of such tragedy.'

'I seem to be finding my way when creating a portrait. I'm careful not to express what I'd like to see, but rather who they really were. The latter is more interesting to capture,' she said.

'Knowing Granny Harper for the extraordinary woman that she was, your portrayal is true and engaging,' Count Flaubert remarked encouragingly.

'Thank you.'

'Your father informed me that the dates for New York coincide with my visit, so I look forward to seeing you in concert there,' he remarked.

Pierre and Philippe pulled up in their red sports car, after the count waved joyously in their direction.

'We sold four paintings before lunch. If you're rich and famous, do climb on board,' Philippe announced.

'The problem is solved and we're back in business,' Count Flaubert clarified flamboyantly.

'I don't think New York is ready for such a spectacle,' Isabelle said as she climbed on board with Count Flaubert.

'One day the entire world may be ready to challenge these artists, but right now let's concentrate on the next exhibition,' Count Flaubert advised.

Mr Chevalier arrived later to join Isabelle for afternoon tea.

'France is the best country in the world but New York is a city of wealth for the artist. We intend to haunt the exhibition with great influences from the past and present,' Philippe advised arrogantly.

'Your art has impressed me greatly, so the preparation ahead is exhilarating. Music also needs to be worked to a pitch then allowed to settle as something greater evolves,' Mr Chevalier clarified, as his eyes shifted to Isabelle with a loving smile.

'My darling mother saw the world differently to me. I understand that now that I'm older and, hopefully, a little wiser,' Isabelle said.

Count Flaubert looked at Phillippe and Pierre's collection of shopping bags.

'I'm presuming the balance is back to zero. Correct me if I'm wrong.'

'Our exuberance is regrettable, but a wealth of art is being created. Another four paintings will cover the spend, I guarantee you,' Philippe promised.

Chapter 27

She opened a lengthy letter from Reverend Durn in which he happily informed her about the birth of their baby boy. He also gave some news about Lorna that Isabelle found disturbing. After Sam Williams's violent outburst, Reverend Harris had asked Mrs Harper to help Lorna. Work and lodgings had been organised for Lorna by Mrs Harper after the gypsies turned against her. It seemed Mrs Harper had stayed in touch with Lorna. Isabelle put the letter back in the envelope.

'You look as though you've seen a ghost, miss,' Elsie said.

'Reverend Harris, surprisingly, asked for Mother's help with Lorna. Of course, he had no idea of her illness or how Lorna had encouraged it,' Isabelle explained.

'Best you know, so now you can dismiss it,' Elsie replied.

~

Isabelle dressed in a fashionable pink evening gown and the children gasped at her beauty as she entered the nursery.

'I love you, my angels,' Isabelle said as she kissed Priscilla and Edward goodbye.

'The theatre awaits us, my darling children,' Mr Chevalier announced as the twins blew kisses in a desperate bid to avoid having the light turned off.

The emotion felt after entering the theatre never failed to amaze Isabelle. As the plush red velvet curtain rose slowly, she glanced in Mary Chevalier and Mr Aubrey's direction, curious to know their impression as the stage came to life and the story of Hamlet unfolded for their first experience of Shakespeare. Mr Chevalier kindly handed her his handkerchief after noticing the tears being shed for her favourite character, Ophelia.

In the interval Mr Aubrey displayed an extreme enthusiasm that could possibly inspire a life in the theatre.

With the applause still ringing in their ears, a light supper at an exclusive restaurant completed a pleasurable evening.

'I'm bewitched and almost convinced that I've missed my true vocation,' Mr Aubrey declared passionately.

'Your expression told that story,' Mary remarked affectionately.

'As the celloist we could dress you in a costume of disguise if that would help,' Mr Chevalier suggested.

'I understand, my good friend. I had the same ardour for the theatre many years ago, but my father would not allow his daughter on the stage. The sheep in the field witnessed many grand performances and my friend Jimmy slept politely so no comment was required,' Isabelle said.

'Shakespeare would not inspire me as much as your remarkable playing which has bewitched me, from the moment I met you,' Miss Chevalier said to Mr Aubrey with keen affection.

'I'm convinced, but I can still enjoy the dream,' Mr Aubrey replied.

~

The daily rehearsal was gruelling, but Mr Chevalier expressed the importance of their success in New York. Many famous orchestras had toured there, so the competition would be formidable. William had arrived with a desire for success as he settled into his first term at the Paris Conservatorium. His parents adored their new life at a nearby chateau and Mr Chevalier showed his admiration as the term progressed. Isabelle had not forgotten her promise to William regarding the Moulin Rouge.

As Isabelle sketched the faces in the street, her fellow traveller arrived at the café.

'I don't wish to intrude on your creative genius, but I felt the need to spend some time with the girl in my dreams,' Count Flaubert declared, holding her hand under the table discreetly.

'How lovely! I was just thinking of you and our wonderful visit to the Moulin Rouge. I did promise William that I'd connect with my fellow traveller and see if we could organise a visit for him,' Isabelle said with a smile.

'Leave it to me, my beauty. But, for now, allow me the pleasure of your company,' he said.

She adored their brief meetings by chance but never involved herself beyond those boundaries. A cherished afternoon followed and the count encouraged her good work.

Another letter had arrived from Reverend Durn, but she'd kept it in her handbag for fear of more distressing news. After politely excusing herself, she took a long walk to the bookshop, browsed carefully and selected a novel to buy. She settled down for a good read, but her fear and curiosity overpowered her better judgement and she decided to open Charles's letter. She needn't have worried; the letter charmed her. A note from Reverend Harris had also been enclosed, apologising for not addressing her mother's illness much earlier and for encouraging her ongoing contact with Lorna. It pleased her to know that his conscience bothered him and he hadn't dismissed the illness that took her mother's life.

~

After arriving home from church with her husband and children, Isabelle felt a joyful sense of belonging. They rested in the magnificent gardens while morning tea was served. Mr Harper rejoiced in his role of grandfather, appreciating young life after such a devastating loss.

Philippe and Pierre made their grand entrance after the elegant lunch which had been served by the waiters under the command of Mr James.

'Do forgive our late arrival. A swim in your enticing river being too good to resist, we dived into the water in our Sunday best,' Pierre confessed.

'You should have informed Mr James. Staff would have attended to your needs at the river,' Isabelle said, laughing at them in their new suits dripping with water.

'The sun will dry us in no time at all,' Philippe replied boldly.

'I hope you have been praying to the good Lord for wealth, success and a fine bank balance,' Count Flaubert said with a hearty laugh.

'We have indeed, sir, and we're confident our prayers will be answered,' Pierre replied.

'Relying on the good Lord is an old habit of ours,' Philippe advised.

'It takes great courage to live the life of an artist,' Mr Chevalier said with conviction.

Mr Aubrey revelled in a splendid sword fight with the children's toys, inspired by Hamlet and the world of make believe. Priscilla and Edward watched keenly as Mr Aubrey lost his lengthy battle willingly to Count Flaubert after irresistible cream cakes were served.

Mary Chevalier intrigued Isabelle by expressing her recent opinion of women's rights after lighting a cigar.

'Women must be much firmer about their rights in the home. If that can be achieved, the rest will follow suit,' Miss Chevalier announced, earnestly.

Noticing Count Flaubert's stern glance at Miss Chevalier, Isabelle felt grateful that her husband had been made aware of women's rights long before she met him, which had made for a blissful marriage.

Mrs Aubrey apologised for her late attendance as she joined her son and his fiancé in the gardens. She appeared distressed and Isabelle noticed Antoine Aubrey's concern. Mr Aubrey senior sat alone drinking whisky from a crystal glass.

Noticing a change in the mood of the afternoon, Mr Chevalier suggested paddling downriver in the canoes.

Isabelle showed a little more understanding of the situation than Miss Chevalier who displayed an impatience as she puffed on a cigar.

'At the risk of sounding old-fashioned, I do believe family disagreements should remain in the home,' Miss Chevalier said.

'A paddle downriver is good for the soul. There's nothing better to dismiss the woes of the day,' Isabelle said caringly, hoping Mr Aubrey could calm the situation as his mother was clearly upset.

As Philippe and Pierre returned in a canoe, displaying shabby suits that had dried in the sun, Isabelle felt a great deal could be learned from their attitude to life. Their joyous laughter mended the day.

'Our canoe awaits you, dear lady,' Pierre announced flamboyantly as he assisted Mrs Aubrey into the canoe. Antoine Aubrey climbed on board.

'Thank you, sir, for your generosity of spirit,' Mr Aubrey said appreciatively.

'There is another passenger, I believe,' Mr Chevalier said with a smile in Mr Aubrey senior's direction.

Mr Aubrey senior nodded his head thankfully, being careful to avoid eye contact with his wife. He stepped into the canoe while his son happily prepared to paddle downriver.

'The beauty of such a tranquil place should heal their rift,' Mr Chevalier whispered to his wife.

'My dear friend feels the importance of his parents' togetherness, being an only child,' Isabelle replied, eager to support his concern.

'Step this way, my darling, and allow me to guide you to a blissful afternoon of happiness. Our friend may need a little help if the river fails to secure a truce,' Mr Chevalier said as he assisted Isabelle into the canoe.

That afternoon, Mr Harper sipped a glass of whisky deep in thought. He looked around him; he was very proud of Isabelle and her very fine marriage. The count reminisced about their Cambridge days and the countess had involved herself in a serious conversation about women's rights. She accepted the offer of a lady's cigar—enjoying the statement made rather than the French tobacco. The count glanced in her direction with a smile but made no comment.

'Will we see much of you on the American tour?' Countess Flaubert enquired, as she puffed on her cigar.

'I'm very proud of being a concert pianist and will continue my career wherever and whenever I choose. I know it sounds a little harsh, but many changes occurred after the First World War. We women must embrace such opportunities with determination, so as never to regress,' Mary announced with pride.

'I would love to emulate a young woman of today, but old habits are very hard to change,' the countess replied.

'Slowly but surely,' Miss Chevalier advised.

~

Isabelle entered the dining room grandly in a magnificent rose-coloured evening gown. Miss Chevalier, Countess Flaubert and Mrs Aubrey also showed a flair for stylish fashion.

After the gentlemen were seated, their intriguing conversation about the future of Great Britain and France continued. Many countries were still rumbling after the First World War.

'Such discussions are vital in achieving world peace,' Mr Chevalier clarified.

'I don't believe world peace is possible. It is a dangerous notion, to be avoided at all cost,' Mr Aubrey senior remarked firmly.

Isabelle, surprised by such an affronting comment, realised that gaining the correct information was of the utmost importance.

'I agree that our history books tell us a different story, but we must make a grand effort to alter the course of history,' Count Flaubert remarked, struggling to disguise his impatience.

'Making sure the information received from other countries is correct would certainly be vital in the first steps towards achieving this difficult task,' Isabelle suggested, in a serious voice.

'My darling girl, your father's legal influence is showing,' Mr Harper declared with a smile and a nod of agreement.

Pierre and Philippe relished in their evening of divine decadence indulging in the best French champagne.

'A reflection of art within our consciousness will create solicitude and care for our fellow beings, therefore acquiring the peace in question,' Pierre said with conviction.

'Well said, my good man,' Count Flaubert replied, contentedly smoking his cigar.

Chapter 28

Isabelle loved New York—a spectacular city with progressive and pleasurable people. After venturing down dark lanes, jazz bands held them spellbound and they enjoyed discovering this music that was new to the ear.

Their concerts received high praise indeed. Isabelle never faltered in performance, and had been met by a full house of thunderous applause each evening. Mr Chevalier presented the beautiful young girl he'd fallen in love with and praised her performance. Not a day passed without a heartfelt thank you to God for such a union. The twins showed such joy playing the flute—an instrument of their own choice—and the nannies delighted in their practice time.

One sunny afternoon Isabelle noticed Mr Aubrey sitting alone in a favourite café near the theatre holding a letter. He had the look of a troubled young man as he puffed on a gentleman's cigar.

'The habit becomes you,' she said, admiring his air of sophistication.

'I would have been very upset if you'd passed by my troubled soul. I love New York and so dearly want to embrace our time here. However, my fiancé appears to be holding my emotions at ransom,' Mr Aubrey disclosed unhappily.

'My father is arriving tomorrow. He will advise you on the best strategy, when replying to such a letter,' Isabelle said, encouragingly.

'Thank you, my dear friend,' he answered.

'We had a remarkable write up in the New York Times, mentioning in particular the violin soloist and the cello duet,' she announced proudly.

'Well, fancy that. The New York Times! We've hit the big time,' he declared.

'We certainly have, Mr Aubrey.'

'Even if I were the king of England, the rapture felt wouldn't be as sublime!' Mr Aubrey announced with pride.

The mayor of New York celebrated with a special luncheon for the orchestra; their excellence had been held in high esteem. Mr Chevalier presented Isabelle and the mayor honoured her with a magnificent sheaf of flowers. He thanked her for the pleasure her music had bestowed upon the people of New York.

Isabelle was enchanted as the curtain rose on her first Broadway show. The city had an energy never to be surpassed. Mr Aubrey had not mentioned his fiancé again as he'd been lured by the magic of New York.

Preparations for the art exhibition in New York were in progress. As they'd envisaged, Pierre and Philippe were turning many heads in their top hats and tails. A crowd of young women gathered daily to catch a glimpse of the French artists.

'The God you were in touch with has answered your prayers,' Count Flaubert declared.

'He usually does,' Pierre answered nonchalantly.

'I live in hope of an introduction when the time is right,' Count Flaubert replied.

'I was unaware that time mattered in this equation,' Pierre said.

'To be in touch with God one needs an intangible knowledge of another dimension not yet explored,' Count Flaubert advised.

Philippe raised his eyebrows, respecting the musings of a very fine mind.

~

Isabelle longed for an old-fashioned ball, and her prayers were answered when an invitation from the mayor of New York arrived. She admired the elegance, grace and style of the grand ballroom as her husband twirled her around the room. Mary Chevalier had been a surprise arrival and, after a strained reunion, Mr Aubrey charmed her again with his glorious playing as their romance blossomed into a new beginning. Isabelle felt blessed to see her father delighting in the company of a charming lady as the evening progressed.

Jazz music certainly seemed here to stay and not a passing fancy. Isabelle was surprised by her father's passion for this style of music. He frequented many nightclubs until the early hours, disrupting his usual habits in life. Philippe and Pierre discovered new venues and invited Count Flaubert and Mr Harper as guests. Their top hats and tails were not unusual; no rules appeared to apply regarding the dress code in New York jazz clubs. The count had been astounded by the bank balance after a very successful art exhibition.

A cream Cadillac convertible was no surprise as the car appeared through the boisterous crowd. Philippe and Pierre parked outside the exhibition, displaying smart cream suits and Fedora hats to match.

'The girls may trample us to death if they catch a glimpse of their heroes,' Isabelle declared, taking Mr Chevalier by the arm.

'Stay close and we'll be safe, my darling,' he replied, highly amused by the spectacle.

Philippe and Pierre made a flamboyant entrance with a gang of young girls following rapturously. Mary Chevalier and Mr Aubrey were amused by the sight until the girls stampeded, urging caution at all cost.

~

Elsie packed the suitcases eagerly; she'd grown a little tired of New York and the speed of its existence. Isabelle and the children entered with a flourish. The twins were thrilled about celebrating American Independence Day; they waved their flags ready for the march.

'I'll miss New York and its extravagant energy. We connected well,' Isabelle confessed.

'Youth can embrace and love such a lifestyle, but we older folk are more set in our ways,' Elsie replied as she closed a suitcase.

Mr Chevalier arrived in his American Independence Day hat. He handed one to Isabelle and the twins laughed heartily.

'Come on, my darlings, or the parade will be over,' he urged.

Rejoicing in the colourful parade, Isabelle noticed that New Yorkers showed a great pride and passion for their country.

The remarkable success in New York had secured another world tour, but for a while Isabelle was very pleased to be home in France. The project she'd envisaged for her mother would hopefully come to fruition, but realised that she'd have to be patient. Her father must be agreeable and choosing the right moment would be imperative.

The next day, while passing a bookshop, Isabelle noticed Miss Chevalier and Mr Aubrey; she observed a lovely connection between them.

'Good afternoon, lovebirds. May I join you?'

'Please do, my good friend. Your assistance in our judgement would be much appreciated,' Mr Aubrey advised, puffing on his cigar.

'I love you both and believe the decision should come from your hearts. But, if all else fails, I will do my best to assist,' Isabelle replied, selecting a novel to indulge in a good read.

'Father agrees that a marriage next spring is possible but the lingering question remains about our careers,' Mr Aubrey remarked seriously.

'Artists who are passionate about their work will experience emotional disruptions, like forever shifting sands. But love will sustain and guide us,' Isabelle said.

'My brother loves in such perfect harmony with the girl of his dreams,' Mary Chevalier declared with a note of despair in her voice, glancing in Mr Aubrey's direction.

'When I arrived, you displayed the look of young lovers in search of adventure. Your love will help you find the answers,' Isabelle replied, wondering if she should have intruded at all.

'Thank you, Isabelle, for your kind words. We look forward to your company immensely. My parents always ask after you with praise and admiration,' Mr Aubrey said pleasurably.

'My brother doesn't mention our parents as he used to. He has his own lovely family now and that makes the difference,' Miss Chevalier remarked.

Mr Aubrey lit his fiancé's cigar with a wistful look into her big brown eyes. He dearly wished they could find the exhilaration they'd experienced in New York.

'As a sprinter there would have been no argument about our careers,' he said in a jovial manner.

'But that would have been a great tragedy for the music world,' Isabelle replied.

~

She sat near the river amongst the secluded trees. The afternoon drifted by peacefully, reading a romantic novel and daydreaming of her beloved. The appearance of Count Flaubert cheered her.

'I had a feeling you'd pass by today and here you are,' Isabelle greeted.

'I don't wish to disrupt your read but, as a fellow traveller, I sensed you nearby,' he said with a smile.

'Father has been in good spirits of late and I would put that down to your fine company as a friend,' she reassured.

'I believe we also have New York to thank for his recovery. By the way, your painting of Granny Harper has been entered in the Paris exhibition,' he advised.

'Your good news has made my day, and I thank you,' she said graciously.

'The countess is a fan of your art. She is also a fan of your sister-in-law, who is certainly influencing her on the topic of women's rights. My wife is puffing away on her cigar, making a statement wherever possible to propagate her cause,' he said with a little firmness in his voice.

'Blame the First World War if you wish but I do believe the change to be necessary,' she remarked boldly.

'Maybe I'm showing my age,' he remarked with a hearty laugh. 'I'd better escort you to the café. Your husband is concerned by your late arrival, so I came to find you,' he said, looking into the deep blue eyes that had bewitched him long ago.

'Time spent alone by the river is a must for any artist. It helps my violin to sing its beautiful song, and the paintbrush to caress the canvas in search of the unknown,' Isabelle disclosed, keenly.

'The words of my fellow traveller have moved me deeply. I'd like to escort you to a faraway place, but the café is your destiny,' he declared.

'Rehearsal ran smoothly so my beloved will be in a joyful mood.'

Isabelle arrived at the café and embraced Mr Chevalier rapturously, his handsome face portraying an enchanting tale, as he welcomed her. She greeted her father, Pierre and Philippe. The exhibition had attracted a greater crowd than expected.

'My darling girl, Granny Harper's portrait was the first to sell,' Mr Harper announced proudly.

'Life is full of surprises today,' she declared.

'Our jealousy has inspired us to create art not yet imagined,' Pierre remarked, with a wicked smile.

'Did you remember to introduce me to your God?' Count Flaubert enquired.

'He's very busy at the moment, but I'm sure we can connect shortly as promised,' Philippe reassured.

William arrived after class; grateful they'd returned from New York. After greeting Isabelle with fondness, he shook hands with Mr Chevalier and Mr Harper as he happily helped himself to afternoon tea.

'The tour next year is a possibility for you, William,' Mr Chevalier advised with a smile of encouragement.

'Thank you, sir,' he said appreciatively.

Isabelle had noticed a pretty, young girl observing him keenly. 'You have an admirer,' she remarked.

'Her name is Anna. She talks of you constantly,' William said.

'Tomorrow you must invite her to morning tea. I insist,' Isabelle urged.

'She had an ambition to be an actress but, like you, it had been forbidden,' William remarked with a charming smile, as he reminisced such a lovely memory.

'Priscilla and Edward are performing on flute this evening. We mustn't be late, my beauty,' Mr Chevalier announced with a sense of urgency.

Chapter 29

The day arrived when Isabelle had to put forward the more serious issue of her mother and her wish to honour her memory. Her father had always been a great strength, but Isabelle felt he might be tested on this issue. He may treat her idea with disdain. Mr Harper had certainly given a great deal of thought to society evolving and he had adapted well, but maybe not where his family was concerned.

Elsie entered with a sheath of yellow roses.

'A secret admirer. How scandalous!' Isabelle remarked, mischievously.

'I don't believe Mr Chevalier would approve,' Elsie replied.

'A lovely gesture from Mary Chevalier. She has wished me luck with my venture for Mother,' she announced jubilantly.

'May I offer a little advice, miss?' Elsie asked.

'Oh dear. I note a tone of concern in your lovely voice.'

'I don't think your father is ready. It may be wise to wait until all sad thoughts have settled.'

'Thank you for your wise words. Maybe you're right. I should harness my ardour and be more considerate of Father's healing.'

'You had the opportunity to forgive your mother, and I believe that meant everything. You allowed her to die in peace.'

~

The recent venture for Isabelle's mother being on hold, Mary Chevalier took a great deal of convincing that it was for the best. Things seemed tense between her sister-in-law and Mr Aubrey. He displayed a loving interest in Priscilla and Edward while his fiancé tolerated them with no visible connection. Mr Aubrey accompanied the twins on piano while they showed the splendour of their talent on flute. Mary Chevalier lit a cigar and drank coffee. Mrs Aubrey arrived late and coughed continuously in the smoke-filled room. Mr Aubrey's discomfort had been noticeable as he looked into Isabelle's eyes despairingly. The look of disdain on Mrs Aubrey's face slowly turned into a cheery smile as Isabelle joined her.

'I pray your good health continues. We've not had the chance to converse of late but your wonderful son keeps me informed,' Isabelle said.

'You are the reason our family is together and I'm forever grateful. I have a few reservations about my son's choice in marriage, but time will tell,' Mrs Aubrey remarked.

Mary Chevalier sat at the grand piano and played an enchanting sonata.

'Your music steals my heart and all other concerns vanish in an instant,' Mr Aubrey confessed. Mary did not acknowledge him and she continued to play, but with a look of disinterest.

Being the same age as Mary, Isabelle felt maturity and marriage would mellow her sister-in-law's temperament. Mr Chevalier took a firmer stand.

'You need to take heed of your behaviour. Graciousness must be shown at all times,' he advised sternly.

'I apologise and promise to make a greater effort. My engagement has reminded me that we're orphans. I miss our parents terribly,' she replied.

'I understand, and I love you, my dear sister,' he said with affection. Philippe and Pierre arrived late, making a grand entrance in their elegant pinstriped suits.

'I believe congratulations are in order,' Mr Chevalier commented.

'We are no longer jealous, dear Isabelle. We have broken all sales records and the expectation for tomorrow is the same,' Pierre announced proudly as he twirled her around the room joyously.

'One thing I do know is that you are absolutely unique and a pleasure to know,' Isabelle said charmingly.

'I believe we should drink to our bank balance. By some miracle it has remained intact,' Philippe announced with finesse.

Mrs Aubrey delighted in the charm and debonair manner of the French artists as they danced with Isabelle flamboyantly. Mary Chevalier and Mr Aubrey puffed away on cigars, laughing heartily at the spectacle. Mr Chevalier surprised their guests by sitting at the piano and playing popular jazz music.

~

When William entered the café dancing the Can-Can Isabelle knew that her fellow traveller had kept his promise. She laughed heartily at the dance routine.

'If you weren't such a fine musician, I would say you had missed your vocation as a dancer.'

'The Moulin Rouge has bewitched me forever. I had such an amazing night. I wished time would stand still so the evening would never end. The picture you painted in my mind was true to expectation, but the action exceeded my wildest dreams.'

'I couldn't allow you to miss the adventure,' Isabelle said passionately.

William's little girlfriend approached with caution. Isabelle welcomed her as William pulled up a chair.

'You must be Anna. I'm pleased to meet you.'

'And I know you're the famous Isabelle. I hold you in high esteem for the glorious music you play,' Anna said admiringly.

'If you're a friend of William's, you are indeed a friend of mine.'

~

Mr Harper arrived with a keen spring in his step to join Isabelle for a delectable morning tea in the secluded gardens. She welcomed him with an endearing warmth and noticed a much-altered demeanour. Mr James served a Devonshire tea while Mr Harper expressed joy at seeing his daughter so happy.

'Your contentment in marriage shows, my darling. I find it a great comfort after the loss of your mother,' he remarked with affection.

'Thank you, Father. I must compliment you on the improvement of your wellbeing. You exude a fine energy that pleases me,' she replied.

'I have been speaking to Doctor Reilly, our doctor in Devon. He's been a client of mine for many years and needed advice on a private hospital he has in mind for women with a similar illness to your mother. I would like to know your thoughts on the matter as our estate in Devon immediately came to mind. The hospital would be built near the woods, well secluded and far away from the manor. Doctor Reilly felt the view of rolling green fields and meadows would play an important role in recovery, along with the best doctors in this line of work of course,' Mr Harper explained.

Isabelle stared in disbelief. Her prayers had been answered without argument.

'My dear father, a miracle has happened today. I support your decision with all my heart. We can make our peace and help others to conquer this terrible demon,' she replied.

'I'm haunted by the memory of those sleepless nights. I didn't understand why or when her mood changed. Her altered mind was so vengeful, but then my loving wife would reappear and all would be forgiven.'

'No man could have handled the situation as you did. We needed help but there was none available. You and I have the chance to make that possible.'

'George sends his love. The marriage is planned for June next year.'

'I owe him a letter, so I'll send my hearty congratulations.'

Philippe and Pierre appeared through the trees as the snowflakes began to fall. Mr James anticipated their passion for morning tea and presented another.

'I would have thought you'd be in front of the fire enjoying a good read,' Pierre said, appreciating the warmth of his fur coat.

'I've been inspired by my father, so my mind is full of expectation.'

'You'll be pleased to hear of our five new paintings, sir. We've said our prayers to God, and our bank balance should be prospering,' Philippe announced.

'Without further ado, a red Cadillac will arrive by the end of the month,' Pierre added proudly.

'Oh dear, a discussion with Count Flaubert may be in order,' Mr Harper said quietly.

'Did I hear my name mentioned by any chance?' the count queried, as he arrived and kissed Isabelle's hand graciously.

'You did, my good friend, but I suggest a quiet drink at the Gentlemen's Club would be a more suitable place for such a discussion,' Mr Harper cautioned politely.

'I had hoped the day would improve as the morning unfolded, but I've the feeling I may have been disillusioned,' Count Flaubert said, managing a smile for his fellow traveller.

~

After the bedtime stories had been read and goodnight kisses given, a rare dinner for two was served.

'I must confess to loving you more than I ever dreamed possible, my darling,' Isabelle said as she looked into her husband's expressive blue eyes.

'Bless you. I thank God for you every day and I will love you until my last breath,' he declared.

The quartet struck the opening notes of her favourite waltz. The couple danced around the elegant room until they were distracted by Mr James who'd been waiting to alert their attention.

Mr Aubrey had not been able to accept his broken engagement to Mary Chevalier and had tragically tried to end his young life. Isabelle and her husband left for the hospital at once; they felt the need to be by his side to encourage him through his darkest hour. Her dearest friend had not been able to find the happiness that he'd yearned for. His heart had been broken, and Miss Chevalier had returned to Germany expressing no desire to return.

His recovery was slow, but his mother's efforts to save her own marriage and show a family bonding encouraged Mr Aubrey's wellbeing. Isabelle, a regular visitor, constantly praised his success and spoke of the wonderful future that awaited him.

Chapter 30

Isabelle rejoiced on Mr Aubrey's first day back at rehearsal. He displayed passion for his music and expressed a desire to reunite with the orchestra.

'I've missed the company of my best friend. Your music has mellowed my soul,' Isabelle said, so pleased with his recovery.

'I'm very happy to be here. I found myself in a very dark place and the road home was very far away,' Mr Aubrey said.

'You are now in control of your wonderful life,' she reassured him.

'I am looking forward to our world tour next year. New York being my favourite city, I may stay a while and play music there, wherever an offer is made.'

'I agree. Rather than wait for the world to greet us, we must take the initiative and meet our destiny with courage.'

'How are Priscilla and Edward?' he enquired.

'Missing you. After preparing a prelude on flute they eagerly await your accompaniment.'

'Tell them to count on me. I must thank you and Mr Chevalier for your love and support. Without you, I don't believe I would have found the will to lift my head off the pillow.'

'I'm so glad we could help,' she replied.

Philippe and Pierre's red Cadillac pulled up at the café. Mr Harper and Count Flaubert followed.

'The Gentlemen's Club may never recover from our morning meeting. On paper, all the finances are sorted. In reality, one must be prepared for the element of surprise,' Mr Harper declared, in a state of exhaustion from the ordeal.

Count Flaubert sat next to Isabelle and held her hand discreetly.

'The day has improved already so my optimism has surpassed my despair,' Count Flaubert announced with a much-improved demeanour.

~

Elsie fussed about the room, removing the toys that were in her path.

'I'm pleased Mr Aubrey has made a good recovery. Matters of the heart take a long time to heal. My husband's brother experienced a similar ordeal many years ago. Sadly, he never married,' Elsie said.

'I pray Mr Aubrey meets a beautiful girl who loves him dearly and forever,' Isabelle exclaimed in earnest.

'Hopefully, the Good Lord will answer our prayers. Your guests this evening will be Mr Harper, Count Flaubert, Reverend Durn, and William,' Elsie announced cheerfully.

'It would have been Mother's birthday tomorrow. I'll wear her favourite pink gown.'

'A little rest before dinner might be advisable. You've been under duress of late, miss.'

~

Isabelle had been glad to hear all the news from the vicarage, and Reverend Durn expressed an eager interest in the new hospital on the Devon estate. As Isabelle listened to her father talk of the hospital's progress, it pleased her greatly that Mr Harper had included her equally. This kind treatment had only been recognised for men, but at last women were able to receive the same cure. Reverend Durn looked caringly at Isabelle, showing admiration for her involvement; he knew how much it meant to her.

'How is Sarah and your gorgeous son?'

'Very well indeed. Oliver is an inspiration to us both, although full of mischief I'm afraid,' Charles replied.

'I'm pleased to hear it,' Isabelle answered.

Mr Chevalier stood to attract the guests' attention as Mr James and the waiters topped up the glasses of champagne.

'If you would kindly stand and raise your glasses. A toast to my lovely wife, Isabelle, and her father, Mr Harper, for their great contribution to the improvement and wellbeing of women,' Mr Chevalier announced with pride.

'My aunty had a similar illness to your mother. Desperate, she asked her doctor for treatment. He advised her to go home and put her mind to more important matters. Aunty died a year later,' William said sadly.

Countess Flaubert caught Isabelle's eye as she puffed on her cigar.

'Mary Chevalier would have been jubilant that your dream has come to fruition,' the countess remarked.

'Thank you, Countess Flaubert. I wrote her a letter and expressed my gratitude for her support.'

After Mr Chevalier had danced her superbly, Isabelle enjoyed the cool of the evening on the terrace. She was reminiscing about her mother's birthday, never expecting it to be her last, as she gazed at the golden moon, in rapture of its wonder. Count Flaubert caught her eye as he stepped through the doorway. He discreetly looked into her eyes with the warmth of a loving friend and she knew he would always be there for her.

'How is Mr Aubrey?' he queried with concern.

'He's much improved, but I believe he would benefit the advice from my fellow traveller.'

'I'll invite him to dinner at my club. There are times when we men need our own company to enable discussions unsuitable for a young lady's ears.'

Mr Aubrey showed a renewed passion for life after a captivating evening with Count Flaubert. As an arduous rehearsal with the orchestra concluded, they retired to the café. William appeared through the crowd with his girlfriend Anna and another pretty young lady. Her blue eyes and long blond hair bewitched Mr Aubrey and he assisted with her chair.

'In case you are wondering who I am, my name is Charlotte Pommier. I'm a student and an admirer of your beautiful playing,' she said.

'Antoine Aubrey. The pleasure is mine I can assure you.'

'The day has certainly improved for you, Mr Aubrey,' Count Flaubert remarked with a wink and a smile.

'It has indeed, sir,' he replied.

~

Miss Charlotte Pommier was in awe of Mr Aubrey's accompaniment on cello as Priscilla and Edward played a well-practised prelude on flute.

The Chevaliers and Mr Harper were spellbound by the music and pleased that the children had found a form of expression through their music.

'I have good news, my darling girl. The hospital opened today and the rooms are fully booked,' Mr Harper said proudly.

'I thank you for enabling such a gift,' Isabelle replied.

'I hope your wonderful husband doesn't mind, but I have a present for you to celebrate this day.'

Opening the box curiously, Isabelle discovered a magnificent diamond necklace that had belonged to her mother.

'Thank you, Father. I will treasure it.'

The warmth from the roaring fire mellowed all other thoughts from the day. Isabelle sat in wonder at her beautiful life. She gently held her husband's hand while dreaming of a glorious future for their children and cherishing the splendid love felt for each other.

Isabelle woke to see Elsie looking out of the window at a spectacular sunrise.

'Good morning, dear Elsie,' Isabelle greeted.

'I don't wish to alarm you, miss, but I heard chanting in the woods this morning,' Elsie cautioned.

'At the very worst, one of your bad dreams may be to blame,' Isabelle replied as she sat down to breakfast.

'Mr Chevalier left early, but advised he'd be home for lunch,' Elsie said.

'He's the love of my life.'

'Mr Chevalier said the same, miss.'

'Father persists that I take an early morning walk in the gardens. He believes exercise is most beneficial to a good outcome for the day.'

'I agree, but please stay away from the woods until Mr Chevalier arrives home.'

'Don't fuss!' Isabelle said in a serious tone of voice.

She was enchanted by the magnificent gardens but a little curious of what Elsie had said. After entering the woods—enticed by the river—her place to dream, she heard the chanting of a pagan ritual through the trees.

Gasping at the sight of Lorna, Isabelle stood proudly, bravely defiant in her presence and overwhelmed by her need to protect her family from the curse. Isabelle wondered if the shadow of the girl she saw in the field that day had been Lorna. Her screams of deranged madness haunted Isabelle.

'Get off the estate!' Isabelle demanded with authority.

'You stole my Jimmy!' Lorna shouted—flashing the voodoo doll at Isabelle.

Darting through the trees as she strove to distance herself from danger, Isabelle was alerted to the bridge that crossed the river. She could see the structure was fragile but took the risk and ran across. As Lorna attacked her on the bridge, it began to collapse. Isabelle leaped onto the riverbank to safety.

Lorna screamed with terror as she fell into the water and the heavy planks of wood landed on top of her, killing her instantly.

Struggling to hang onto a tree trunk in a semi-conscious state, the sound of Mr Chevalier's voice gave her hope.

'Isabelle,' he called anxiously.

'I was afraid to die alone and here you are,' Isabelle confessed. The curse of Jimmy being foremost on her mind.

'Elsie told me where you were. I panicked when I heard the timber crashing. Reverend Durn will have the answers to save you from the curse my darling,' Mr Chevalier promised as he embraced her into his arms, striving to hide his tears.

A month had passed with little change to Isabelle's health. Rehearsal for the next New York tour had resumed and Mr Aubrey was overjoyed as he welcomed Isabelle; her music being his inspiration and saviour. Mr Chevalier had been moved to tears by the lovely duet being played.

'Your music reminds me that there is a God after all and glorious goodness will prevail,' Mr Chevalier said and turned away to hide his emotional state. The loss of Isabelle was unimaginable.

Arriving at the café the joy of seeing her fellow traveller lifted Isabelle's spirits. Their treasured connection never wavered; knowing how blessed she'd been as he held her hand discreetly. Philippe and Pierre made a spectacular entrance, proudly presenting paintings for payment.

'I assume the bank balance is zero,' Count Flaubert announced in a nonchalant manner.

'It is indeed, but the wealth of New York awaits us,' Pierre declared with polite arrogance.

Isabelle had glimpsed Pierre's painting and covered the art with her coat; astounded by what she saw.

~

William had been chosen to play in a well-known orchestra in Russia and desired a celebration with Isabelle. Elsie greeted him at the chateau.

'I'm looking for Isabelle,' William advised courteously.

'Is she expecting you?'

'Yes. I have wonderful news.'

'Good news will be most welcome,' Elsie said, showing a brave smile.

He walked a distance along the river as there was no sign of Isabelle in the gardens. William had almost given up the search when he saw a canoe floating down river. He ran to the riverbank and could see Isabelle lying in the canoe. She had picked wildflowers to thread through her hair. He was shocked by her pale and lifeless face.

'I've been chosen for the Russian orchestra, I wanted you to be the first to know,' he kindly advised, hoping the news would lift her spirits.

'I'm so happy for you, William. My thoughts will always be with you,' Isabelle confessed.

'Are you all right?' he queried.

'No, William. I've been cursed. You can thread wildflowers through my hair but you must never mention our secret to a living soul.'

'I promise. I've heard what happened,' he said.

'There was no choice. I had to save my family. How do I look?'

'Very beautiful,' William said with sadness in his heart as he threaded the last of the wildflowers through her hair.

'Children's voices keep haunting me through the wilderness and I pray to God that my family can bring me home.'

'I can't imagine a world without Isabelle,' he replied.

'You must leave me now.'

'Please stay,' he urged.

'Goodbye, William,' she farewelled.

He watched the canoe drift far away into the mist and knew he would keep his promise to Isabelle for all eternity.

CPSIA information can be obtained
at www.ICGtesting.com
Printed in the USA
LVHW031229220323
742255LV00004B/65